FAITH: ASCENSION SAGA - BOOKS 4-6

INTERSTELLAR BRIDES®: ASCENSION SAGA

GRACE GOODWIN

PREQUEL

Twenty-seven years ago Queen Celene was forced to flee Alera with her unborn child. Read the story of her escape to Earth in The Ascension Saga prequel — for free!

Click now to find out how the adventure began...
www.ascensionsaga.com

BOOK 4

PROLOGUE

Q ueen Celene of Alera, Transport Room, Location
Unknown

THE MALE I'd begun to think of as a hyena shoved me onto the
transport platform, all pretense of trying to play nice... gone.

I hid my smile. There were few things in the universe that
could put that look on an arrogant male's face—and being
bested by a female—or three—was one of them.

"Where are you taking me?" I asked, trying to keep my
voice mild and sweet.

"Do not speak, or I will wrap my hands around your neck
and squeeze until you can no longer bother me."

I should have held my tongue. I wasn't stupid. But I was
proud of my daughters. Proud of my people. Proud of the fact
that I'd not only survived this monster and his master's evil plot
to eliminate my entire family's bloodline, but had returned to
Alera with not one, but three daughters. Strong young women.
Stronger, even, than me. "Four spires light the sky. A new
queen is poised to take the throne," I commented, not

remaining silent at all. "Your master has failed. Do you really think he'll allow you to live to speak of it?"

With a shove, he pushed me down onto the cold, black surface of the transport pad, flinging me so that I fell to my hands and knees before I could catch myself.

It hurt, but I placed my palms on the smooth surface and pushed myself into a sitting position so I could look up at him through the long strands of blonde hair hanging, unkempt, over my face. I'd been healed from their last bout of... evil. I was uninjured, but a bathing tube was a distant memory.

His face was pale, the blood gone from his lips. The hooked scar that ran from the corner of his mouth down, past his jawline, was an old one. Faded and puckered, I doubted the mercenary could smile, even if he wanted to.

"You know nothing, female," he hissed, spittle flying from his mouth. "Not my name, nor the identity of my master. You have no idea where you are."

That was true, and not true. I knew I was being transported off this ship. I knew we were orbiting above my home plant of Alera. And I knew that my daughters continued to defy the odds and survive. And keep peace on Alera. Was he truly that surprised by my words?

"Have you not thought this through? What did you think would happen to you in the end?" I asked.

"And what do you think will happen to you if my master does not acquire the royal jewels?"

I gave a bland shrug. "It no longer matters." That was also the truth. My daughters' spires were lit above the royal city. The entire planet knew of their existence, and their place in line to the throne. Trinity, Faith and Destiny. They each knew where the royal jewels had been hidden. There was no way I would betray my people and hand over such a powerful symbol to an enemy.

"Perhaps not. But since you won't cooperate with me, you're being relocated—to a less hospitable prison."

I could only imagine. There were ancient dungeons beneath almost every family palace as well as the police and Optimus unit. Also, larger temples run by the Clerical Order. Dozens of possibilities pushed to the front of my mind, all equally likely and impossible to monitor from the outside.

But at least I'd be on the ground on Alera.

Standing on shaky legs, I crossed my arms and remained silent.

He chuckled as he walked off the platform toward the control panel that would send me goddess knew where. All I could do was lift my chin and hope for the best.

I would not give up the jewels. They were a powerful symbol of sovereignty, passed down generation after generation from the original queen of Alera. They were thousands of years old, and had graced the neck of every queen since our history began.

No ruler could appease the people without the black gemstones proudly around her neck. The gems had been fashioned into a necklace, designed for female rulers, and I knew, one day, they would rest against Trinity's warm skin and would sing to her in welcome, as they had to me, part of the citadel's life force, or energy, or awareness. I never truly understood exactly *what* lived in the citadel's walls, or perhaps, the ultimate term would be spirit. The spirit of the gems would sing to her in welcome.

They would not sing for a stranger, nor for anyone deemed unworthy.

They would be categorically useless to anyone who stole them, or wore them if they did not have royal blood.

But as a symbol to the people? I could think of nothing on Earth that was powerful enough to compare. A queen without these gems was like the mighty comic book heroine, *Wonder Woman,* without her sword and golden lasso. The people would resist accepting anyone as their ruler without one of the spires at the citadel coming to life.

But, even if my enemies could convince the people that they had no choice, that all true royal females were dead, they would never accept the absence of the royal jewels.

Hard to break thousands of years of tradition and crown a king, especially without the iconic symbol of power around his neck. A male? Wearing the jewels?

Never. I had seen to that. And now my daughters would carry the bloodline, defend our planet. The citadel would help them. They would become powerful beyond what these fools could even imagine. The three of them together? Unstoppable.

.

I stood tall as the blinding cold agony of transport enveloped my body.

The last thing I saw and heard over the hum of the machines was the scarred man's laughter.

But I would laugh last, from this life or the next. Of that, I was certain.

1

F aith, *the Jax mansion*

I HOPED my sisters fared better than I did. A princess, a maid and a nun. What a combination.

Trinity was all over the news on the screens. The dress she had on the day she went public was spectacular. She'd never worn her hair in much other than a braid or ponytail, but as she walked up the stairs of our mother's palace, she looked like a queen.

She looked so beautiful that I'd cried, and I rarely cried. And if that hadn't been enough, Zel, the unconscious guard we'd saved that first night turned out to be a really, really bad guy and had kidnapped her at her big welcome-to-the-throne reception. He'd almost gotten away with it, too. Boy, did I cry after that. It was one thing to know there might be some danger, but actual, *real* threats and bad guys? I freaked. Cried, then cried some more. But I had to stop, to pull up my big girl, princess panties. So now I found it much easier to make a joke and move on.

Move on. That had been my life motto until my sisters and I came to Alera. Now I was a prisoner of my own design. A *servant* in the Jax household. The place that was under Optimus unit investigation because of Zel. That, too, was all over the news. And it made me a little nervous since I was snooping around where other people were investigating. I was not CIA trained and wasn't doing all that well at my mission.

"Bring me another drink, would you, dear? I'm about to die of thirst." Lord Jax, the elder—as I liked to think of him—had his feet up in front of the fireplace in his office, despite the fact that he was fully dressed in riding gear from his late afternoon outing, and he had two creatures that looked like very large cats with zebra stripes lounging in his lap. "And some of those little snacks, too."

He held his empty cup into the air and I took it from him. "Of course, my lord." The cat creatures were fascinating and gorgeous, and they didn't purr—exactly. But the sound reminded me of an idling diesel engine, just not quite as loud, nor smelled as bad.

Carrying the cup to a sideboard, I filled the glass—not with water, which would have actually quenched his thirst—but with wine. The lord did enjoy his wine. And his pets. And bragging about his son, the magnificent, perfect paragon of all male specimens. To hear the older man speak, you'd think his son, Thordis Jax, was on a level with *Superman* himself.

I'd seen a portrait in the hall. And yes, he was gorgeous. More like the actor who played *Captain America* in the movies back home than the dark-haired Adonis from Krypton. But I'd never met the prodigal son. And I had no desire to, especially since I'd learned he'd grown up with Zel, been BFFs as kids. He lived in his own home on the other side of the city which was just fine with me. If he was as intelligent and attentive as his father claimed, I'd never get all my tasks done in this house just ogling him. But he could be a traitor. Anyone in this house could be out to finish off my family.

I stuck to the tasks I'd been *hired* to do. These tasks included staying under the radar and hunting down a traitor.

No biggie, right? For a princess disguised as a serving wench. Actually, it wasn't all bad, and no one had ever used the word *wench*. I didn't have to wear a rough cotton dress and scrub laundry until my fingers cracked and bled. They took great advantage of their advanced technology. The Spontaneous Matter Generators, or S-Gen units, created new clothing from nothing every day. Perfectly sized. Clean, which meant there was no laundry to do. No food to clean up. The S-Gen recycled on an atomic level, breaking down everything into a basic unit of energy, the building blocks for the next item that might be requested.

I was a servant. A maid. I *served*. God forbid these nobles had to actually *walk over to the S-Gen unit* and order something for themselves. But the wine? That was special. Imported from a planet called Atlan, or so I'd been told.

The lady of the house had very clearly informed me that *no one of any worth* drank wine from an S-Gen unit.

Fuck that. I'd done it almost every night since I got here, and it tasted just fine. Took the edge off when it was time to lock myself in my tiny little room and try to sleep. Most nights, it helped, but not enough. I'd wake in a cold sweat with visions of the assassins who'd tried to kill us, of my hands covered in blood...

Shit. I was shaking now. Where was a good joke when I needed one?

I took the glass and the small plate of food the cook left out for him every afternoon—some kind of chopped fish on crackers he enjoyed eating...and sharing with his cats.

"Here you go, sir. Filled to the rim, just the way you like it." And he did. So full that one misstep would spill large quantities of wine onto both my hand and the plush, ivory carpeting. "And your favorite snacks."

"Excellent. You're a good one, Faith. Very good." He picked

up a cracker with the chunky white topping and popped it in his mouth. "Mmm, have you tried the fish yet? Delicious." He took another from the plate and fed it to the cat."

"Thank you, my lord, but no. I don't eat meat."

"Oh?" He glanced up at me. "Yes, I can see the animals like you too much for you to eat them."

He grinned and took another cracker and fish, then washed it down with the wine.

He was a likable man. As far as I could tell, he was nearing sixty, and didn't do much these days. He told me his son had taken over the business side of their empire several years ago, so he was free to ride and drink and—in a more drunken moment—supposedly fuck his gorgeous mate. *'The old cock still works, I tell you. Fills her right up and makes her scream just like it did when I was a younger man. Oh yes. My cock never fails her. Never!'*

That had been *way* too much information, but he'd been very pleased with himself. And he was utterly devoted to his wife of more than thirty years. So, I had to smile, take him his drink, and tell him that his cock must be very great indeed.

He'd glared at me, and we'd both burst out laughing, just as the object of his undying affection strode into the room.

One look had passed between them and he'd hauled her off to their bedroom, leaving me alone to clean up the wine he'd spilled in his haste—and search through the drawers and cabinets.

Every chance I got, I went through everything. Read notes. Looked for clues as to who might have kidnapped our mother. I eavesdropped on conversations and asked questions, hoping someone would tell me *something* I could use. So far, I'd found nothing.

Nothing that connected anyone else in the Jax household to Zel, any information about Mother. Zel, God, he made me so mad, it was a good thing he was dead. I'd actually helped the asshole! Yet my mother was still missing, meaning the jerk wasn't working alone. Of course, he wouldn't be, especially since the Optimus unit was supposedly still all over investigating the Jax family like white on rice. It couldn't be Cassander, the consort who had miraculously survived. He'd been sent to some stupid southern estate where a young lady in the Jax house was entering her Ardor. Why would he want to harm the princess when all he had to do all day was have sex with eager females? God, what a life. No doubt, Cassander would have her naked and beneath him for days. Lucky girl. "Cue the eye roll."

"What's that, dear?" Lord Jax rubbed his nose against that of a preening zebra cat creature and watched me from the corner of his eye. He wasn't completely stupid, he just didn't pay attention, content to just be happy in the moment and trust his son to take care of everything. I did not want to do anything to change that.

"Nothing. Mumbling to myself." Shit. I had to control myself. I wasn't used to watching my mouth. I liked to let things fly as they popped into my mind, and that habit was *not* serving me well in this house. Hell, on this planet.

"Me, too, my dear. I've found that I am the only one who truly enjoys my sense of humor." He chuckled, as if he found himself funny, and nuzzled the second creature, who had risen onto its hind legs, front legs on the lord's chest, and was licking his cheek. Both creatures were rumbling loudly, and I wondered if they were a mated pair. The female was larger, but the male was more aggressive with making his desire known to their master, wanting constant attention.

I wanted to pet them. Nuzzle them. Bury my nose in their fur and enjoy their snuggly attentions. And affection. But that wasn't why I was here, and I'd been informed by Lady Jax that the creatures were exotic, extremely expensive, and no one but the lord himself was allowed to touch them.

Whatever. I had bigger fish to fry. A traitor to find, because while Zel was dead and buried—someone else had our mother, Queen Celene. They'd dragged her out of her bed back on Earth, and there had been no sign of her since. None at all. And as much as I hated to admit it, that made me very, very nervous. If her spire wasn't still lit—the light somehow linked to her life force by ancient alien technology no one on this planet understood—I would have given up hope of finding her. I was a realist. She'd been gone for almost two weeks now. In the hands of god only knew who. Murderers? Killers? Traitors? Were they torturing her right now?

I had yet to search Lady Jax's room—if the lord's mate would ever stay out of it long enough for me to search properly. I had hoped to do it when they were at the royal reception that had served as my sister Trinity's introduction to the nobles on the planet—and to everyone else. But no such luck.

They'd sent the prodigal son in their place, hoping he would be awakened by the future queen. What good it would do them, I had no idea. Not when it had been made clear on the news that Trinity already had a mate. Leo. And I knew my sister. She wasn't the cheating kind, especially since the Jax household was supposedly the epicenter of the huge investigation. Leo was hers now. And she was his. I'd met him. Talked to him. He was a regular overly-protective alpha male. I had no idea what the hell my sister was thinking, but she seemed happy. Perhaps she wasn't thinking... that her lust and love ruled. And, she was alive. Score two points for the princess squad.

But that didn't stop a power-hungry mother from hoping her son could turn Trinity's head. The woman probably needed some good news for the family name.

Speaking of the devil herself, Lady Jax chose that moment to walk in. She saw the creatures, the wine spilling over onto the floor as the larger of the two cats pushed at the lord's arm with her paw, jostling his hand and the drink he held. "My lord, you are making a mess on the floor again." Her voice was stern, like an angry nun at Catholic school. Her stress level was through the roof since the whole Zel fiasco came to light.

"It's not me, love. It's her fault." Lord Jax rubbed his cheek along the face of the female creature. "Isn't it, kitten?"

Lady Jax crossed her arms with a tolerant smile. It was clear that she cared for her mate. But then, he was likable. Unlike his cock's choice of mate. "I think you love those creatures more than you love me, mate."

He raised a brow and looked up at her. His gaze took in the floor-length pale green dress she wore, the small slippers on her feet, the softly coiled hair. She was clearly in her fifties, but still gorgeous. "Is that so, female?"

"You know it is."

He was already rising from his chair, pushing the protesting creatures from his lap. She took a step backward, too late. "Come here, mate. It sounds like you're a little stressed and need some... *relief.*"

She shook her head, but her eyes were bright with interest. "No."

"Obey your mate, female."

"Make me." With that, she laughed and ran from the room, the older lord hot on her heels.

I grinned. I couldn't help it. I didn't much care for the lady of the house, except when she was with him, and she did deserve a little relief. With the servants, visitors, everyone else, including the investigators who'd been through the house often enough, she was cold. Calculating. Vindictive. The word *diva* didn't come close to doing her justice. But with her mate?

I took his cup and watched the creatures leave through their own special door with a sigh. They never stayed. Never let me touch them. Too loyal to their one true master, or so I'd been told.

Walking as quietly as possible to the hallway, I followed the lord and lady, eager to discover where they might end up. Most of the time, he carried her to her chambers, leaving me no hope of searching them.

But today?

A door slammed ahead of me, her squeals of laughter clearly heard through the thick panel.

Yes! The library. Her room was empty!

I ran to the side cupboard, put down the partially full glass of wine and made my way to the lady's room as quickly as possible. She locked herself in here for hours and hours. Now was my chance!

Closing the door quietly behind me, I took in the high ceiling, the large bed covered in ivory material even softer than silk. The carpeting was so thick I would have to rough up the floor on my way out to cover the evidence of deep footfalls with each step I took.

I started in the closet, opening and closing everything. Searching pockets. Shoes. Decorative boxes. Nothing.

Moving on to her desk, I pulled at the drawer, found it locked. Damn it.

"Key. Key. Where's the key?" It looked like an old-fashioned lock. The lock on the lord's desk had been much more advanced. I'd had to copy a fingerprint from one of his wine glasses and record his voice to gain access. But I'd found nothing there. Business and banking documents. All public and confirmed by hours of research I'd done on their version of the internet.

But Lady Jax? She was much more of a mystery to me, and my instincts told me she knew a lot more than she let on.

Lying on my back on the floor, I slid under the desk and saw the key jammed into a small space between the wooden braces in one corner. "Gotcha."

I grabbed the key, slid out from beneath the desk and unlocked the drawer. Before I could open it, a woman's cutting voice stopped me cold.

"What do you think you are doing?"

Frozen in place, I slowly looked over my shoulder to find Lord and Lady Jax staring at me from the now open bedroom door.

"Just tidying up in here." God, I really needed to work on my lying. Even Lord Jax didn't believe me. I could see it in the scowl on his face, the way his lips tightened into a thin line.

"Well, my lord, it appears we have found the one leaking information to our enemies."

Who, me? She couldn't possibly be talking about me. Right? Wrong.

Lord Jax's face turned red with anger. "Guards!"

Whirling to face them, I kept my hands behind me and relocked the drawer. "I was cleaning the room. That is all."

"I don't believe you. The way the Jax name is being destroyed in the media? The way we're losing our integrity, our honor? Because people like *you* and your evil, wicked ways." Lady Jax walked to me and yanked me away from her desk. Boy, she could be strong! I took the opportunity to flick the key under the chair behind me. It was the best I could do. At least I wouldn't have it on me.

"You dare enter my mate's quarters without permission?" Lord Jax was no longer soft or amiable. Now he was a male defending his mate, and I was screwed.

Two burly, well-armed guards were at the door and he stepped aside. "Lock her up in my office and summon our son and the police."

Lady Jax went to his side, shaking like a leaf at the great *danger* I was to her. I didn't think it was in fear, but fury. His scowl deepened and he wrapped his arms around her protectively. They were both flushed but it hadn't been long enough for even a quickie in the library. I had to assume they'd decided to take a bit more time here in her bedroom. Lucky me.

"Shouldn't we summon the palace guard? The Optimus unit? They're the ones investigating. She is the mole, love. She is the reason so many of our guards are dead. She probably sent that traitor, Zel, to kidnap the princess at the royal reception!" She sounded as if she were on the verge of a complete breakdown. Tears. Trembling. Jeez. The woman deserved a freaking acting award.

But then, maybe she really *did* believe I was the mole in the Jax household. I was here, looking for him—or her—myself. So was the Optimus unit.

The guards stormed in and grabbed me. Their hands were rough, and I couldn't blame them. If they believed what Lady Jax was saying—and they had no reason not too—I was, most likely, the reason their men had been killed the night of mine and my sisters' arrival on Alera.

Double screwed.

"I want Thor to talk to her first, but I want the police as well, just in case she turns violent. Thor can decide what to do with her... and whether or not he wants to hand her over to the police or the palace."

The palace guard would be easy. I could just ask to see Trinity. She'd rescue me from her own guards. But the police? Assuming I was the mole, would they just torture and kill me? Lock me up? Make me disappear?

I could tell them that I was a princess now, but they'd never believe me. Everyone on the planet was looking for me and my sister, Destiny. Everyone, although no one knew what we looked like, or even that we *were* princesses. And I'd been cleaning bathrooms and waiting on them hand and foot? Yep. Not exactly royal behavior. And besides, maybe this way the real traitor would show his face, or at least come at me so he could gloat.

I'd have to let this play out.

When the guards led me away, I didn't fight. And when they stood guard around me in Lord Jax's office as they awaited Thor and the police, I refused to cry.

I was a fucking princess.

Lord Thordis Jax, Mytikas City, Planet Alera

"My Lord, you've been summoned to the family mansion." My head of household, a stern and highly efficient female, spoke from the doorway of my office.

"My mother?" I asked. Mother sent for me often. If she was lonely, or bored, or wanted to discuss the latest female she hoped to parade before me. Always scheming, my dear mother, hoping the right female would come along and awaken my dormant cock, inspire me to be more. She believed a mate would force me to increase my interest in politics and the family finances. I was in no hurry to be dragged around by the balls, crawling after a female. And in no mood to entertain my mother today.

"No, my lord. Your father. The traitor has been caught and detained. He has ordered you to come at once."

The traitor? Caught? No wonder they called me. The two of them had been stressed and bothered—understandably—by the weight of the investigation on the Jax family. They thought us traitors. Zel, fuck, Zel had been one. I'd grown up with him, his father a guard for my grandfather. We'd gone to school together, been best friends. Until we'd grown apart. So far apart that he'd gone down a dark path, a path that led to his attempt at kidnapping the princess. And it had occurred right after I'd been seen talking with her at the royal reception, which only fueled the Optimus unit's interest in us.

The traitor had been found. Thank fuck. I set the crystalline drink glass down on my desk and grabbed my coat. The air at this altitude was cold.

Dancing with the princess at the reception had made two things abundantly clear. One, Celene's daughter was highly intelligent, not the uninformed, spoiled twit I'd been expecting.

And two? She knew a lot more about what was going on in Mytikas than she let on. And she was doing everything in her power to protect the identities of the other two females, both of royal blood if the spire lights were any indication—who had arrived on Alera with her.

Princess Trinity was a step—or ten—ahead of me, and I didn't like that feeling. Not one bit. For despite what my mother believed, I'd been running the family estate for several years now. My father, not wanting to lose face in front of his beloved, pretended, and fed her bits of information that I provided to him. As I lived in my own apartment closer to the city center, it was easy for us to keep up the charade. My mother always worried overmuch about status, and money, and power. Best if she believed everything was going as it always had. That her mate was taking care of her, was still a competent, ambitious male.

He was old, he said. Tired. He wanted nothing more than to spend time with his expensive and exotic pets, drink a bit of wine, and fuck his mate. The last, I didn't even want to think about. But he doted on her, and I had to respect at least that. This whole mess was wearing on all of us and I was glad to know it just might be over.

Especially since I'd agreed to accept the responsibility for the family. I had no mate, and my cock, after all these years, countless parties, and what felt like an infinite number of females paraded before me—had yet to be awakened. My mate nowhere to be found.

Things used to be quiet. Simple. At least until three spires randomly lit up the Mytikas sky just a short time ago. All of Alera probably thought the same thing I had, that our lives had changed overnight.

For most, the arrival of Princess Trinity gave hope, curiosity and even eagerness for the future. But for some, the lighting of the spires made decades of scheming and maneuvering for power suddenly irrelevant. The fights between the warring houses interested in taking over Queen Celene's reign had gone suspiciously quiet. Just a week ago, the royal guard, including Princess Trinity's mate, Leoron Turaya, had fought off another incursion into the sacred city.

Each time, the attacks on the capital city had been carried out by mercenaries carrying no banner. They were notorious for brutality in battle, and taking their own lives rather than surrender. I had spoken to my father's own men, those who had fought beside the royal guard in the last battle, and they all said the same thing.

The mercenaries never talked. They fought to the death, or they vanished into the night. No injured men were left behind. Only the dead. And dead warriors told no tales.

I strode out to the street and slid into the seat of the EMV waiting to take me to my parents' mansion. The Jax household had always been loyal to the crown. For thousands of years, we had served the bloodline of the ancients. So, too, had the other families. But they had yet to realize they had no fight left to win. Not with three new spires lighting the Aleran sky.

But the Jax household had plenty of fight at the moment. Not for the crown, but for a different reason entirely. There was a mole among us and we wanted to know who it was. A traitor willing to destroy the age-old name and the honor associated with the Jax family name. That made me want the EMV to move faster, to find out about this traitor they'd captured first hand.

When the princess first arrived, a group of Jax guards had been trusted to keep her, and her mystery companions, safe. All of the Jax guards had been killed, except Zel, who'd been seriously injured and in need of a ReGen pod for healing. Our most valuable and well-loved consort, Cassander, had been injured as well.

We'd believed the attack had come from someone outside the family, a group of assassins hired to kill our men.

But the night of the princess's reception, we'd discovered a much more disturbing truth. It had been Zel who had been part of an ambush to kill Princess Trinity and the two females she'd transported with. When he hadn't succeeded, Zel, the bastard, had kidnapped the royal from her own welcome reception.

Wearing a Jax family crest.

If he weren't dead, I would kill him myself. Slowly.

Thankfully, Princess Trinity had been saved. Zel had been killed. While I wasn't sorry to see him dead, I did wish I could interrogate him. Even though we'd grown up together, known each other almost like brothers, I didn't know him now. I'd wanted to find out who he'd worked for. It was obvious now he'd just been a pawn. Not too intelligent. Highly disposable.

Without knowing who was leading the evil faction against Queen Celene's daughter, the princess was not safe. The tension within the walls of the family mansion was incredible. Were all of the Jax family foes of the royal family? Did we wish them harm? Death? Those were the questions tossed about in the Aleran press.

No fucking way, but words weren't enough to prove our innocence. With our honor tarnished, nothing less than the traitor's head on a platter would prove our innocence. I was eager to see it done and had spent more time than usual with my parents. I had my own responsibilities, handling the financial fallout of our family's newly tarnished name. I could not afford to hide in my apartment. There was too much at stake for my anxiety ridden mother, or my doting but irresponsible father to handle this fiasco alone.

There was another reason for my frequent presence in the Jax mansion these past few days. Someone within the household stirred something in me. A scent lingered in the air, something I could only describe as hypnotic in nature, tantalized my senses in almost every room. My cock stirred. Not fully awakened, but... no longer fully dormant either. I was in an agony of inertia.

It happened for the first time several days ago when I stood in the empty dining room. I'd eaten meals there my entire life and my cock never thickened, never swelled in my pants. Arousal became an instant hunger in me, as if I were hungry, but not for the food I knew would be served later in the day, but instead, for a female's wet, willing pussy.

What the fuck had been wrong with me? A female was meant to awaken me, and only one at that. My mate.

I'd had to excuse myself, seek the privacy of my old bedroom to open up my pants to alleviate the growing ache in my balls, to see for the first time how my cock was now like a club, thickly-veined and broad-headed. Eager. I'd stroked it, felt the powerful pulse of desire that coursed through me at the contact, but it had been unfulfilled.

The arousal had faded. I had begun to wonder if, after reaching nearly thirty years with no mate, my body had simply gone mad. For there was no mate to be found, only that scent. Elusive. I caught the barest whisper of it here and there.

I felt as if I were hunting a ghost. Or, worse, losing my mind.

And so I'd been curious to know the answer. Eager to find the one who had awakened me. Every time I searched my childhood home, I could only hope to breathe in that elusive, addictive scent.

And in the days since, I'd grown frustrated—my cock only grew harder each time I caught the scent—my body more and more eager to fuck. To mate. To satisfy the female who'd been mysteriously taunting me.

The EMV came to a stop at the mansion's entrance and I stepped from the vehicle into the cold air, my cock once again as it had always been, asleep. But there was a newfound eagerness in my steps as I made my way to the front door.

The servants greeted me and I handed my coat to a familiar face. Sometimes, it was good to be home.

Home. Perhaps, if I found a mate, I would return to the mansion and raise my children here, where my father could spoil them and my mother dote on them, lavishing them with a bit too much attention.

The idea of finding my mate consumed me, even now, as I went to face a traitor, I thought of her. Wondered what she looked like. What noble family she had been born to. For I had come to believe it was, indeed, a female who eluded me, for the scent of her mocked me from everywhere in this home. The library, my old bedchamber, even the coat closet. I was constantly aroused at my parents' home and that made me crazy. I should be worried about this mole who had been caught, not eager to breathe in that mysterious sweet scent and have my cock rise once again.

For the first time in my life, I wanted to fuck. The desire had been dormant because... well, because. An Aleran male didn't have his cock awaken until he found his mate. Before that moment, he felt arousal, but never got hard. I could stroke my cock and never find satisfaction or completion because my body was waiting for The One. But who the fuck was she?

I ran my hand over the back of my neck as I walked down the ornate hallway. My parents didn't go for simple when they could show off their fortune.

I followed the sound of voices to my father's office, strode in ready to beat the shit out of the traitor with my own fists. My pent-up energy needed an outlet and I was pleased a male without honor would provide one. Zel was dead, but this other... he would answer for his sins, or else.

I took in my father, my mother and three guards with their backs to me, all facing the long sofa positioned in front of the now-cold fireplace. If he wasn't working at his desk—situated before the tall window that looked out over the property's back lawn—he often sat there to read. This was his sanctuary and it was strange to see so many people within.

My mother heard my entrance and turned. "Thordis, I'm so glad you're here." She came over to me with her usual grace, put her hand on my upper arm. Her gray hair was pulled up into the customary bun, the lines in her face deeper than usual. Her lips were pinched. Her normally stoic face showed a mixture of worry and anger. "She was found searching through my bedchamber."

I heard the word *she* and scented the dark forest at the same time. But this time there was much more than a hint of the erotic scent. My cock stirred, swelled. My body hardened into aching stone and my mind went blank. No longer just a male, I felt an instinct rise in me I'd never felt before. Powerful. Dominant. Ready to hunt...

Fuck it. Inwardly, I growled. I had to regain control. This wasn't the time for my cock to—

"She?" I asked, confused, pulling myself together enough to pick up on that one word.

My mother turned and pointed. At *her*.

Long brown hair was coiled around her shoulders like the finest silk. Her eyes were large, a deep color that looked like sun-dried honey. Her lips were pink, and full. Ripe for kissing. And her gaze, when it locked on mine, was defiant. Rebellious.

My body, my mind, everything became consumed with one

word. Mine. All I could think, all my brain, my body could consider was *mine. Mine. MINE.*

My mother stood between us, blocking my path to the female I was meant to claim, to fuck. And she was talking. Why was she still talking? "Yes, son, it was one of the maids. It was obvious she wasn't cleaning beneath my desk in my bedroom, and when I asked her what she was doing, she said she was tidying."

As my mother spoke, I stared at the maid. Her long hair was tucked behind her ears as if she weren't vain, if style wasn't a requirement. She was garbed in the simple household uniform, but it didn't hide the swells of her breasts, the narrow waist. With her sitting, I couldn't gauge her height, but she looked slight, as if I might be able to pick her up and carry her off to my bed without any strain.

It was her eyes though, the color of nature, that hooked me.

I didn't see fear in their depths, as if she'd been caught and was afraid for her life. No, I saw defiance and a hint of... peace. But after a few seconds of staring, they widened, as if she hadn't been surprised to be caught, but to see me. Something passed between us, some... current I didn't understand, but my cock liked.

Her full lips parted and a pink flush crept into her cheeks. Goddess, she was lovely. My cock agreed. There was no question, no doubt, that she was my mate. The one I would keep safe and whole... mine. Forever.

And fuck! She was the mole, the traitor who'd been trying to have the princess killed. Her. She was responsible for the deaths of several Jax family guards. The one to drag our name through the mud with the media. It seemed impossible by looking at her. She was a *maid*, for goddess' sake. Or was she?

My cock didn't care who she was. *What* she was. My mind though, needed answers. And since the police had supposedly been called for, I needed them now before she was taken away.

I strode over to her, the Jax guards stepping back to clear

my way. Taking hold of her arm, I tugged her to her feet and then across the room.

"I want to speak to her myself. Alone," I called, but not turning to look at either of my parents. I didn't give them time to argue, for we were through a side door and into the library before they could say a word. I shut the door behind me, spun her about and pressed her against it. Capturing her wrists, I lifted them up so they were by her head, my body keeping her pinned.

Fuck, she felt good. Soft in all the right places. Warm. And her scent. Yes, wild gardens, damp forests. She was what had been taunting me, awakening me.

My cock pulsed as it pressed against her belly. Lengthened. My balls drew up, ready to empty my cum into her. She'd awakened me. She was my mate, but I knew nothing about her.

"Who are you?"

Her eyes were wide and I watched her pupils dilate. I felt her warm breath on my face, felt the way she was all but panting. Her little pink tongue flicked out and licked her lower lip and I growled.

She whimpered in response.

"Tell me your name."

I couldn't help but roll my hips, my cock rubbing against her. Pre-cum seeped from the tip for the first time. I ached to be balls deep in her. To feel her pussy clamp down on my cock, to watch her face as she milked the cum from me. Fuck.

"You're going to jail, you little snoop. Or should I call you murderer? If you don't answer my questions, you'll answer theirs. Their tactics will be much less pleasant than mine."

I couldn't help it. Couldn't resist a second longer, so I kissed her.

Sweet, lush, her lips were perfect. She responded instantly, as if a fire had been smoldering, but now had the oxygen it needed to rage. Her lips parted and I took, my tongue finding hers, tangling.

She writhed against me, which only had my cock hardening impossibly further. The friction she created almost my undoing.

What was I doing? Kissing a traitor? I pulled my head back, never feeling so aroused in my entire life. "I want my cock so far inside you we won't know where I end and you begin."

A moan escaped her lips, which were now red and swollen, glistening from our kiss. I wanted to see them stretched wide around my cock, to feel that same lush tongue laving the crown and licking up every drop of my cum.

"If I'm going to jail, why are you kissing me?" she asked. Her voice was soft with a lilt to it. It called to me as if I'd heard it before. As if I'd heard it forever, even though it was the first time.

I pushed off the door, paced, ran my hand over the back of my neck. Stared at her. She was right. Why the fuck was I kissing a traitor?

I spun about, stalked close—but didn't touch—and asked, "What is your role in my parents' home?"

She looked down at herself in the bland uniform. It did nothing for her, only meant for her to blend into her surroundings, to disappear, like all servants should. But she could have worn a sack and she'd be beautiful.

"Maid."

"Ah, you answer a question," I replied, angry. Riled. I would never touch a woman in harm, especially not her. I wanted to fuck the questions right out of her and if that didn't work, deny her the orgasms I could wring from her body until she gave every one of her secrets to me.

I closed the space between us—she hadn't moved away from the door— and kissed her again, this time cupping her lush ass, pulling her up so her feet barely touched the floor. My cock was now aligned with her pussy and I rocked into her. Only our clothing separated us.

"You are pliant when aroused," I commented, noting she

was just as eager for me as I was for her. Our breaths mingled, our foreheads touched.

That made her still, her mouth close. Her little hands pressed against my chest to move me away, but I wouldn't give her an inch. "And your mate doesn't mind you fooling around with me to get answers?"

I stared at her, saw the hint of fire mixed with desire in her eyes, but there was outrage there as well, as if she thought *I* was in the wrong.

"Only awakened males get hard like you are. That means you have a mate out there somewhere... yet you're touching me. How dare you?"

She thought I was already mated, that I would cheat? That made my anger simmer, for I was too honorable to do such a thing. *She* was the one without honor, the one destroying the Jax name. And why?

Clearly, she didn't imagine that my cock was hard because of her, that she was the first woman I'd touched like this. Kissed. No, she thought me worse than a consort.

She had no idea she was mine, and for now, I would keep it that way.

"If you don't talk, then I won't either."

Her silence only implicated her further and I owed her nothing. An innocent would spout like the courtyard fountain, trying to save her pretty neck. I would not turn this interrogation about and let her get any more information from the Jax family. Or about my cock.

Her lips pinched together into a thin line. She thought me a cheat, an adulterer.

My cock was not happy about this, for it wanted me to strip her bare, tug her to the soft carpet and fuck her senseless. I would not use my first time with my mate as an interrogation tool. It would not be like that between us.

But what *would* it be like? Was she duplicitous? Dangerous not only to my family but all of Alera? She didn't seem like a mastermind to bring the downfall of the crown, but perhaps she was another pawn, like Zel. If she were being used falsely, blackmailed, I wanted to know.

Fuck, I wanted to know everything about her.

"The police are here." My father's voice carried through the thick door.

I stared at her, but she did not seem fearful of the threat of a Mytikas jail cell.

"Last chance," I offered. I could delay the police, even send them away if I had answers.

She only crossed her arms over those full breasts I'd felt, the hard nipples I ached to feel against my palms.

Stubborn thing. Perhaps seeing the team of law enforcement would entice her to talk. The idea of others pressuring her, even laying their hands on her, made me see red. Made every protective instinct flare to life. But I would not bed this female—my fucking mate—without answers. Without the truth. If she wouldn't give them to me, she'd have to give them to the police.

"So be it." I took her wrist, pulled her away from the door so I could open it, led her back into my father's office where he and my mother stood not just with the family's security detail, but with three police officers. They wore the familiar dark uniforms, ion blasters on their hips along with other paraphernalia related to law and order.

One stepped forward and the female backed up a half a step, then stood her ground. Her chin tipped up in defiance.

She was a brave little thing. I wanted to reach out, tug her behind me and protect her from these officers, to take her away and get her to tell me her every secret with soft persuasion.

But when the officer put his hand on her shoulder my thoughts changed. No, they scattered. Stalled.

Between one breath and the next, she'd widened her stance, reached across and took hold of the officer's hand, then used the other to strike up and out into his neck.

He bent slightly at the surprising contact, gurgled because her fingers had whipped into his throat. The hand holding her loosened and she twirled about, lowered to one knee and grabbed his ion pistol from his holster on his hip.

With just a flick of her finger, she shot him, the guard falling to the ground. There was no blood; she'd somehow set the weapon to stun.

Spinning on her heel, she aimed the weapon at the other guards, clearly ready to shoot.

Holy. Fucking. Shit.

She was no maid. No mild, forest-scented female. She was ruthless, cunning and wicked with advanced training in hand-to-hand fighting skills.

My mate was some kind of trained assassin. The fact that she hadn't killed the officer was a surprise. Or the rest of us. I didn't care that my cock had awakened because of her. Clearly, she was guilty. We needed answers from her more than I needed to strip her naked and bury myself balls deep.

My body disagreed. My cock didn't care who she was. It was practically ripping the fabric of my pants because they were so tight. It needed out, needed to be inside her. Now. Her little scene only made pre-cum slip from me, made me stifle a groan of desire.

She turned her head, looked up at me. That was her downfall.

The other officers took the opportunity to storm close, to retrieve the weapon from her. To subdue her. She fought, valiantly in fact. But her size was against her and she was quickly subdued. Cuffed. Lifted to her feet.

Her heated gaze held mine the entire time.

Perhaps I was her weakness. Perhaps she was mine. The attraction between us—from her side—was unmistakable. I hadn't had an unwilling female pressed against a door or my hard body. She had kissed me back, melded her heat to mine.

When I finally took her, the heat would be explosive.

I was torn. Grab her? Save her? Carry her off? She hadn't gotten her hands on my balls, but it felt like she had them in her grasp.

She had attacked an officer of the law. Stunned him with his own weapon.

For the moment, her fate was out of my hands. I had to watch her be dragged away. I knew she would be interrogated like the ruthless assassin she was and rot in jail, my cock be damned.

3

F *aith*

MY ENTIRE BODY felt like it was on fire.

Two men were manhandling me. My wrists were locked behind me in fancy alien handcuffs. My shoulders were torqued too far, aching.

Even with that discomfort, all I could do was stare at Lord Thordis Jax. At his lips, still wet from mine. At the huge cock tenting his pants. The feel of it as it pressed against me. At the dark urgency I saw in his eyes.

He wanted me, and I wanted to let him have anything he wanted. Which made absolutely no sense.

"You should let me go." I wasn't addressing the guards, or Lady Jax—who stood next to her mate with her chest heaving. I had to assume it was pure rage running through her body. Rage that I'd been in her room, digging through her things? Or rage that her son had had an erection the size of Texas in his pants and couldn't take his eyes off me?

"You're going to tell them everything you know, who you

work for, and why you are here." Thor, as I'd come to think of him since that was what his father called him, was looking down at me like he cared, like I mattered to him in some mysterious way. Which was total bullshit. He took a step forward, raised his fingers to trace the line of my jaw. The look in his eyes was contemplative. Unsure.

"How did you learn to fight like that? You took down a guard twice your size in seconds." His gaze dropped from my eyes to my lips, and if I didn't know better, I would have sworn that knowledge was making him hotter, not cooling him off.

"I don't know. I've never done that before." Another truth. Seemed my pussy wanted to keep this man happy, and *she* was currently in charge of my mouth. Nothing was affecting the pure, needy lust pulsing through me. Not even the two guards standing on either side of me, their meaty hands on my arms, holding me in place.

Hell, maybe that's what was turning him on? Did he like to tie up his women and have his wicked, wicked way with them?

A shudder passed through me at the thought and I licked my lips, needing to taste him again. He was so damn close. So close. But I couldn't move. Couldn't kiss him. Couldn't rub my body all over his. This Aleran Ardor was going to be the death of me. One stupid kiss and I had literally lost my freaking mind.

"Lies!" That was Lady Jax, and she was in a full rage. Her face was bright red and swollen, her eyes bulging from the sockets as if they would pop out of her head at any moment. Talk about needing a chill-pill. "Why are you destroying the Jax honor, a position in society we've had for centuries? Why?" she shouted the last, livid.

But being so harshly scolded did get my attention off her son long enough for me to regain a hint of dignity—and get my mind out of the gutter. But it was difficult.

First, that holy-hotness kiss from the only son. No heir and spare here. Thor was everything to this family, their future, and they thought I was jeopardizing it all. I'd thought him attractive in the portrait his father hung so proudly in the house. But up close and personal?

God. He smelled like heat and sex and raw manpower. I wanted to climb on top of him, under him, all over him. Peel off my clothes and just go skin on skin for hours.

Days.

He'd kissed me, his cock hard as a rock. Which meant he had to have a mate. I knew enough about Aleran males to know their cocks lay dormant until they met the right woman. Then... ping! The never-ending hard on. I'd seen it with Leo's instantaneous reaction to Trinity, and they'd barely been able to keep their hands off each other. And since I'd met Thor all of five minutes ago, I doubted all of that alien hotness was aimed at me. More likely, he was a spoiled aristocrat's son who thought the world owed him something—including all the women he wanted. I was a challenge, a hot piece of tail I could fuck, or fuck with, and forget. Or, in my case, send to jail.

Seemed things weren't all that different here on Alera than they were at home on Earth.

But then, Earth wasn't home anymore either.

I felt like I had no home. Not really. Not anymore. Especially with Trinity blatantly in the palace standing in for Mom. It wasn't like she was heading back to Earth anytime soon. Even if Mom was found, Leo wasn't going to relocate to suburbia. Even with Dad still there, it wasn't going to be the same. I knew too much. Understood there was more *out there* than just Earth.

And that lack of foundation made me weak. Vulnerable. Especially without my sisters, without anyone to know who I really was, what I was going through, the fears, the worries about Mom. God, just Thor's touch made me... feel, his kiss, and everything else. And that made it worse. I didn't care how freaking hot he was, I was *not* this week's plaything. Just because I was pretending to be a servant didn't mean I wanted his hands all over me.

But I did. Fuck and damn and shit and every other curse word my sister Destiny knew and I didn't. I *did* want him. Kissing me. Touching me. On top of me. Behind me. Under me. *Inside me.*

This stupid Ardor was ruining everything. Ever since I'd arrived on this planet, my body had decided that it was time to wake up. And not in a slow, I'm so sleepy, kind of way. No, this was a full on, zero-to-sixty, explosion. And my pussy was driving the car. Not me. Not. Me.

Still reeling from the kiss, adrenaline so thick in my bloodstream I could barely see straight, that damn cop, or security guard, or whatever the hell he was *put his hands on me.*

I had taken the basic self-defense class at the local Y. Mother had insisted we all could, at the very least, put up a fight. But I wasn't Destiny, especially since I lasted all of six months and took up tennis instead. She'd studied for years, obsessed with learning multiple styles of martial arts. Mastering all of them.

I could break a hold, use someone's weight against them, go for the soft spots. Knew to hit the groin, gouge eyes, break fingers. But that was about it. I did have an impressive back swing, but that did me no good.

What the hell had just happened? I'd gone all Kung Fu Master, Jackie Chan and even a little Jean Claude Van Damme on him. I'd actually assaulted a police officer. *Shot* him, as a matter of fact, with one of those fancy space guns I shouldn't even know how to use. I'd even flicked a button on it to make sure it only stunned him. I'd never even held one of those weapons before!

But somehow, I *just knew.* Just like I'd known how to shift my body weight and throw a stiff-handed strike to his windpipe.

I'd hit him *hard.* Looking around me, I jerked my head to the side to break the sexiest male alive's hold on my chin and found the guard staring at me like I had two heads. He was awake now, still sitting down, his back against the wall. He'd woken up from the stun mode he'd been blasted with and was rubbing his neck like it hurt.

I hated hurting things. Destiny and Trinity made fun of me, but I even let spiders go when I caught them in the house. "Sorry about that," I said to him. "I didn't mean to hit you so hard. Or stun you. You just startled me."

Was that shock on his face? The guard seemed nice enough. Just a regular guy doing his job. In his late thirties, maybe forty. He probably had a mate and two kids at home. "It's all right, miss. I'll be fine. Not a scratch on me."

"Oh, good. I'm so sorry. I really am." I smiled at him, a real smile, and he smiled back. Great. He really was going to be okay.

"Who are you?" The voice was deep and slid over my body like melted chocolate. Already, I'd recognize that voice anywhere. Good god, this Ardor stuff was for real.

For. Real.

"Faith. My name is Faith." I told him the truth but I didn't look into his eyes. I wasn't falling into that trap again. And no sense not using my real name since that's what his father knew, what I'd shared all along. None of these people knew who I was. No one was looking for Faith Jones from Earth. Other than my sisters, no one knew I was here.

Well, they knew Trinity came with two other royals because the spires had begun to glow the moment Destiny and I put our blood on the sacred stone. However, no one but Leo had seen my face.

Take that back, Leo, and the assassin who'd almost killed us.

I had no doubt if people knew who I really was, I'd be in danger, just like Trinity had been in. But Mytikas was a very big city. Millions of people. And I was quite sure whoever had kidnapped Mother and sent the assassins to kill me and my sisters would not even be looking for me here, in the Jax palace. Behind enemy lines, so to speak.

Perhaps, if I weren't Princess Faith Herakles of Alera, I'd be a bit more worried about being arrested. But the truth was, I knew all I had to do was name drop my sister, Trinity's identity, and I'd be free faster than I could snap my fingers.

The guards thought they held a prisoner. Lady Jax thought she'd caught a thief. A traitor.

I had no idea what Thor thought, but I really, really wanted to know.

Whatever it was, he was wrong. So wrong. And whatever this hot, kinky sex thing was between us, that wasn't happening either. I didn't have time for that. And my stupid pussy was just going to have to simmer down and wait.

Trinity's Ardor had hit while she was on Earth and she'd lasted months. *Months!* Surely, I could last a few weeks.

Lord Jax, the elder, a man I thought of as a friendly acquaintance, if not a brother at heart for the way he treated his pets, moved away from his frigid mate and came toward me. Thor took a step back out of respect, and I noticed the small movement with approval. His mother was a real piece of work, but his father? His father reminded me of Dad back home. Solid. Warm. No pretenses and no bullshit. Lord Jax wasn't as smart as my dad—the brilliant lawyer—but he was kind, eccentric even. I liked him. Which made this moment a lot harder than I'd imagined something like this might be.

"I'm surprised by this, Faith. I am. Even my pets liked you, and they don't care for anyone but me."

That brought my chin up with a snap and I realized I'd dropped it in shame, just like when *my* dad had come to give me a stern talking to. Usually well-deserved, but still, not fun. "They did? How could you tell?"

"They don't normally appear for others."

"She's seen those precious animals of yours?" Thor's shocked voice barely registered as Lord Jax and I were sharing a smile that felt like a secret handshake, like I'd just been granted membership to a secret club.

"They don't?" I asked. I'd spent hours in their presence. More than once, they'd actually looked at me, nearly come close enough to pet. The only reason I hadn't touched one was because I didn't want to ask permission, and I was afraid to anger Lord Jax.

"They do not. They are very selective, young lady. But I trust their judgment. So, tell me, who are you really and why were you snooping around in my home?"

"My love, she refuses to talk, so let the police take her away," Lady Jax intervened. "Lord Wyse and his team will get the truth out of her, which will certainly get the media attention off of us. The Jax family name can now be vindicated." She was as severe and uptight as I'd thought her before. I had to respect the one thing she had in spades, absolute love and loyalty to her family. I'd fucked with them and she disliked me for it. I couldn't really fault her for that. I'd watched her, listened to her conversations. She was like a lioness when it came to her son and her mate. No one fucked with them. No one undermined their position or their power. I respected her, for that alone.

But I'd also learned that the Jax family was more closely allied with the Wyse family, my cousins, as my mother had told me. Lord Wyse himself was the head of the Royal Guards' Optimus unit—which, as far as I could tell, was like the head of the FBI back home. The Inspector Optimi were detectives and district attorneys all rolled into one. They investigated crimes, examined the evidence, and prosecuted the guilty in the Aleran courts.

He was old, but sharp as a tack. He'd been to the house for dinner twice already in the short time I'd been here, spending long hours holed up in either the living area or library with either Lord or Lady Jax, or both. I'd learned that Lady Jax had once been an inspector herself, and a damn good one. The other servants told me that she was brilliant and was often consulted on cases now that she was retired.

So, basically, I'd just been caught snooping around in an FBI agent's bedroom.

Dumb. Unlike her distracted husband, she was too clever and too aware of everything going on around her. I should have waited for her to go to the market, or to a meeting. I should have waited until she was out of the house, not having a quickie with her mate just down the hall.

Oh well. Faith zero, Ardor one. I had a hard time waiting for anything the last few days. My patience was, well, non-existent.

"I'm sorry. I'm not your enemy. I promise you that." The words were for Thor, but I spoke to Lord Jax, whose disappointment was palpable, like a heavy fog pressing down on me, making it hard to breathe.

So much like my dad. I hoped he was okay, back on Earth. Giving those stupid alien chasers a run for their money.

"We will discover the truth. Have no doubt of that." Lady Jax stepped forward and slid her arm through her mate's to stand in solidarity with him. In that moment, she reminded me of my mother. "Take her away and be careful with her. She's obviously more dangerous than she lets on. Not only spying, but resisting arrest. I'll contact Lord Wyse at once."

The guards gripped my upper arms behind my back, pushed me toward the door and I didn't resist. Not this time, not with handcuffs on. The wild Kung Fu moves I'd used on the other guard still upset me. It was like an alien had taken over my body and I'd just been along for the ride. It had been real sci-fi movie kind of insanity, and I wanted no part of it. Except I was all "it."

The ride to the police station, or whatever they called it here, was shorter than I'd hoped. Less than twenty minutes later I was being led inside, scanned and scowled at and generally disliked instantly by anyone who saw the handcuffs. I was used to being adored by human and animal alike.

But they weren't human, no matter how much this looked or felt like home. I had to remember that.

They didn't take me to a cell. Instead, they dumped me into a room I recognized from watching one too many thriller movies. Dum-dum-dah—the interrogation room. Cold table. Stark white walls. One chair, presumably mine, bolted to the floor.

I thought they'd chain me down, but apparently, they didn't think I was much of a threat because the cuffs were removed and I was told to sit.

Sit. And wait.

4

F aith, *police headquarters, interrogation room #3*

I'D NEVER BEEN to a police station before, even on Earth. I hadn't really ever met a police officer. One had come to my second-grade classroom to give a talk about stranger danger, but that was as close as I'd ever gotten. I just never felt the need to break the law. Laugh at the rules? Push the envelope. Every day. But actually break the law?

That was more my twin sister, Destiny's, style.

Trinity had been the one to steal some of the neighbor's flowers to make a bouquet for Mother's Day. While it had been taking something that hadn't belonged to her, and our mother had required her to confess her transgression to poor Mrs. Kluger while holding a handful of the old woman's prized daffodils and tulips, it hadn't been serial killer level problems

Destiny had stolen a lipstick from the dollar store once. Mom had dragged her back, made her tell the manager, bought the lipstick, and then my poor twin had to wash dishes after dinner every night for a month to pay Mom back. Ridiculous since it had only been a dollar, but at ten years old, she'd learned tough love.

Yet here I was, the most innocent of the trio, and these people thought I was an assassin? I was the one sitting in police custody. I couldn't really blame them since I'd attacked the one officer. But what was going to happen now? I'd been sitting here for at least an hour—it felt that way since there was no clock—waiting. I had to pee and I wondered if making me uncomfortable was part of their scare tactic.

Deny me a bathroom, food and water, sleep. Was I in for waterboarding, too?

Lord Jax had been disappointed. I'd seen the sad, resigned look in his eyes and the slump of his shoulders. He wasn't going to rescue me. He wanted answers.

Lady Jax? Ha! Enough said there. She lived to make me feel small.

And Thor? God, my body heated just thinking of him. I raised my hands to my lips, felt them still tingle from his aggressive kisses. My nipples had a mind of their own and formed hard points beneath my bra. Instant attraction wasn't going to save me. He might want to fuck me, but he hadn't been thinking with the head in his pants there at the end. It felt good to know he wouldn't fuck anyone, especially a potential planetary threat like me.

His cock had some discretion, or at least his mind did.

And as for me, did I have *any* discretion left? I had no idea if he were mated, widowed or what. He might even have kids at home and I'd been ready to climb him like a monkey. I wasn't a virgin, but I was careful. Until now. Until this stupid Ardor.

I shifted in my chair. No, I *was* selective. I'd found other household staff attractive, had a few of the hotter Aleran males make my Ardor simmer, but I hadn't been ready to ride them like a cowgirl. It was Thor who made me forget everything except all that hard, thick length he had in his pants.

I licked my lips, wondering what his skin would taste like. It was hard to remember *he* could possibly be the traitor himself. Someone had sent Zel to kill us that first night, and then again to kidnap Trinity at the reception. All signs led to the Jax family, and yet I was thinking about a possible suspect taking me slowly, or shoving me against the wall and fucking me like a wild man.

I was trying to decide which I would prefer—slow or hard —when the door of the interrogation room opened and in came one, two... four men.

My cheeks heated, although I knew they couldn't read my thoughts.

"I am Inspector Wyse," the first one said. Based on his outfit and demeanor, it was clear he was in charge. "Lord of the Wyse family and the Inspector Optimi in the Optimus unit. Do you know what that means?"

Shit.

I had heard about them from mother for years. They were the detective, judge and jury all in one. He could decide I was guilty and lock me away for years, especially being Inspector Optimi, fancy title for head honcho.

All of a sudden I wished I was back home with an over-worked public defender. My dad was a judge. He loved the rule of law.

This man clearly loved power.

Inspector Wyse appeared to be in his late sixties, maybe even early seventies. Graying hair, deep lines in his chiseled features. But his spine was straight, his bearing, no nonsense. I got not one bit of kindness off him. He was all business, and his business today was me.

Based on their uniforms, two of the males with him were police officers. Their clothing matched those who came to the Jax house and took me away. The other guy looked like an evil sidekick. His eyes were deeply set and looked dead. No hint of laughter or amusement there. A deep scar slashed down the side of his face in a hook-like shape from the corner of his mouth down past his jaw. His uniform was clearly military, but basic black. No insignia or house symbols. He could have been anyone. Anything.

Or nothing.

Everything about him made me think of mafia enforcers or black ops. I really, really hoped it wasn't the first.

Scarface looked me over, and from his standing position, made me feel small. I knew it was intentional, but it was working anyway. I wasn't anything exciting to look at. My brown hair was tucked behind my ears, I had on no makeup and I wore the simple Jax maid's uniform.

"You have one opportunity to talk. To tell us who you really are, why you were in the Jax household and why you were snooping around. I recommend taking it, for if you don't..."

He let that hang, like a dangling carrot. Sing like a canary and put my mother and sisters in danger, or else.

"If I don't?" I countered.

His salt and pepper brow went up and Scarface crossed his arms over his chest. He didn't need to do that to be intimidating. He was scary as hell just by breathing.

The corner of Lord Wyse's mouth tipped up. He flicked a glance at the police officers. "This is just a basic interrogation room at a precinct of the Mytikas police. They handle minor crimes, simple thugs. You recognize my uniform?" he asked.

"You just said you're with the Optimus unit." I didn't want to deny it. I had no doubt all of Alera knew of this elite group. It would be like denying knowledge of the FBI. I didn't have to be in their custody to know of the FBI's existence, and their power in the US.

"Yes, and the Optimus unit has enough intelligence data power to know that you do not exist. There are no fingerprints, no eye scans or birth records. Nothing about you, Faith. Why is that? You must have very interesting friends, indeed. Friends with a lot of money. Connections." He leaned over the table and stared down into my eyes like he was examining an insect. Creep. "Power."

Yeah, the identity thing was a problem. I wasn't born here, didn't have a driver's license, bank account, own or rent a house. I had no idea how they tracked people on Alera, but I assumed it was all the same kind of things. Birth certificate. Medical records. Schooling.

I didn't exist in planetary databases because I hadn't existed on Alera until recently. I just had to hope they wouldn't do a DNA analysis or something because then it would become obvious who I was. DNA didn't lie. My lineage would be verified. My mother would be instantly identified as the queen and myself as Trinity's sister.

I slid my hands off the table and folded them in my lap. Clenched my fingers together. Maybe I could string him along for a while? Buy myself some time to figure out what to do next.

"What intelligence are you trying to gather on the Jax family?" he asked, leaning even farther forward and putting his palms flat on the table. This close, I could see his eyes were a dark blue.

I lifted my chin, remained silent. They'd found me in the Jax mansion. He thought I was interested in the that family. He believed that I was seeking intel on them specifically. I was, but it was because they'd sent bad guys to kill me and my sisters. Almost accomplished the task, too. Fortunately, there was no reason for him to make a mental leap from a maid to the royal line. And no one outside of the Jax family and the men who'd died knew what had happened the night of our arrival on this planet.

It wasn't like they put all those dead guards on the news. I knew. I'd been watching.

For once, I was grateful that I looked more like my dad, with my brown hair and eyes, than I did like my mother or Trinity. They were both beautiful blondes with fair skin and blue eyes. There was absolutely zero family resemblance. Thank god.

"I have nothing to say to you." I couldn't say I wanted a lawyer. I had no idea what the rules were on Alera. Were people innocent until proven otherwise? Were they provided legal counsel? I wasn't going to give myself away by asking.

Those laws were set in place by the queen, but they had been operating without one of those for almost thirty years. Who knew what kind of insanity they had created in my mother's absence.

He stood to his full height, glanced at the officers and snapped his fingers. They moved and stood on either side of me.

"Very well. We will continue this conversation in an environment that is more conducive to... talking."

I didn't think he was referencing a comfortable sofa and a few glasses of wine.

Scarface laughed. "Optimus cell level C will get her talking within an hour."

My blood went cold at the thought of what might happen on this infamous level C, but I wasn't going to relent now. I couldn't share about Trinity, about my status. Nothing. I had to keep quiet at all costs. I had to buy them more time. Talking now could endanger my mother. Scared people did stupid things, like kill hostages to hide their tracks.

The Jones sisters needed more time. My mother needed more time. I just hoped it didn't cost me too much.

The guards grabbed my upper arms and tugged me to my feet, the chair beneath me sliding across the smooth floor.

I didn't think, but acted, a flood of energy pouring into my body like hot water filling me from the feet up.

I felt powerful.

Invincible.

Pivoting on my serviceable maid shoes, I straightened my arm and angled up, my heel palm catching one officer in the nose. The sound of crunching bone was loud in the room. The other officer tugged me back and I used that momentum to elbow him in the solar plexus, causing him to bend over. I grabbed the back of his head, pulled him down as I raised my knee and got him in the face.

Neither guy was subdued entirely, but definitely stunned as I kept at them, trying to get them unconscious and on the floor. They had at least fifty pounds on me and several inches. They weren't going down easily. It was Scarface who stopped me and only with the stun of an ion pistol. I went rigid and began to tip over, but I was grabbed and held upright. I was just thankful I didn't pee myself as I felt handcuffs going back around my wrists behind my back.

It was a low stun setting, for I was paralyzed for all of twenty seconds or so. Long enough to totally freak me out and to get me in bigger trouble than ever.

Why had I attacked the two officers like hell-raising Destiny? I hadn't even thought, just reacted. I didn't like them touching me, manhandling me. I had no interest in going to wherever the hell Optimus cell level C was. But now I was absolutely headed that way. Alone. Cuffed. No one was going to help me, especially since they now probably considered me a tad dangerous. No one was going to save me. I'd have to figure something out myself.

Trinity and Leo didn't know I was here. Destiny was a flipping nun somewhere. The only way I was getting out of this was to talk and that wasn't happening.

I'd rot in jail for a while if I had to. Destiny needed time to finish her mission. Trinity needed time to solidify her claim on the throne. They needed more time to hunt for our mother.

And I still wasn't done with my task. There was a traitor in the Jax house, a traitor who would lead me to our mother. And I really hoped it wasn't Thor, that the traitor himself hadn't just kissed all good sense right out of me and then watched me be dragged away by my mother's enemies.

∖⫯∕

THOR

THE MINUTE FAITH had been led from the house, settled into the backseat of the police vehicle and driven away, I'd gone insane.

I didn't go berserker in my parents' home, but I wasn't rational either. Someone had my mate. In handcuffs. And she was being taken away from me.

There was a very primal part of me that didn't care who she was, what she'd done or why. I wanted to protect her, keep her safe from anything the police planned to do to her.

The thought of her in the big building downtown had me panicking. There were real criminals there. Thugs. Those who might want to hurt her. She was slight. Small. I remembered every soft inch of her. Someone could take advantage, *touch* her.

Hurt her.

Instead of going back into the house and talking with my parents, I left without a word. Went home. The peace and quiet of my apartment only made me crazier. I paced, as best I could with a fucking rock-hard cock. In the middle of my living room, with views of the city in two directions a dozen floors below, I opened up my pants and pulled out my cock. Looked at it. Stroked it. Watched pre-cum slide down the crown and over my fingers.

I'd never seen it this hard before, never knew it could get this big. Never knew the pleasure I'd feel as I stroked up and down the length. I hissed out a breath and thought of Faith.

I groaned, pulled my hand away.

No! I shouldn't think of the female who was so obviously an enemy of my family. After Zel had attacked Princess Trinity— and him being from the family's squad—I'd had to be vigilant.

There was still a traitor in my family home, and I didn't believe the female I'd kissed was capable of such evil. I just couldn't imagine Faith giving Zel orders to kill the princess.

It wasn't impossible, but highly improbable.

That wasn't my head talking, but my heart. My body. I didn't want to believe the female destined to be mine was part of such a diabolical plot.

But then there was my cock, angled thick and long up to my navel. Bobbing as if it were seeking out a mate. Looking for Faith.

She was my mate. There was no question. It was as if my cock were an arrow, pointing right at her. The only more obvious sign of our connection would be if the goddess had a tree fall from the sky and knock me out.

Faith was mine. And she was in police custody. Mother had called for Lord Wyse the moment the guards disappeared with Faith. Lord Wyse meant the Optimus unit. And that meant—

"Fuck," I growled, shoving my angry cock back in my pants and heading for the door.

If Lord Wyse—who was the Inspector Optimi of that ruthless organization—got his hands on Faith, he would not be gentle. He'd treat her like one of the most dangerous criminals, especially with all the media attention on the Jax family. Having a suspect would make the Optimus unit look like it was doing its job—which it was possible it was—and settle unrest throughout Alera. A suspect had been caught in the attempted murder of the princess.

Big news.

Perhaps she was, but I was getting her out of there. If she needed to be punished, I'd do it. I'd spank her ass until she talked, until she gave me everything. Her pleasure, her secrets and her body.

Twenty minutes later, I stormed into the station and asked for Lord Wyse personally. The officer, I could tell, recognized me. Probably from the fucking media. I was the heir apparent to the Jax name. The family who'd masterminded the attacks on Princess Trinity. We weren't well-liked, vilified in fact. And the way this officer looked at me with such scorn and distaste, he believed the reports.

Instead of offering me help, he turned away. Ignored me. Snubbed me and the Jax family.

Before I could lose my shit, the Optimus leader came down the long hallway. Faith was with him, her hands cuffed behind her back again. She looked unhurt. Not happy, but whole.

My cock practically worked its way out of my pants at the sight of her.

Mate.

Claim.

Fuck.

Possess.

I could barely see more, the need that consumed me narrowing my focus to her. Only her. The need that ached and drove me to step in front of Lord Wyse, blocking his way, blocking the path of one of the most powerful males on the planet.

"Thordis Jax," he said in way of greeting. "We are about to take the prisoner to Optimus headquarters. Do not concern yourself; we will gain all information from her before we're through—and pass it along to your father, of course. I have no doubt your family's name will be cleared quickly. Once she talks."

Faith stood stoic, eyes on me as he spoke of the vile, unspeakable things they might do to her once they took her to their *headquarters*. Only the most violent criminals were interrogated there. It was a prison, nothing less. If they took her there and locked her up, it would become much more difficult to secure her freedom, and I'd have to fight this arrogant asshole every step of the way.

"That will not be necessary," I said.

"You don't want your family's honor back? She has not told

us anything," Lord Wyse said. "She was combative. Violent. She might look meek and mild, but she is a threat to society. To your *family*."

That was obvious based on the way I'd been treated at just approaching the fucking front desk.

I took a moment to look at the two officers who had their hands on her shoulders. One had blood stains on his face, his nose swollen. The other didn't look injured, but neither looked happy. In fact, they looked furious.

She'd attacked two more officers? I stifled a smile, for Lord Wyse was correct. She wasn't meek at all. No, my mate had a fire in her that I ached to see expressed in *other* ways. She would be full of passion and I longed to awaken it. To see it. Hear it. *Feel* it.

"The Jax family will not be pressing charges. Release her at once."

Faith's mouth opened in surprise, but she remained silent. Once I had her beneath me, she'd talk. I wanted her to tell me every secret, but I had no problem starting that particular conversation with her saying *more* and *harder* and *yes*.

"Excuse me?" Lord Wyse asked, as if he hadn't heard me.

"We are not pressing charges; therefore, you can remove the handcuffs and set her free."

"Your mother will not agree. Your family name has been—"

He spoke to me as if I were a child, and it only made me more eager to get her the fuck away from him. "I am well aware of the perception of my family." I glared at the officer who'd snubbed me. "My mother is not here. I am. I represent the Jax name. I am not pressing charges," I repeated. "Set her free."

"She attacked two officers," he countered.

"Did they touch her?" I asked, ready to punch them myself.

Lord Wyse lifted his chin. "They helped her from her chair."

I narrowed my eyes. "No one touches my mate."

"Your *mate*?" Lord Wyse's eyes widened, then lowered to

take in my cock. Yes, it was completely hard and obvious. Proof I was not lying.

"I will not be denied her. You have a choice, Lord Wyse. My mate is set free or I will be the next person to attack your officers for denying me what is rightfully mine. Set. Her. Free."

The officers must have noticed something in me—more than my huge cock—and took a step back from Faith, their hands falling from her shoulders. It had never happened to me before now, but everyone knew a newly awakened Aleran male should not be denied his mate in any way or all fucking hell would break loose.

"I assure you, Faith will not be out of my sight, or out of my bed, for at least a week."

He had no choice. Even the law was on my side in this. Without a Jax representative pressing charges, Faith was just a snooping maid. As for resisting arrest, I could easily argue to a judge that she did not wish to be parted from me, her awakened mate. My cock was as irresistible to her as her pussy was to me.

Lord Wyse's face turned a mottled red and veins stood out on his temples. He wasn't happy uttering the words, "Release her."

The cuffs were immediately removed and I pulled Faith into my arms. Thank the goddess she did not resist but melted into me as if she belonged there. Was part of me. Fuck, she felt good. The ache in my chest at being separated from her lessened, but my need to protect was running rampant. I was ready to beat the shit out of Lord Wyse and the guards, even those in the lobby of the police station who had nothing to do with the entire mess.

It seemed finding one's mate made mere mortals totally irrational.

She remained silent as I led her from the building. One glance over my shoulder and I saw Lord Wyse, watching. His sidekick with the scar on his face right beside him. They weren't happy.

But my cock was. And soon, it would be even happier because it would be buried deep in Faith's pussy. She was mine. I would seduce her. Kiss her senseless. Make her feel safe and wanted and protected. And she would tell me the truth. I would find out if she was a traitor just as I would learn every inch of her body.

Before I was finished, she'd trust me with everything. She was mine, and I would accept nothing less than her complete surrender.

5

F *aith, Thor's apartment*

"THANK YOU." I said the words quietly, tentatively. While Thor had yanked me from the ruthless intentions of Lord Wyse, I couldn't say he was thrilled about it. He hadn't said a word since we left the police station. But he'd said one word *at* the station that had my brain swirling until I was dizzy.

Mate.

He'd called me his mate and he'd behaved as I'd seen Leo act around Trinity. Like a lunatic. Thor had to be crazed with lust to drop the charges against me and bring me to his apartment. I'd been caught red-handed snooping in his mother's bedroom. I hadn't stated my reasons or given him any information whatsoever to clear my name. And yet he'd pissed off Lord Wyse—that had been quite obvious—and pulled me into his side.

God, that had felt good. For once, I'd felt as if someone had my back, that I wasn't alone. From what he'd said, he'd have my front too. And everywhere in between. He had no plans to let me out of his apartment, or his bed, for a week. His words.

Mate. Bed. Week.

My Ardor liked all of those words very much. And my Ardor liked Thor, too. Every tall, blond and muscled inch of him. It would be like having Captain America eager to fuck the Ardor right out of me.

But Thor was a Jax. Someone in his family had sent Zel to kill me and my sisters. Someone in the Jax family had known we were arriving on Alera, knew we were threats to... well, we didn't know who. I'd been snooping in Thor's house to find out.

Was I truly mated to the heir of a family who wanted mine dead? Could I use him to soothe my Ardor like a consort? He was willing—his cock blatantly gave him away. Could I let him inside my body, give him something so personal, so intimate, when he thought I might be a traitor?

I wasn't a nun. I liked sex. But I didn't do well separating the act from my emotions. Inevitably, my heart got all tangled up in the transaction, whether I wanted it to or not. I didn't know this male. I knew *of him*. His father had talked non-stop about his precious son. His perfect, precious boy. A stranger I'd allowed to kiss me.

A stranger I did want inside me. Badly. My body trembled with the urge to run at him and pounce like a wild animal. This fucking Aleran Ardor was *serious*. I felt like I was coming out of my own skin. I hurt everywhere. Hungered.

Needed. I needed his energy to sustain me. His intensity. His body.

He believed I was his enemy, and yet here I was in his apartment—he hadn't taken me back to the Jax mansion, but to his own home—standing in front of Thor, who looked at me as if he were the wild animal, a tiger ready to pounce on a tiny, fluffy bunny. Not because I was innocent of wrongdoing, but because I was his mate.

His mate!

Holy shit balls.

This relationship soooo wasn't going to work.

But couldn't that be discussed *after* my Ardor was soothed by a virgin alien hottie? He *was* a virgin. He had to be. Based on everything Leo had said, the way he had behaved toward Trinity, Thor had all the signs. Okay, the huge cock. The protectiveness, the possessiveness. The laser sharp focus. The words. Mate. Mine. Bed. Week.

Yeah, he wanted sex. His cock was hard. Eager. Ready. If I were a virgin, I'd want to finally... *finally,* have sex.

My pussy clenched and I rubbed my thighs together. My clit throbbed, all but saying *JUMP HIM NOW.* If I stared at him for another moment, imagined him rubbing his huge cock inside me, his body covering mine. God, *his scent*—

"Come," Thor ordered.

I shivered and let my lids fall closed, for I did just that. A baby orgasm, because his voice was deep, commanding and well... I was *primed.*

When I opened my eyes, I saw Thor staring at me. I'd never seen such heat, such need. He knew what that one word had done. But he had his hand out. He hadn't ordered me to climax, he'd wanted me to go with him.

That worked, too.

There was an electric sizzle when our hands touched. And that was just our palms. Our fingers. What would it be like when he put tab A in slot B? If he could get me to come from one word, I'd probably pass out from his cock deep in my pussy.

He led me into his bathing room, stopped me directly in front of the shower. Bathing tube. Whatever.

"If I kiss you, I won't stop. I'll press you up against the wall and fuck you until you scream my name," he admitted.

Yeah, that was probably true, and I'd totally let him.

"So no kissing." He paused, eyed me. "Yet. I'm sure you want to wash off the feel of the police station."

I nodded. Thoughtful, too? I was totally fucked.

Well, soon, I hoped.

He reached past me so his chest brushed my shoulder and he pushed a button on the wall. The shower turned on behind me. He didn't move away. I breathed in his scent, male and dark and screaming of sex.

Everything about him screamed sex.

I swallowed hard and slipped past him. He was using restraint. I would need to as well, at least until after I felt clean again.

I started to unbutton the front of my uniform, glanced at Thor. His gaze was on my fingers, but raised to mine when I stopped. He turned to face me and the shower tube, crossed his arms over his chest.

"I'm going to watch."

If I got in the shower, I couldn't get much wetter. Oh. My. God.

Even in a serviceable maid uniform, he wanted me. I toed off one shoe, then the other. I lifted the shirt up and over my head, let it fall to the floor. My hair slid long over my bare back and I felt exposed. But the way he dropped his arms to his sides, his hands curling into fists as if he were trying not to reach out and touch me, I felt... powerful.

And I knew he'd never seen sexy lingerie like I was wearing. It wasn't as if I'd had time—or Aleran money—to go find a store that sold sexy underthings. No, in my free time in the Jax household, I'd played with the S-Gen machine in my room and gotten it to spit out some fancy, totally sexy bra and panty sets. What else was I going to do? Read? Watch the screen with images of Trinity wearing fancy ball gowns and having fun at the palace while I mopped floors and skulked around in a maid uniform?

Ummm, no.

"What the fuck is that?" Thor asked, stepping closer, his gaze squarely on the swells of my boobs. I had on a black push-up bra made of shiny satin cups, with accent ribbons on either side of my breasts that went up to the strap, leaving sections of my curves bare. The nipples were covered, but the thin material did nothing to hide how hard they were. The underwires—that had taken a little time to program successfully—lifted the girls up so they looked more C cup than B.

I glanced down at my chest, smiled. Hot lingerie for the win. I playfully ran my hand along the ribbons and Thor groaned. "This?" I asked.

"Holy fuck," he growled.

I worked off my pants, let them fall to the floor, let him see the matching bottoms—which didn't cover my bottom at all. It was a satin thong with ribbons in the back that went from the center string out to the waistband in a way that matched the bra.

I didn't have time to blink before he slapped the button to turn off the water and then tossed me over his shoulder like a sack of potatoes and carried me out of the bathing room. I smacked Thor's back playfully, and felt all the tense, hard muscles.

"Thor!" I cried and grinned, although he couldn't see it. I watched as his butt muscles flexed and moved as he did. It had to be the Ardor that wanted me to take a bite out of one taut cheek.

"I am only so strong, mate." He dropped me on his bed and I bounced, but then he pounced.

He caged me in with his body and I looked up into his eyes. A gorgeous blue flecked with gray, the color reminding me of my favorite pair of jeans. His skin was darker than mine, as if he'd spent the summer outside. His nose was long, regal even. His jaw was square and rigid—I assumed from his unrequited need—and could cut diamonds. His hair fell over his forehead and I wanted to reach up and brush it back, but he had my wrists pinned beside my head.

"I can't wait any longer to make you mine," he said.

I may have taunted him with the lingerie, but I was teasing myself, too. Why was I stalling, waiting a second longer?

"Yes," I breathed, and that was all it took for him to lower his head and kiss me.

His hands roved over me, warm and gentle, yet with a fervency I felt myself.

He was wearing too many clothes. Tugging at the hem of his shirt, I worked it up. He lifted his head long enough to pull it over his head and we both groaned at the contact of skin on skin.

"Please," I begged, my leg bending so I could slide it along his. My hands went to the opening of his pants.

He pushed off me, stood at the foot of the bed, stripped. Naked. He was magnificent. All sharp angles and bulging muscle. His chest could grace the cover of a thousand romance novels, and his washboard abs? I wanted to lick them. Rub my nipples over them. Rub *me* all over them.

I came up onto my elbows to watch as he shucked his pants. "Wow," I said when his cock bobbed before him. Thick, long, bulging veins and a glorious crown.

His hand gripped the base and he stroked the full length. "Those scraps of fabric are sexy, but I want you bare, mate. I want to see what belongs to me."

Well, I didn't want to have the whole mate-not-mate, this is never going to work out argument right this moment. I wanted that hard, long, rigid cock filling me up. I sat up, undid my bra, worked off my panties until I was naked before him.

He took a step closer, ran a knuckle over one nipple, then pushed me back with a gentle nudge to my shoulder.

I fell on my back, knees bent. He climbed onto the bed, parted my thighs and stared.

I wasn't usually that self-conscious naked, but I was now. I was wet, ridiculously so, and he wouldn't miss it glistening on my thighs, my pussy. I shaved... there, keeping it neat and trim. I refused to go completely bare, but I hoped he liked what he saw. Pussies came in all shapes and colors and god, did I look appealing to him?

He groaned and practically dove between my legs. His mouth was on me, like my juices were the sustenance that he needed to stay alive.

I arched my back and wrapped my knees around his head. "Oh shit!" I cried.

The feel of his mouth was like dumping kerosene on a fire. Hot, intense, brilliant heat.

My temperature rose to a feverish level. I could feel the shudders passing through me, the ache intensifying as the energy built between us.

I needed him, not just to fuck me, but to cover me, burn his energy into me. I needed to absorb it, fill myself up with him.

I'd been primed and ready to come forever, it seemed. This Ardor thing had me on the brink of coming in seconds. I'd had a guy go down on me before, but it hadn't been like this. It was like Thor was learning my taste, every curve and hot spot.

The Ardor went from simmer to explosion and I twisted my fingers in his hair, pulled him up my body. "More." I needed. That was all I had to give him.

"Tell me what you want," he commented, kissing and licking his way up my body. Every touch was like a brand, his hot breath fanning my needy flesh.

He pushed up onto his elbows, hovered over me, moved so his hips were between mine. He looked down at me with slick lips, a slight grin.

"You. Thor, please." I arched my back, squirming under him, trying to take him in, get him where I really, really needed him to be.

"You're beautiful," he commented, not lifting his eyes from mine. His cock slid over me there, the head circled my core, taunting me, teasing me. Though I knew he was a virgin, he definitely wasn't acting as if he'd never touched a pussy, or seen one before. Then I remembered Leo stating he'd taken some sex-ed classes, that all guys on Alera were required so their mate—when found—would be well-pleased.

"Stop making me beg," I pleaded, squirming and ready.

"Need a big cock filling you up?" he asked, lowering himself so that our lips touched, our breath mingled. He settled his cock at my entrance. The hard, yet hot, tip pressed against me.

"Yes. Now!" I cried, frustrated. I hooked a foot behind his back and tried to pull him down.

"You're mine. My mate."

I knew what he wanted, but I couldn't go there. Not right now. Tears of frustration leaked from the corner of my eye. He saw it, kissed the wetness away.

"You're mine. Whatever is between us, we will figure it out. I'm not letting you go." He didn't wait a second longer, just pushed in, one thick, long inch at a time.

He wasn't breathing, just watching my face as he filled me completely, connecting us.

"Fuck. You feel so good," he finally said when he bottomed out, when I'd taken all of him.

My inner walls clenched, trying to adjust to him. I rocked up, taking him a touch deeper. I used my heels on his back once again to push him in. "More. Please."

He grinned, but it was hard-edged, as if he were still holding on to his control. "As my mate wishes."

He settled his lips on mine, taking everything, giving everything, and fucked me. There was no other word for it. Hard, deep, thorough. He moved as if learning what felt good, watching to know what I liked, what made my back arch, made moans slip from my lips.

My Ardor rose with a roar to claim what it wanted, pulling his heat inside my body everywhere our skin touched. I rubbed my legs on his, buried my hands in his hair, held him to me, taking his kiss. His touch. His heat.

It was as if my body was starved for him, literally starved. Dying. Needy.

"Goddess, yes. Take it. Take it all." He groaned as his heat filled me and I knew, somehow he could feel what I was doing to him. It was kinky and weird and I felt like a vampire, but I didn't think I could stop. They called it the Aleran Ardor. But I had a new name for it.

The emptiness. I needed him to fill me up. With his kiss, his body, his heat and his cum. I wanted all of him. And then I wanted it all again and again.

And again.

"Thor, god, please!" I needed to come, but my body was his. So hot. So fucking hot. I needed him to talk dirty to me. To get me off.

"Do you want to come?"

I nodded against the soft bed. "Yes."

"Are you mine?"

My pussy clenched down on him and I gasped, sobbed.

"Your pussy knows you're mine." He thrust hard. Deep. Stopped moving. My pussy was so swollen and sensitive, so hot. I could feel every inch of him. His cock. His body. Mine. He was wrong. *He* was *mine.* I was a fucking princess. Surely, I could figure out a way to keep him if I wanted to.

I squeezed my inner muscles, teasing both of us. His growl made me feel very feminine. Powerful.

And I drank him in, skin on skin. The Ardor a greedy bitch at the moment, but he didn't seem to mind. In fact, the more I let go, the more he gave, his tongue in my mouth, his body rubbing along mine, his cock inside me.

"More."

"Are you mine?" he asked again.

He was going to be stubborn? Fine. Two could play that game.

Reaching down around my hip, then my ass, I found what I was looking for.

His balls hung thick and heavy. Exposed.

I touched them gently. Held them. Rolled them between my fingers.

"Female, you are my undoing." He groaned but gave in, fucking me hard. Fast. Deep. Giving me what I needed.

"Come now. Fucking come."

So dirty. So fucking hot. He was wild, out of control, his balls jerking and spasming in my hand as I held them, his cum filling me up.

I dropped my hand, took the sheet in my fist and screamed as I shattered into a thousand pieces, the orgasm so hard and fast, so intense that I lost all sense of where I was.

But I knew who was covering me with protective heat. Whose energy was somehow merging with mine, making me hotter than I'd ever felt in my life. Whose cock was inside me. Whose cum coated my inner thighs.

Thor. Thordis Jax.

Enemy.

And I wanted him again.

6

T *hor*

SHE CAME ON COMMAND, her hot pussy pulsing around me like a heated fist. I could barely catch my breath. My muscles were lax, my bones having melted sometime while I came. Goddess, my balls had tightened and I'd emptied myself into Faith. Not just my cum, but my very being. She was my mate and what we'd shared for the first time had been incredible.

My cock hadn't flagged. It was still just as hard as the first moment it awakened. I'd come and come hard, but it wasn't done. Just looking down at Faith, seeing her skin flushed and slick with sweat, her nipples softening into plump pink tips, her legs parted casually to fit my body... it was enough to make me crazed to lean down and kiss her, tease her, touch her, make her needy. And do it all again. But feeling her pussy, all rosy and swollen, my seed slipping from her delicate folds, had my need rushing back with all the intensity of a no-longer-a-virgin male.

"I want you again." Her husky voice went straight to my

cock and the self-satisfied bastard pulsed into instant iron, so hard I clenched my jaw on a sharp intake of breath.

It hurt. I wanted her so fucking badly that I was in pain. I never knew it would be like this. To feel so amazingly good. That the top of my head felt like it was going to blow off; that when I came, I thought I'd gone blind. That my balls would ache with a desperation I'd never imagined. I had one focus and one focus only.

Fuck.

Shifting my hips, I pulled out of her body, leaving her with just the head of my hard cock inside her. She moaned, locked her ankles around my thighs, tried to lift her hips up off the bed, impale herself.

I held her down. "I'll fuck you, mate. I'll fuck you until you're used up, until you can't move, until the need you feel is sated."

"Gaaawd, yes." She wrapped her hands in my hair and pulled my mouth to hers, kissing me like she'd never get enough.

Goddess help me, she was going to kill me. I'd never be able to deny her. Never.

But she mustn't know that. Not yet.

Pushing into her, I felt her body open up, take all of me. She groaned as I bottomed out inside her. Cried out when I pulled back once more.

"But you're going to give me answers." I thrust hard, deep, much faster than I had the first time and she arched up off the bed, panting. I could give my body what it needed—and hers— as I interrogated her.

"I can't." She rubbed against me like a wild pet, eager to be touched. "Too dangerous."

Fuck. Was she protecting me? That didn't make sense. It was my job as her mate to protect her. But my body didn't care about semantics right now, neither did my cock, pulsing inside her, growing even larger, swelling with the need to come again.

She felt it, she must have, for she tossed her head back on the bed, exposed her neck to me in a long, delicate line. She had no idea how much trust was in that simple gesture, but I did. And so did the instinct raging in me to claim her, tame her, make sure she stayed with me forever.

I lowered my lips to the soft, exposed skin and nibbled, kissed, suckled, leaving my mark on her there as I thrust in and out of her hot, wet pussy. She offered and I took it all, every moan, every whimper, every sound she made was mine.

The heat between us rose once more and my dominant, male energy responded, covering her with heat, energy, the life force she needed to take in and be whole.

The sensation of flowing into her was terrifying and thrilling all at once. I couldn't stop it. She could drain me dry, and I'd give her everything I had without thinking twice.

That was the terrifying part. I knew nothing about her but her name. No history. No surname. I didn't know where she was from, how old she was, if she was alone in the world or was already promised to another. Why she'd been in my mother's bedroom. Why she thought talking to me was dangerous.

Nothing. I knew nothing.

No. Not nothing. I knew her pussy was hot. Wet. Swollen. I knew her skin tasted like heaven on my tongue, so soft it would put the petals of the Aleran flower to shame. I knew the wild, needy sounds she made as I fucked her drove all rational thought from my mind. I knew I'd die, if I had to, to fill her up. To ease her Ardor. To make her mine.

Insanity was too mild a word. This was obsession.

Males had been doing this for females in Ardor for thousands of years, so I wasn't worried that her Ardor would actually kill me.

But goddess, the pleasure might. A virgin fucking the need out of her. Laughable. But my cock was up for the task.

I'd been told it would take a while for my need for my mate to settle, for my body to be assuaged enough, to know that she was truly mine forever. Good thing I told Lord Wyse I'd have her in bed for a week. I'd spoken then with the need to fuck, but now, with that first time out of the way and my body even more inflamed that it had been before, I spoke from surety.

Faith wasn't going to be more than a few steps away from me anytime soon. I'd have to feed her. Bathe her. Take care of her body so she could take what she needed from me.

She had the Ardor. How a woman so advanced in age could just now be coming into her body's need, I had no explanation for. If I had to guess, I would say she was in her mid-twenties. A good five to seven years after most Aleran females suffered the Ardor.

But thank the goddess she'd saved all that delirious need for me. I'd felt the drain of energy, the heat pulsing between us as my body did what it was made to do—give her what she needed. My life force filled her, made her strong. Whole. Mine.

An Ardor only came once, and I was ridiculously pleased that no other male would ever know what it felt like to give himself to her in that way. Not just the seed from my body, but my true self. It felt like I was giving her part of my soul.

She was my mate. My body knew it. After this? Keeping my head on straight was going to be a very serious problem.

If she beckoned me, I would fall at her feet like a conquered fool at the mercy of her soft skin, heated kiss and hot, wet pussy. And if she were truly a ruthless traitor not only to the Jax family but to the crown itself, I was screwed... in more ways than one.

I fucked her. Filled her. Kissed her. We moved slowly this time, the rolling motion of our bodies rocking together like the brazen embers of a freshly banked fire.

We came together, her cries driving me over. The greedy massage of her pussy around my cock pulling both seed and energy from me in a violent wave that left me collapsed on top of her. Buried deep.

Unwilling to leave her.

She owned me. I was so fucking screwed. Because the fact remained, I'd taken her body, given her my life force, soothed her Ardor, at least for the moment. And she hadn't told me a damn thing.

Why had she been in my mother's room? What was she doing in my family's home? Was she a traitor to the new princess? To Queen Celene? Was she just a petty thief, looking for a bit of jewelry to sell? Or was she something much, much worse?

The most disturbing question? Did I care what the answer to that question might be?

Not only did I have to learn every inch of her body, what made her hot, made her moan... hell, made her come, I needed to get the truth from her.

She was mine, body and soul, and I would get answers. I would protect her, no matter who she was, what she'd done. But I couldn't do that blind.

I needed answers, needed them now, while my cock was on a temporary break and my mind stood a fighting chance. It wouldn't be long before my body, or her Ardor, took over and all I'd want—or need—was to satisfy her. Feed her Ardor. Fuck her.

I lifted my hand, stroked her dark hair back from her face. The long strands were softer than silk. A smile crept onto her face.

"More," she purred and arched her hips up and into me. It felt good, but my mind was still in charge. At least for the moment.

I was all for pleasing my mate, but even I wasn't quite ready. Her demand confirmed my suspicions about what I'd felt happening between us. The only way a female would be so eager was—

"You're in Ardor," I said. It wasn't a question.

Her eyes opened, met mine. If I hadn't been braced on my

elbows I would have fallen forward, into those eyes. Drowned in them.

Her smile made my breath catch and my heartbeat race anew. She was beautiful.

"It works out well, since you've been awakened."

Frowning, I looked at her again, confirming my earlier suspicions. She had to be mid-twenties, at least. Ardor came upon females around twenty or so. There was no way she'd had it for over five years. It was impossible. She'd have gone insane.

Then why had there been such a delay? It was different for each female, but this old?

"How long have you had it?"

She shrugged her slim shoulders, the action dragging her still taut nipples along my chest. I bit back a groan.

"Not long."

"How long?" I tipped up her chin so she couldn't look away. The thought of my mate in pain, that she may have suffered and I hadn't been there to soothe her... unless, someone else had. Cassander perhaps? Or one of the other males in my parents' palace. I saw red. If I hadn't been buried balls deep in her body, I would have been pacing the room. Fighting the urge to rage at anyone who looked at her. "How many have there been?"

Her eyes widened at my sharp tone. "What do you mean?"

"Who else have you fucked?"

Her mouth opened but no other sound came out. Then, in an instant, I watched the heat disappear from her eyes and be replaced by anger. She pushed at my chest, but I wasn't moving. I had her just where I wanted.

"Don't you dare do any of that self-defense on me," I warned. "I promise your ass will be well-spanked if you even think it."

"First you insult me and call me a slut and then you tell me I shouldn't be offended? Or defend myself from a bully?"

"A bully?"

"You're keeping here me against my will."

"Mate, my cock is still buried in your pussy. My seed is slipping from you. You pleaded with me for more moments ago. I am not fucking you under duress. You begged me to get inside you."

"That was before you were acting like a jackass."

"And it was after you were caught snooping around my parents' home."

She stilled then, let her hands fall to the bed beside her. "So why am I here? You should have let Lord Wyse take me to his Level C death chamber."

I stilled, blood running cold, the potential threat from Lord Wyse very real. "Is that what he said to you? Did he threaten your life?"

She rolled her eyes and shoved at my chest again. I did not move. "No. Not exactly. Get off me. You're a Neanderthal."

"You are my mate," I said. "If Lord Wyse threatened to kill you, or even harm you, he will be dealt with."

"Seriously? You're a banker, not G.I. Joe." She shoved, hard, and I reluctantly pulled my cock from her body and rolled to one side. She sat up, pulling the sheet to cover her perfect breasts. I noticed, with some satisfaction, the dark red marks on her neck where I'd suckled her skin, marked her as mine.

"I am the heir to one of the wealthiest families on Alera. I do not know what a G.I. Joe is, but I assure you, I do not run a banking facility."

She burst out laughing, the first real laugh I'd heard from her, and the sound was musical. Enchanting. "You are a strange duck, Thordis Jax."

"I am not a duck. I am Thor. Call me Thor. I am yours." I lifted her hand and placed it over my chest, locking it to me, skin to skin, both to reassure her and because I could not tolerate the lack of contact this new position on the bed provided. She was inches away from me. Naked. But it was still too far. "I am yours and you are mine. This is one truth that can't be denied. That we can both agree on. Everything else doesn't matter."

I saw something in her eyes. Doubt, perhaps? "Nothing else matters? You think me a traitor, at least your parents do, and it has been proven your family housed a traitor."

"Zel, definitely." I couldn't deny the soldier's guilt, nor the fact that he worked for my family. "Sadly, he was my friend when we were children. I hadn't spoken to him in years, until the royal reception. I can't believe I left the princess alone with him there. I would kill him all over again for what he did to Princess Trinity. But what about you? Why were you in my mother's room?"

He let that hang.

"You don't know anything about me."

"Exactly. I will learn, if you would cooperate and actually answer my questions."

"And I don't know anything about you."

I sighed. We were getting nowhere fast. "Ask and I will reveal all. There are no secrets between mates."

Those words were a complete lie, for it seemed we each thought the other was made up of only secrets.

Her gaze clouded further and she bit her lip, studied me with a quiet intensity I had never experienced before. Her attention was absolute and set about a strange sensation in my stomach. A fluttering I'd never felt before. The sensation was making me nauseous and I took a deep, calming breath to rid myself of the uncomfortable feeling. But her next words were no help.

"What do you know of the traitor, Zel?"

My blood turned to ice. Was she the mole? Had she been working with that male? Was she guilty of plotting to kidnap the newly returned princess, Trinity? "I just told you he was a friend of mine when we were younger. What do *you* know of him?"

She sighed, and I wished I could take back the words, but I

could not. Nor would I. "That's what I was afraid of." She turned to the side, swung her legs over the bed, as if preparing to leave me behind. "This is soooo not going to work."

I reached out, wrapped my hand around her arm to stop her from leaving me. I couldn't bear to see the sadness in her eyes, hear the defeated sound of her voice. Her shoulders slumped with weariness, and I was the cause. I had hurt her somehow. I had to make it right. "I do not know much, mate, but I know you are not evil. We will, as you say, work out. You will trust me with the truth and I will protect you."

She laughed then. "You make it so simple. So I should just let you make love to me over and over, let you soothe my Ardor, pretend we're going to last forever. You want me to give you everything. You want me to trust you, even though your family wants me imprisoned?"

"Don't you see? You've already given me everything," I countered, wrapping my arm around her waist and slipping my hand down so that my fingers could slide through her slick folds. "All of those things. But I need more."

She gasped and her skin flushed pink with heat. The Ardor rose in her once more, I could feel it through her skin, her energy pulling at mine, enticing me to come closer, to feed her body with passion and fucking and heat. "I can't give you more."

"Yes, you can. And you will. I can't protect you if you don't trust me with the truth." I found her still swollen clit, rubbed the nub gently with my finger. Played until she swayed toward me. Lost to sensation. To lust. To need.

"Zel was from your house," she murmured, the words thick with desire. Clearly I wasn't doing a good enough job if she thought of Zel as I teased her pussy. "One of your guards. I'm not the enemy, Thor. You are."

Her words bypassed my thinking mind and went straight to the animal she'd created. She believed I was a threat to her? An enemy?

No. This could not be allowed. I would break her with pleasure if I had to, force her to surrender completely. But she
could not be allowed to believe this of me. If she could not trust
me, I was doomed. If she did not trust me, she would leave me.
Abandon me.

She was my mate, but I was not hers. Any Aleran male
could soothe her Ardor. She had to *choose* to stay with me, to be
mine. Forever.

I needed forever.

Desperate to erase such vile thoughts from her mind, I
kissed her side. Her thighs. Her shoulders. Pressed my fingers
inside her wet core—dripping with my seed—and worked
them in and out in a slow rhythm calculated to make her beg
me to stay. To fuck her. To belong to her.

My beautiful mate must have felt my urgency for her hands
lifted to cup her breasts, to pinch her nipples. I pushed her
arms out of the way. "You want stimulation, mate? You want
them in my mouth? Some suction? What about a little nip with
my teeth?"

I scooted closer and bent down, licked one hardening peak.
I groaned, taking the tip fully into my mouth and sucked.
Marked. Every time she looked in the mirror I wanted her to
think of me. Of this.

She moaned, her fingers tangling in my hair.

I lifted my head. "Who are you?"

"Faith," she replied immediately.

I believed her.

"Do you belong to me?" I asked as I kissed between her
breasts, pushing her back onto the bed. She would not be
leaving me. Not now. Not ever.

I took the other nipple into my mouth.

"Yes. For now. Yes."

I believed her again. How could I not when she was so
perfect? When *we* were so perfect for each other. I would
accept even this small victory. For now was better than a flat

out denial. It gave me time I needed to win her over. To discover the truth about her. "I am yours, Faith. Forever. And I will fuck the answers out of you eventually," I vowed.

With a surprising leg sweep, Faith rolled us so she was on top. I didn't feel threatened, only surprised. She looked down at me with a sexy grin. I didn't think my cock could get any harder, but I was wrong.

"Perhaps I will fuck the answers out of you?" she countered.

I arched a brow, studied her. From her pert breasts, soft curve of her belly, the flare of her hips. Even the groomed hair that shielded her pussy. But I felt the heat of it, how wet it was as she straddled me.

Gripping my cock, she had to use two hands to get most of it.

I bucked, then hissed. "What do you want to know?"

"Your favorite food."

I stilled then, even as she continued to stroke me to the brink of orgasm.

I laughed, then groaned. "My favorite food?"

"Fine, your favorite position for sex."

I opened my mouth to answer, stumped, but she continued. "That's right, you're new at this. Then I will have to show you all the possibilities."

She lifted up onto her knees, hovered over my cock before she lowered herself down, took me inside her body. "Starting with this one."

"Oh fuck," I breathed. She was going to be the death of me. But what a good way to go.

7

T *hor*

DAWN's first rays turned my bedchamber into a softly glowing nest. Faith was curled against me in bed, her leg nestled between mine, her head on my chest.

I could awake this way every day for the rest of my life and be content.

My worst fears had come to pass. I would, no doubt, be led around by the balls by this female for the rest of my life.

The shocking realization was that I did not mind in the least. I'd be honored to serve this female, for as long as she'd have me. And she could lead me around that way, as long as she caressed those same greedy fuckers after. Let me fill her up with my cock and my seed.

I placed my palm gently over her flat abdomen. Perhaps she'd allow me to fill her womb with my child as well. But not yet. There was much to be settled between us.

Finding a mate was supposed to be simple. While the fucking was incredible, it was the only time when both Faith and I were in sync. There was no outside world. No traitor. No family honor. No Optimus unit. No threat to the crown. All the politics and drama existed beyond the walls of my apartment. Here, in my bedroom, in my bed, it was like a cocoon, a secret world where the truth was only that we belonged to each other.

Our bodies knew it. But our minds?

I looked down at her, dark tousled hair spread across on my pillow, her pink lips parted slightly. A little whiffling sound escaped as she breathed. Did my mate know she snored? I smiled, eager to tease her about it later.

And lower, her pale shoulders looked softer than the sheets tucked around her to warm her. I imagined the rest of her naked body beneath the sheet. I knew exactly what it looked like, every inch. We'd fucked practically into unconsciousness. To say my mate was inventive, fun and a little daring in bed made me proud. The sex education classes I'd taken as required for Aleran males hadn't taught some of the things she'd shown me. It was probably a good thing, for if I'd known, I would have tossed her over my shoulder the first time I saw her in my father's office and carried her away. Guards be damned.

My cock stirred with the memory. It wanted her again, even after only two hours rest. I'd woken her throughout the night, taken her over and over. Even with her Ardor, I imagined her sore.

Perhaps I should check and see. With a sly smile, I carefully maneuvered out from beneath her, slid the sheet down from her gorgeous body. In the morning light, her skin looked creamy, pale, except for the little love marks I'd left. I'd started at her neck, leaving pink spots of remembrance there, then lower on the curve of her breasts, lower still to the inside of her thighs. I moved down the bed, settled between those gorgeous thighs and parted them.

I breathed in the scent of her pussy, of fucking and I grinned, eager to make her gasp with pleasure, to shock her into wakefulness with my mouth on her body, worshipping her, feasting on what was mine.

I rocked my hips into the bed, rubbing my hard cock to ease the need to sink in her once more. Not yet. First, I would soothe the ache I knew my eager cock must have wrought on her pussy.

Lowering my head, I kissed first one inner thigh, then the other. Then between right on top of her tender, swollen flesh. It was hot against my lips, wet against my tongue. And sensitive, for Faith moaned in her sleep. I smiled against her clit, then flicked it with my tongue.

"Thor," she murmured dreamily. My name. No other. Mine. She knew who touched her, who pleasured her. Even in her sleep she called for me.

Content that she was aroused, honored that she trusted me enough to practically sleep through my mouth tending to her pussy, I worked her. Gently, carefully, slowly as to pull her from one set of dreams to another. I wanted to be a dream for her, fantastic and sensual and necessary to her, as she now was to me.

Her hand went to my head, fingers tangling in my hair. Her knees fell wide in welcome and I had all the access I wanted to the sweetest, stickiest part of her.

Heaven.

All of a sudden, there was a loud crash, then another. Foot-steps, my bedroom door ripped from the hinges as a team of men in black rushed in. Their ion weapons were raised, their sights aimed at me and Faith. I startled and Faith was wide awake, afraid.

She pushed up to her palms at the stunning surprise, but we were in a very compromising position. There was no doubt these guards could see exactly what we were doing. Nothing covered us. Everything was exposed.

They could see Faith's body, every glorious inch of her, as well as the red flush on her cheeks at her awakening desire from my ministrations. The love bites, even her pussy with her knees spread wide. My body couldn't both shield her from the danger that had burst through my door and protect her modesty.

I yanked the sheet from the foot of the bed and quickly covered Faith, turning so she was safeguarded behind me, but her legs were still parted, my body blocking any chances of her closing them.

I was naked, in bed. No weapons at hand. I had no way to protect her against the guards who were heavily armed. But I would die before I allowed them to hurt her.

Who the fuck were they and why were they in my apartment? Now, of all fucking times. Was Lord Wyse behind this? Had he found a way to take my mate away from me?

Behind me, I heard Faith scramble to her knees, heard the rustling of the sheet as she pulled the rest of it out from beneath me. I lifted my knees, one at a time, at her insistent tugging, glad to know she was covering herself, recovering.

She'd been open and content as I played with her pussy. This had been a very rude awakening for both of us. I now knew what would make my cock flag.

Drawing the guards' attention away from her, I cleared my throat. "Who are you and why are you in my home?"

"You are under arrest, Lord Jax, for abduction and torture of a member of the royal family." That was the oldest guard who spoke, a man near the door, and I recognized him as Travin Thuraya, Lord Leo's father. The well-respected royal guard and father to Princess Trinity's mate.

"What the fuck are you talking about? Where is Princess Trinity? Has she been kidnapped again? Zel is dead. I have been hunting for the traitor. You speak nonsense." I lowered my hands to my sides, slowly, but the old man shook his head in annoyance.

"Hands up, Thor. Don't make us shoot you."

"This is insanity. Get out of my home."

Another guard entered the room. Tall, thin, he was death walking. Even from my layman's eyes, a killer. Ruthless in his role as some kind of special guard. Behind me, Faith gasped.

"You!" Faith leapt off the bed, as if to attack the man. Moving quickly, I jumped to my feet to block her into the corner with my much larger frame.

"Stay where you are!" I ordered.

She pounded on my back, pushed against me. Enraged. "Move! Let me at him. He tried to kill us." Her accusation was a snarl of pure feminine rage, and I looked at the large guard with new eyes. He grinned at her words, as if her anger amused him.

I'd calm my mate and then kill him myself.

I took one step forward, but Travin cleared his throat and lifted his own ion blaster in my direction. That made five blasters and six men. The odds were not in my favor. "I'd think twice about making that move, young man. Let the female go. We will not harm her. You have my word."

Faith moved around me and with all the blasters pointed in my direction, and Travin's order hanging in the air, there wasn't much I could do to stop her. Not without getting us both killed.

Thank the goddess she didn't go far, but stopped directly before me, as if using her body as a shield. Which was insane. "Faith, get behind me. Now."

"No." She stood proudly, unafraid, and I was proud of my mate in that moment. She might be a commoner, a servant in my parents' home, but she was magnificent. Fearless. Proud. Mine. She was mine. "You." She pointed at the tall one, the killer, yet looked to Travin. "Who are you? Are you in charge of this disaster?"

Travin bowed to her with a deference I did not understand. "Yes. I am Travin Thuraya, commander of these men."

"Thuraya? Are you Leo's father?" she asked.

"I am."

How did she know Leoron, Princess Trinity's new mate? Of

course, his face had been all over the news feeds for days. The common soldier who had risen in the world and managed to mate the princess. He was famous, almost more so than the princess herself. Every male on the planet wanted to be Leo right now.

I looked at Faith's shoulders, her shining hair, and shook my head. No. Not every male. I was content with what was mine. Faith was more beautiful than the new princess, softer, more alluring in every way. Even her scent drove me to distraction—

"If you are Leo's father, then you will arrest this man. He tried to kill me and my sisters."

What the fuck was Faith talking about? I didn't know she had sisters. I knew nothing about her, other than the fact that she brought my body and my heart to life. That I couldn't bear to see her hurt or in pain. That I would die to protect her.

I didn't recognize the guard she pointed out. I didn't recognize any of them but Leo's father. It wasn't a surprise, for I wasn't involved with the police or the Optimus unit. But I did know their uniforms were from neither organization. They wore the uniform of royal guards. Travin Thuraya had been the head of the guard for years before he retired.

I had to guess with his son's rise in the ranks as mate to the newly returned princess, he'd decided to go back into a more active role. Especially with the threat to the princess at the reception. But why now? Why *here*? There was no explanation for why they were in my home at dawn, interrupting a fabulously perfect round of pussy eating.

"Zel is dead. I've been searching for the traitor in my mother's house. I promise you. It is not me." I put my hand to my bare chest.

The killer snorted at me like I was an idiot. A complete and total idiot. "Now that Faith is safe, I can assure you we will get to you, my *Lord*." He said the word Lord like it was acid on his tongue. "You have kidnapped and held a member of the royal family without permission. You allowed the princess to be in danger. You plotted with your friend, Zel, a soldier in this house, to kidnap and murder Queen Celene as well as Princess Trinity. You will pay for your mistakes."

Holy fuck. He was dead serious, and so was the look on Travin's face. But Princess Trinity was fine. Alive. Whole. I'd seen the news, at least yesterday. Zel had been one of my father's guards, it was true, but he was dead, and the trail had gone cold the moment his traitor's heart stopped beating. Yes, we'd been friends as children, run through my parents' mansion with wild abandon, raiding the kitchen and stealing treats from the cooks. But that was two decades ago. As we aged, we settled into our roles, me as a Lord and him as a common soldier. I hadn't spoken more than ten words to him in the last ten years. This was madness. "Faith is safe with me. She is mine. My mate. I saved her from interrogation by the Optimus unit. I don't know what you are talking about. I haven't spoken to Zel, more than to say *Hello,* in years. *I* would never do anything to endanger Princess Trinity. You have made a mistake."

Faith shivered, holding the sheet to the top of her breasts like a shield as she stared at the most dangerous man in the room. "You were there that night," she continued. I could see her hands shaking. "You were after us. Killed the Jax guards. You laughed when my sister shot you. *Laughed!*" Faith was shouting now and I was no longer convinced the shaking I saw in her was from fear. Her skin was glowing with her rage, her stance light as if she was ready to fly into an attack at any moment.

What the fuck was she talking about?

"And you kept one of those traitors alive," he countered. "You healed the traitor, Zel, with a ReGen wand so he could go back to the palace and finish what he started. He nearly murdered Princess Trinity."

Faith froze, as if she'd been slapped. All color drained from her cheeks. "Oh my God." She swayed on her feet, as if he'd physically struck her. Another reason to kill him later. "So what now?" she asked, her voice much calmer, as if she'd figured something out. "Are you trying to convince me you aren't here to kill us?"

The other four guards had their weapons trained on us— no, on *me*. They hadn't moved a muscle, hadn't blinked, probably hadn't even breathed.

"If they were, we'd already be dead," I told her, my voice grim. Whoever the fuck these people were knew where I lived, knew Faith would be here. Knew things about her I still didn't. Which made me want to rage and scream like an idiot. She was mine. My mate. And I knew nothing about what was happening here.

She'd been keeping secrets.

But then, she *had* been caught going through my mother's things. Snooping around my home. To what end? I'd rescued her from the Optimus unit when they proved a bit too eager to interrogate her, but never gotten any real information out of her. I'd been too busy fucking her. Feeding her Ardor. Practically begging her to drain my strength and my seed often and well. My cock had woken up and I'd lost my fucking mind.

"What the fuck is going on here?" I asked, putting my arm out, dragging Faith back so that her body pressed to my chest, my arm around her waist. She didn't resist, but Travin and the other guard, the dangerous one, scowled at the move. Faith wasn't going anywhere without me, and I was a fucking Lord, one of the most powerful, wealthiest males on the planet. They could start answering my fucking questions. "Why are you in my apartment? You cannot think, even for a moment, that I am a traitor to the queen."

"I can answer that," a female voice called from the doorway, the distinct tone carried a regal bearing I recognized.

Princess Trinity was here?

In confirmation, her mate, Leo, entered my bedroom first,

in a uniform matching the others. Her Royal Highness, Princess Trinity, walked in behind him. No longer in the large blue gown she'd worn to dance with me just days ago, she had donned a soldier's uniform, and she was livid—if the glare she sent my way was any indication.

"Get your fucking man-paws off my sister, you asshole. How dare you?"

My brain stalled and I tried to process. To understand. To *think*.

"Leave him out of this, Trin. He didn't do anything wrong." That was Faith's voice. Defending *me*. And referring to the heir to the throne by a nickname of sorts I'd never heard before.

"The Ardor fried your brains, little sister. Step away from him. He's a traitor. We've found evidence that the Jax family was involved in the plot to kidnap Mother."

"What?" Faith stepped backward, pressed her body to mine, just for a moment, as if she couldn't bear to leave me. But then she did the unthinkable. She pulled free of my embrace and walked to her *sister*.

The princess wrapped her arms around my mate and Faith melted against her as if it was right, as if they were trusted allies. Bonded in love. Family. "I'll tell you all about it once you're safe... and away from *him*."

Sisters? My mate was Trinity's *sister?* A princess?

And here I'd treated her as a servant. Believed her to be common. Been proud of myself for accepting her lower status. I'd been an arrogant prick.

Fuck. Fuck. Fuck.

As one, they turned to face me and my knees threatened to buckle.

They looked nothing alike, the two females. One dark, one light. One with blue eyes one with brown. But there was no denying the straight lines of their shoulders, the noble bearing of the heads, even with Faith wearing nothing but my sheet, and my seed.

Unlike my mate's, there was no pain in Princess Trinity's eyes. No torment. Only rage.

"I am not a traitor, Faith. I promise you. This is a mistake." I held my hands out at my sides, practically begging her to believe me.

Faith blinked away tears, as if this was ripping her in two, as if her heart and body believed me, but her head didn't. Princess Trinity had no such qualms. "Nix, take him to the palace and lock him up. Nix will get answers out of him. And for Pete's sake, put some clothes on him."

I had no idea who Pete was, but he probably wasn't a nice guy.

"It will be my pleasure, Your Highness." The tall one, the killer, Nix, bowed to his princess and smiled ruthlessly at me.

Fuck.

BOOK 5

PROLOGUE

Q *ueen Celene of Alera, Optimus Unit Headquarters, Solitary Confinement*

HAD I known where they were going to transport me when I was taken off Scarface's ship, I might have put up more of a fight.

Then again, probably not, for I was getting what I wanted now. My daughters were safe, as far as I knew—he'd probably look a lot happier if something had happened to any of them—and searching for me.

At last, I knew the name of at least one person who had betrayed me and my beloved mate all those years ago.

Lord Wyse, or Inspector Optimi, of the Optimus unit stood before me, his cheeks flushed, his eyes shining with a fever I recognized as fanaticism. He hated me, apparently.

We had grown up together, he just a few years older. I'd considered him a big brother of sorts, even though he was not a brother by blood, but a cousin.

When he had decided to try to kill me, or why, I had no idea. How far back did his hatred go? I would find out.

Scarface stood with his back to the door. He hadn't beaten me, yet. Not since I'd been sent here, under lock and key in the private interrogation rooms saved for the most defiant and dangerous prisoners.

Defiant? Yes.

Dangerous? More than he could possibly imagine, but not for the usual reasons. There was no way I could defend myself or fight back—I thought proudly of Destiny who would be able to whoop his ass—but there were other ways to be ruthless.

"I see your lack of success has forced you to show your face, cousin," I said. How very brave of you." I made sure to sound amused, as if his presence were no more of a threat than that of a worm under my shoe. Of course, I had bare feet, I was starving, freezing cold, and fairly certain I was becoming ill. But he didn't need to know any of that. I'd taunted, goaded and acted unaffected ever since I'd been transported from Earth. I had to *fake it 'til I make it* as the girls would say.

I was a queen, after all. Even being on Earth for all these years, didn't change who or what I was. I could handle anything. And if I couldn't... Lord Wyse would have to deal with my daughters, and they were so much stronger—mentally and physically—than me.

"It's not bravery, dear," he countered. Dark eyes blazed, but he kept his calm reserve. "But the assurance that you'll soon be too dead to talk."

I'd already figured that one out myself, but now that he was here, I knew something else as well—he wasn't in charge. He was a pawn. A more powerful pawn than the man with the scars, but one all the same. A much needed tool to wield since he had royal blood flowing through his veins. I didn't care about minor players in this game; I was hunting their master now. His presence proved I was one step closer. He wouldn't be here—he'd let his underlings guard me—if things weren't heating up. Were their plans falling apart? Was my remaining silent affecting their schedule? Were my girls' plans so effective that theirs weren't? I hid the small smile that was about to curl my lips as I thought of them being bested by a bunch of Earth-born females. But Trinity, Faith and Destiny would not be safe until I found the mastermind, and planned a way to destroy him.

Or her. I supposed their master could be a woman, but a female, in my experience, was much less into frontal assault and much sneakier than the attack had been twenty-seven years ago on me and the king. To them, my mate had just been collateral damage. I was the one they'd wanted, the one who'd gotten away.

A woman would have been more cunning in her attack—less fists and more finesse—taken the jewels from my neck and put herself on the throne in due order. I'd had plenty of time to think, to wonder who it might be. Male or female.

No. This was a man's personal vendetta, I was sure. There had never been a ruling king on Alera and someone wanted to be the first. My mate, obviously, had been the king before he'd been killed, but in title, not by power. Not that the law forbade a male to lead the planet, but the royal family, those in the direct line of succession, by chance or design, did not give birth to sons. My three daughters were proof of that. I had a suspicion the intelligence within the citadel that gave us our gifts had something to do with that as well. A suspicion, but no proof.

Other than the fact that, through all of recorded history, a royal heir had never given birth to a son.

A daughter had the power to rule within her. A son would need the jewels so desperately to have any hope of claiming the throne, for they provided a different kind of power, but enough to rule nonetheless. The spire would not light for a king, yet with the sacred stones, he'd be able to control the planet. No doubt the arrival of my girls and the lighting of their spires only added to the mastermind's plans. Get the jewels, kill me and rule the word. Simple enough, but he hadn't considered I'd had daughters. Heirs and future rulers.

Whoever he was, he was ruthless. Lacked a conscience. Had the biggest balls ever. Only a very aggressive—or desperate—male would attack my mate and I with an entire squadron of soldiers in plain view of the entire city.

Lord Wyse was watching me closely now, his inspection unflinching, as if he could read my mind.

I knew for a fact he could not. He had none of the gifts. He was a cog in a war machine. Nothing more. "Why are you here, Coburt?"

I wanted to call him *bastard* or *dumbass* or a whole bunch of other names, but I went with his given one.

"Where are the royal jewels, Celene? Tell me and I'll let your daughters live."

I laughed. I couldn't stop myself, and I enjoyed taunting him. It was the same question I'd been asked ever since I'd been snatched from my bed on Earth—until the spires lit and my daughters' existence was brought to light... literally—and then they added the additional threat of harming them. "If you could kill my daughters, you would have already done so," I countered. "I suspect you've tried and they slipped through your fingers like water. How embarrassing for you, *Inspector Optimi*." I used his title as a taunt, as a reminder that if the leader of the most ruthless protective unit on Alera couldn't be successful in ridding the planet of three females, then he probably shouldn't hold the position. "I'm sure your master was very disappointed."

"I have no master, Celene," he replied.

I hadn't seen him in twenty-seven years. He looked older. That cunning look he'd always had about him when younger was understandable now. He'd had evil running through his veins all along.

"You have always been lesser, Coburt. That's why you cower

in a corner and send others to do your dirty work for you."

That earned me a slap across the face, but he was nowhere near as strong as the man with the scarred face. Not even close. It hurt, but was nothing compared to what I'd become accustomed to. I very nearly laughed.

"Where are they?" he shouted, spittle flying from his lips.

"Who?"

"Your other two daughters. Faith and the other one. The ones who lit up the other spires. I'm not stupid. I know they came here together. I had Faith in my clutches. In custody. No records of her birth or her fingerprints exist. Of course, she was one of the mysterious females. A fucking princess. But Thordis Jax saved her, took her away." He growled, beyond livid. To know he held Faith, had her life in his hands and then she slipped away... "Trinity might be in the palace, but the other two are on Alera. I will find them and kill them both."

I didn't want to panic at the thought of Faith being held by Wyse, so I thought of how proud I was of her, of all three girls, instead. Yes, without any Aleran records, it had been easy for him to take the mental leap about Faith and Destiny. Not hard to put together. But now, he had no clue where either of them were. I smiled. "I don't know what you're talking about. Tell your master that."

"I *do not* have a master." He towered over me, his hand raised as if to strike me again, his voice low and each word clearly enunciated. I did not flinch or turn away, but stared him in the eye and dared him to do it.

"Lord Jax has one of them, Celene. Not the old man you once knew, but his son. It has to be her. I had her in my custody. No birth records. No schooling, bank accounts. Fingerprints. Nothing. I am sure she is one of yours."

He began to pace. "But Thordis Jax took her away. I would have guessed his apartment, but since my team checked *thoroughly,* no. Tell me where they would go, where *she* would hide, and I'll save her from him and his... attentions."

The lewd innuendo was obvious, but I wasn't taking the bait. I knew the elder Lord Jax, and his mate. Lady Jax was a shrew. Calculating and brilliant, mean to everyone but her family. For them, for her small son—a strapping young man I remembered as a sweet-faced toddler—she would bring hell down on anyone. Well, he wasn't so small now, but a full-grown male and clearly interested in Faith.

Lord Wyse didn't understand Earth women. Faith didn't *need* Thordis Jax. She didn't need his attentions, or anyone saving her from them. If Faith wanted Thordis Jax, then she'd have him. Or not. The fact Lord Wyse thought my daughter needed protecting from a male made me want to laugh.

I thought of Lady Jax, then her mate, Lord Jax. I remembered him fondly. No one loved to laugh more than he did. And he adored his mate, at least all those years ago. I doubted that would have changed. If any of my daughters were in that house, they'd be safer there than they would be with Lord Wyse, that was for damned sure. He'd had Faith in custody—in his evil grasp—but she'd somehow slipped through his fingers. No wonder he was pissed.

"Better Lord Jax than you, cousin."

"Where are the jewels, Celene?"

God, he was like a broken record.

"They won't do you any good, you know," I said again, even though he knew all this. "Even if you had them, they're useless now with four spires lit at the citadel. Killing me does *nothing*." I looked him over, from head to toe, slowly, with as much disgust as I could muster. "And you're not the most attractive male on the planet. You'll look like a complete idiot with a pretty necklace on your greedy neck."

He did not respond, but stared at me for a full minute before speaking. "Not when you're all dead, Celene. I'll wear them to your burial ceremony. Yours, and all three of your daughters'."

F aith Jones Herakles, *The Royal Palace, Planet Alera*

"I HAD sex with a bad guy. A really bad guy." I moaned, ran my hand through my tangled hair. The sheet I'd been wrapped in when I arrived lay in a crumpled heap by the bedpost in my sister's royal bedchamber. Seeing it was a reminder. Of *him.*

I kicked it in frustration, narrowly missed stubbing my bare toes on the large wooden frame of the bed. The fabric smelled like Lord Thordis Jax, the sex-on-a-stick, sexy as hell, too damn good looking for his own good, male claiming to be my mate. The Aleran rotting in my sister's dungeon—well, technically, it was my dungeon too—right now for trying to have her kidnapped and killed. The male Trinity believed had betrayed the entire family.

And I wanted him again anyway. I felt achy. Needy.

Empty. My pussy. My chest. My skin. I *needed* him to touch me in a way I'd never needed anyone.

This Ardor was serious fucking business.

"Look on the bright side, Faith, at least it wasn't Zach

Richardson." My sister, Her Royal Highness, Princess Trinity Herakles, had the good graces to look sympathetic. She *had* her mate. Her Ardor was over. And she was so blissfully in love, every time I saw her and Leo together my heart hurt.

Jesus. I had it bad. For a traitor.

Despite the rambling nature of my thoughts, I couldn't believe what she'd just said.

"What?" I stared at her, thought of Zach, the total loser from high school, then burst out laughing, which only added to my emotional roller coaster. Sad, mad, angry and now laughing like a lunatic.

I'd been quiet on the ride to the palace. Was quiet still—which was very unlike me. I talked smack as a general rule. But then, the last few days of sneaking around, lying low, and *cleaning* a *traitor's house,* had taken the proverbial wind right out of my sails. I felt as if I'd been stunned by an ion blaster. *Again.*

Only this time they'd aimed right for my heart and somehow skipped the rest of me.

When the guards had burst into the bedroom in Thor's apartment, I'd been confused. When I saw the assassin who had tried to kill us—no, who I'd tried to kill us the night we arrived on Alera—I'd been terrified.

But finding out Trinity was there to save me from a traitor?

That had broken me somehow. Seeing Thor standing there naked, willing to defend me, had made me love him, just a little. But then those eyes had darkened with betrayal when he realized who I was. When we'd shared so much and I hadn't told him I was a princess.

It was as if *I'd* betrayed *him.*

The man had balls of steel. I'd give him that.

But then, he was a spoiled lordling, raised in a fancy mansion. A traitor. Was it any surprise he believed the same way an entitled rich kid would back home on Earth? Thinking the world owed him everything? Believing he had the right to do whatever he wanted, whenever he wanted?

I kicked the sheet again. He'd taken what he wanted from me as well.

And I'd let him.

No. I'd *begged him* for more. Begged. And whimpered. And let him take me over and over and over.

Fuck. I was an idiot.

"Stop trying to kill the sheet. It didn't do anything." Trinity's words were meant to lighten the mood, but they were too soft. She knew. Somehow, she knew exactly how this was tearing me in half.

Her mate, Leo, had escorted us up through dark secret passages—which would have been pretty darn cool if I wasn't such a hot mess. They'd ushered me into their private quarters on the second floor, and I'd promptly burst into tears. I had no idea how long I'd cried, but when the crying jag had stopped, Trinity and I were alone.

No doubt Leo had taken one look at me, a sobbing mess, and run for his life.

Trin had given me a robe, and I'd dropped the sheet like it burned.

Thor's scent, of hours of sex, still clung to me. Even without the sheet, I could *smell him.*

I needed a fucking shower. With a power washer strong enough to take off my skin. Maybe then I could get him out of my head. Maybe then my body would stop screaming at me to go crawl into his arms and ask for more.

At least all my tears had run out. When that happened, I'd switched to being mad, pacing the sitting area in her suite with a furious fervor that would surely wear a path in the sumptuous carpet. I'd muttered to myself, swore that all men were assholes and not worth anything. How dare Thor fuck me, all the while being a traitor! How could he be a murderer and get hard at the sight of me? It made no sense. How could one be so evil and then be so intent on giving me pleasure when he got between my thighs?

None of it made sense and probably, to Trinity, neither did I. Thankfully, she'd remained silent, just letting me vent. Between me, Trinity and Destiny, one of us was always having some kind of meltdown. At least once a week back home. We'd agreed when Destiny and I were thirteen, and Trinity sixteen, that only one of us could lose our shit at any given time. Clearly, it was soooo my turn.

Trinity had Leo. She was known and recognized as the princess. Not working as a maid, arrested and accused of being an informant or traitor. Clearly, I was off the hook for that. I wanted to give Lord Wyse and his scar-faced friend in the Optimus unit a middle finger salute, the asshole.

No luck there either. Which was fine. But instead of a fancy entrance with a gorgeous gown and tons of press—like Trinity had during her grand entrance into public life on the front steps of the palace—I'd been sneaked in so only a few knew I was here, and the rest didn't know who I was, that there was another princess.

I was the naked woman in the sheet. For now, that was it. The *crazy* naked woman in the sheet, because not only did I not exist, I had a mate who was a traitor. Who had helped kidnap my mother. Had he been in on the plot to kill Trinity's biological father, the king of Alera, as well?

No. He would have been about three or four years old at the time. Like a mad super-genius villain from a comic book.

Even if he *were* a traitor, he was still better than Zach Richardson. That jerk had called his penis "Big Z" and talked to it like it was his best friend. Shit. I hadn't thought of that in years...

I laughed again until tears rolled down my cheeks. It wasn't really that funny, but I couldn't throw myself on the ground and have a tantrum like the wounded little girl inside of me wanted to do, so I laughed instead.

"I can't believe you would compare Zach to Thor. They're like... light years apart." And not just literally, but in every possible way. I wondered if Aleran men named their dicks like human men did. Thor's would need a better name than "Big T." Maybe something like, *miraculous-fucking-machine*. Or, *make-me-forget-my-name-and-betray-my-sisters*.

Trinity tapped her chin, then grinned. "I am the princess now. I can order guards to go to Earth and transport Zach here for round two if you want."

I smiled, sighed. God, I loved my sister. She could spin humor from nothing. Thor vs. Zach, the guy I'd slept with the summer after graduation? No contest. Except...

"So you think having sex with Zach in the bathroom at Ty Konwinski's party an hour before I find him getting head from Sarah Moore in the back of his car is worse than fucking a traitor who tried to have you murdered?"

Trinity shrugged. "When you put it that way... Tell me this —who was better?"

As if there was any comparison. Zach had been a nineteen-year-old asshole who thought his dick was God's gift to women. Thor was an attentive, protective, possessive alien whose cock had awakened for me and who had claimed me as his mate. Who also, even as a virgin, had given me more pleasure than I ever imagined. And yet...

And yet my pussy didn't care that he might be evil. My pussy needed him. Craved him.

"Stupid Ardor," I muttered.

"Welcome to the club," Trinity countered.

"Yeah, well, yours is all done and you've still got Leo to give you a happy ending every night. I've got Ardor and the only cock that will satisfy me is rotting in your dungeon."

"He's been there a couple of hours, Faith. I doubt it's falling off already."

And thank *God* for that. It would be a complete and total waste for all women in the universe.

My sister continued. "There are plenty of guys who can soothe your Ardor here. The males in the queen's guard are, as far as I can tell, all good ones, if they've been awakened. There's the Royal Consort. I've met him. I can, for a fact, say that his cock is quite large and his balls... well, his balls might be a little sore if you decide to play with them."

My mouth dropped open as I stared. She was sprawled, very un-princess like, on one of the couches, hugging a pretty blue pillow to her chest.

"How do you know so much about a consort's balls? Isn't Leo enough?"

She grinned. "Long story. And yes, Leo is totally enough."

I walked around the couch, dropped down onto it so I faced my sister. "God, I'm naked. I smell like sex. And I had to sneak into Mom's palace wearing a stupid-ass sheet." I tugged at the collar of the robe I wore and pulled it more tightly around me. Even covered now, I felt more naked than ever. "I need a shower."

"You have crazy sex hair. So, yeah, I was wondering how long it would take you to realize that."

I took a breath, then another. "Trin, what am I going to do?"

She cocked her head to the side, smiled, but this time one that was laced with sympathy. "Leo and his dad are looking into Thor and his parents."

"You said you had evidence against him. What kind of evidence?"

She nodded. "Leo's dad—the older guy who burst into your little love fest this morning—retrieved data that showed Zel had a comms call with someone in the Jax household just a few hours before he tried to kidnap me. The call went to Thor's bedroom, to be exact."

"He doesn't live there anymore, which you are well aware of since you burst into his apartment like a SWAT team." I wasn't really upset that the guards had come. If Thor was bad, it was better he was caught. But I hadn't really needed those guards to see me in such a compromising position. The first time I saw Leo's dad I had Thor's head buried in my pussy.

I groaned.

"True, but security data shows that Thor was at his parents' mansion at the time. He has a history with Zel. They were best friends. Leo said they grew up together. They were close, Faith. That's two strikes against him."

I remembered back to my conversation with Thor the night before. He'd told me the exact same thing as Trinity, that they'd been childhood friends, but he'd also said he hadn't spoken to him in years. "I don't think... I don't think he's bad," I replied.

When he'd mentioned this, Thor's cock had been in me at the time, or pretty darn close to it. Unless he was a really good actor, I believed him. He'd thought I was a maid then. And that we were mates. He'd said it over and over, touched me like I mattered. Naked, in bed, sated after hours of sex? It would be a difficult time to lie. And if I really had been a maid, he would have had no reason to avoid the truth. What did I care about some man I'd never met before? "He told me they hadn't spoken in years. I don't think he would have lied to me. He didn't know who I was. He thought I was his mate, the household servant."

"*Think* he wouldn't lie, or *hope*?" she countered.

I harrumphed, because I hated when she thought logically. Damn her linear brain.

"He's the one who left me with Zel at the reception, Faith," she continued. "He said I was in good hands and patted Zel on the shoulder before he walked away. He practically handed me over to a ruthless bad guy on a silver platter."

"Thor has no reason to do this." I said it, but I didn't quite believe it. Not anymore.

"Did Zel?"

I shrugged, thought of the unconscious guard whose life I had been determined to save. Remembered the irritated look on the assassin's face when he told me I'd saved the life of a traitor and nearly gotten my sister killed. Shit.

I licked my lips, tried to condense everything I knew about

Thor down into feelings. "It doesn't make sense. I mean, he rescued me at the police station from being taken off by the Optimus unit." I shivered and lifted a pillow off the sofa, hugged it to my chest. "That would have been bad. You saw how he protected me from you."

"Faith, I know you want him to be innocent. God, if it were Leo we were talking about, I'd be freaking out. But Nix and the others broke down his door while he was eating you out."

"Don't remind me. I don't think I'll be able to look Leo's dad in the eye. Ever."

"Thor fed your Ardor. I know what that feels like. It's a really deep connection. Trust me, I know what you're going through right now. I really do. And I don't think you can be impartial. Especially not while your Ardor is still going strong. All I could think about was getting Leo in bed again."

She was right about that; all I could think about was Thor. Over me. Inside me. Kissing me. Fucking me. But I couldn't go there. It hurt too much. "But, Trin, if Thor were truly evil, he'd have left me to Lord Wyse's interrogation and some creepy place called cell level C. I would have taken the fall for his crime. Why would he rescue someone who could divert all attention away from him?"

"You're his mate." She was quiet for a moment, clearly thinking hard, but those three words had the force of a baseball bat striking my rib cage at full swing. Things were breaking. Not literally, but this hurt just as much.

"So, he saved me because his cock got hard, and not because he's a decent human being?"

"They wait years to find a mate. There's no way he could walk away from you once he found you. I don't think it's biologically possible for them. He's not human, Faith. Don't forget that."

"Neither are you."

"Ouch."

I was turning into a bitch. "I'm sorry. I don't know why I said that."

"I do. He hurt you. I don't know how or why he's involved in all this, but the queen's guard will figure it out." She reached over and took my hand. "We'll figure it out. I promise."

I laughed, or tried to. It came out as a sad little squeak of sound. "Why does he have to be so freaking hot? It was like being in bed with *Captain America."*

"True. I noticed, when I came in. I mean, some guys don't look too great naked, but he was like—"

"Captain America," I cut in.

"I was going to say a guy from the *Thunder From Down Under* calendar."

"He's hotter than that."

She waggled her eyebrows and grinned. "Not as hot as Leo, but not too shabby. Especially when his head's between your legs."

I flushed hotly and my pussy clenched at the memory. I couldn't help but smile. "My new favorite way to wake up."

Trinity grinned. "Yeah, mine, too."

I sighed. "God, I missed you."

"No, you didn't. You were busy fucking your brains out."

I rolled my eyes. "Fine. Before that." I sobered, felt the ache in my heart. And the rage. Why me? Why did I have to be the freak of the family? The one who things never worked out for? Why did I have to want to be with Thor, even knowing what I knew now? God dammit. The whole thing pissed me off. "What am I going to do? I need him."

She sat up, reached out and put her hand on mine. Her blue eyes held my gaze like a tractor beam from *Star Trek.* All playfulness was gone. "It's the Ardor, right? Or did you fall in love with him?"

"I'm not sure." I sat up, knocking her hand away. "How bad is it down there in the dungeon? Rats and stuff? Medieval torture devices? The rack?"

Trinity shrugged. "I've never been, and Leo said I should stay out of there." She made quotation marks with her fingers. *"No place for a princess."*

That made me roll my eyes. Obviously, Leo had a thing or two to learn about my stubborn, buttoned-up sister. She was deceptively mild on the outside, but pure steel beneath. If she wanted to go check out her creepy basement prison, she would. End. Of. Discussion. "Men. So bossy."

"Especially when you're sleeping with them." She did laugh then, and it was a contagious sound, full of happiness I seriously envied at the moment. I was happy for her and Leo. Thrilled, actually. But a bit distracted by my own pile of stinking dog-poo at the moment.

Didn't help that I remembered exactly how bossy Thor had been, in bed. And when he'd saved me from Lord Wyse, from the extra-special interrogation that old jerk had planned. Thor was a lot like Leo, but also like Dad. Alpha male, protecting women while letting them run the show. Oh, Dad wasn't a chump. Hell, no. He just knew how to respect and appreciate women. Like Thor. God, Thor.

He'd protected me—as best he could while being stark naked—from the guards when they burst into his apartment. He'd stood up to the creepy assassin guy, and I ached for some of that bossiness again.

I ached for Thor, and it wasn't just my pussy that missed him, but my heart, too. I'd started to think we had a real chance at a happily-ever-after. Having that taken away? Like ripping candy from a baby. I wanted to cry, but I wasn't a two-year-old. I was royal. A freaking *princess*.

I stood. Determined. This was total bullshit. I wasn't going to wait for the queen's guards or whoever else to get answers out of him. He said he was mine. Well, he was going to prove it. Right now. "I'm going down there. He's going to talk to me. If I'm his mate, and he really believes that, then he's going to give me some answers whether he wants to or not."

"Or what?" Leave it to my sister to call my bluff. She was good like that.

"Or I'll rip his balls off and shove them down his throat." That was a bit much, even for me, but I'd been feeling particularly aggressive lately, especially when anyone threatened me or mine. The kung fu badass who somehow exploded out of me these days was wiggling her way into my mind as well. I blamed it on Destiny. Years of listening to her go on and on *and on* about fighting, and self-mastery, and all that Eastern philosophy stuff was finally sinking in. Had to be. There was no other explanation.

I looked at Trinity, who'd been quiet a bit too long.

"Well?" I waited for her to try to talk me out of charging into the dungeon in her typical lawyerly style. Logic and all that analysis jargon she wielded like a weapon.

"Okay."

That was *it? Okay?*

"I'm going down there. Right now."

"Okay," she said again. "But maybe you should get dressed first?"

L ord Thordis Jax, The Royal Dungeons

No matter how hard I tried, I couldn't stop thinking about Faith. The look in her eyes when her sister, her fucking *sister*, Princess Trinity, had named me a traitor.

I'd been in the palace prison for a few hours. They'd taken me from my apartment, naked, hosed me down like I was a piece of equipment, shoved some coarse clothing at me and chained me to a wall the moment I had the pants and tunic on.

At least I was sitting down. But the chains attached to my arms were on runners. I could move them up or down the track, but not more than a few inches from the wall itself. I could stand, or sit, or sleep with my back to the wall, but that was all.

The cuffs attached to my wrists and ankles were unnecessary. There was no escaping this cell. It looked like it was a thousand years old with stone walls and a stone floor, the black graphite bars across the front of the square space were stronger than the centuries old metal they'd replaced. And beyond that?

An energy barrier used on the planet Atlan to control the beasts scheduled for execution. Males who'd lost control and could tear through graphite like ripping a piece of paper. Males without a mate to soothe them.

Males like me. I wasn't going to go into beast mode, but that didn't mean my cock wasn't hard, aching for her. With the shackles, I couldn't even get myself off to ease the need. Not that I wanted to. I wanted *in* Faith's pussy.

In Faith.

Her name was a dagger in my chest. She'd lied to me. Lied about who she was and why she'd been in my parents' home.

I was no Atlan beast. I wouldn't literally lose my mind and need to be executed after being separated from her. I could survive without her. But I did not want to.

Her Ardor was not over, and the thought of another male pleasuring her, heating her body, giving her his energy as he pumped his thick cock into her—

Fuck.

I yelled in frustration and yanked and pulled against my restraints once more, rattling the chains that hung from the manacles around my wrists and ankles. Those were special gifts from the bastard, Nix, and they'd worked like a charm, the heavy weight reminding me every second of how hopeless this situation was.

Not that I could blame him. He thought I wanted to kill his queen and the princess. They believed I'd kidnapped Faith and held her against her will in my apartment. That I would hurt my mate! Leo. Travin. Nix. They all believed it.

If I were going to hurt her, I wouldn't have had my mouth on her pussy when they burst in.

Never. She was mine. And she was upstairs above me right now, somewhere in this massive palace, with people she trusted telling her lies about me.

I was no traitor. Not to my own family or the Queen's. Never had been. Never. But Faith didn't know that. She didn't know anything about me because we hadn't really *talked about anything*. I'd been determined to get her to talk about herself, and,' of course, I'd been so busy getting my cock inside her, making her come, congratulating myself when she screamed my name and begged for more, that I hadn't done the one thing I should have. Let her *know me*. Made her fall in love with me.

Me. Not my body.

I couldn't contain the turmoil in my mind and yelled again. If anyone touched her... I'd kill him. I'd cut his cock off and hang it around his neck. I'd—

"Not happy, I take it?"

That voice. *Her voice*.

I looked up to see a beautiful stranger standing just outside the dark bars of my cell. Was that really Faith? She looked exactly the same, and yet, so very different. She must have turned off the energy field already to be standing so close. I'd been too caught up in my own misery to notice.

But seeing Faith now was a blow I wasn't ready to take. I couldn't breathe.

I barely recognized her. She wore a gown that shimmered when she moved. The material was a dark, wine color that made little bits of red shine between the gorgeous strands of brown on her head. The ones I knew felt like silk between my fingers. The gown fit her from the hips up like a glove, outlining every curve. Every inch of which I knew very well. Below, it fell straight as rain on a windless night to cover her feet.

The neckline dipped just low enough to tease me with her skin. I could bury my face there and be blissfully happy kissing and tasting for hours. Forever.

If she would allow it.

Which, from her crossed arms and foul expression, she most definitely would *not*.

She was breathtaking. Stunning. So beautiful I couldn't think, her regal bearing and noble bloodline obvious in every graceful movement of her hands, her chin. Even the square set of her shoulders.

Goddess, I'd been an idiot to think she was nothing more than a servant. A complete, cock-blinded idiot. I tugged at the restraints wanting to reach for her. "Faith. Please, listen to me. I'm not a traitor. I don't care what your sister—"

"Her Royal Highness, Princess Trinity, you mean?" she scolded me, and I dipped my chin in apology but didn't dare break eye contact. She was listening, although definitely pissed. That was a start. My mate, the fucking *princess*, was willing to hear me out.

"I don't care what Her Royal Highness, Princess Trinity, has said about me. I am not a traitor. I had nothing to do with Zel's scheme."

"How am I supposed to believe you? Trinity said you handed her over to Zel at the reception practically gift-wrapped." Her tone was one I'd not heard from her before, and the monotone recital of facts made me nervous. That wasn't Faith. Not the Faith I knew. It was like she was being forced to swallow something extremely unpleasant.

"A coincidence," I explained. "We had just shared a dance and she was thirsty. I have no idea how many Alerans she'd danced with, but I was the last. I escorted her to the refreshment table and she saw Zel before I did. Recognized him. She hugged him in front of everyone, clearly thinking he'd tried to save her from the queen's guards who'd come to do the actually rescuing." I sighed. "Goddess, what a fuck up. Look, I acted the gentleman and left her to entertain her next guest. Why would I think she needed protection from him?"

She shook her head slowly. "I don't know, Thor. That's why I'm here. I don't know what to believe." She pressed a button on the wall out of my line of sight and the door to my personal prison swung wide. She stepped inside, leaving it open behind her. The closer she approached, the thicker the air in my cell became. My body reached for hers, desperate in a way I'd never experienced, but I couldn't reach her. Not a chance with the fucking chains. My cock was a painful rod in the coarse pants, the rough fabric rubbing the sensitive head. Even that discomfort was not enough to tame my lust. With her before me, precum seeped from the tip. I could smell her now. That dark forest scent—and more—that made me wild. Her skin. Her hair. Her wet pussy. Desire filled the room. I breathed it in, and I recognized it now, as unique to her.

Unlike me, who I knew smelled of a harsh cleanser, she smelled like flowers and perfumed lotions. Like she'd soaked in a bath of Aleran flowers and they'd melted into her skin. I recognized the scent as partly the result of her bath, but mostly, just her.

Mine.

Yet here she stood before me, inches away and completely beyond my reach.

She licked her full lips but stopped walking forward when the hem of her dress brushed my bare toes. She should have towered over me, but even seated as I was, we were nearly the same height. With my arms spread wide and chained to the wall, I could not touch her. Only gaze upon what I'd had and lost.

"My sister and Leo are convinced you had something to do with kidnapping my mother." No monotone now. Pain. Regret.

What was she talking about?

Princess Trinity's words came back to me from just hours earlier in my apartment. *The Ardor fried your brains, little sister. Step away from him. He's a traitor. We've found evidence that the Jax family was involved in the plot to kidnap Mother.*

I put my soul into my eyes, willed her to believe me. "I would never betray the true queen. I vow this to you as your mate."

She cleared her throat and looked away from me, a blush creeping into her cheeks that I had learned meant she was either embarrassed or aroused. With the scent of her Ardor, her desire, driving me mad, I was hoping for the latter. "I release you from that whole mate thing."

My heart stilled, a chill seeped into my bones. "What?"

She shivered and wrapped her arms around her waist as if she were freezing. Which was unlikely. The cell was temperature controlled to be habitable. "I said, I release you from the whole mate thing."

I shook my head. "No. Fuck no."

She froze, eyes wide. "What do you mean, no?"

"No," I repeated, my voice louder. I couldn't say the one word any more clearly. "You are mine."

It was her turn to shake her head. "You don't know anything about me. And even if I believed you, which I'm not saying I do, but even if I did, I'd need proof. My sister is convinced you are involved, Thor. And her head's a lot clearer than mine at the moment."

"I do not like hearing you speak poorly of yourself. Why would you say such a thing?" She was intelligent. Highly so. I'd seen it myself in our brief time together.

"Because." Her gaze drifted to my cock and it was like she'd stroked me. I hissed in shock at the violence of my reaction. A spurt of pre-cum stained my pants.

There was only one explanation for her words. Her Ardor. My body was responding to hers, to her need. It was my job to soothe her, to ease this discomfort. To keep her from doubting herself. So she could *be* her true self again.

"I said no. You cannot refute me. I have never lied to you. *Never*. Can you say the same, *Your Highness*?"

Her dark eyes widened, then narrowed. "That's not fair. I couldn't tell you who I really was."

"Why?" She'd kept the biggest secret of all. I hadn't known. Obviously, my parents hadn't either. No one on Alera, except for a select few, knew who she really was. A female from Earth who was the daughter of Queen Celene. One of the lit spires belonged to her. Her life force illuminated it, and it would stay that way until she took her last breath. Which, if I had my way, would be at a very old age and in my arms.

"You know why," she replied. "There's a traitor in the Jax house, one who sent Zel to kill me and my sisters within hours of our transport from Earth. My mother is missing. Kidnapped. They dragged her out of bed and transported her to god knows where. They're probably torturing her right now. We have to find her. I couldn't tell you any of that."

She was riled. Angry. Sad, too. Clearly, she loved her mother and worried for her. Because she was not happy, neither was I. I wanted to hold her, ease her upset and at the same time, go track down the fuckers.

"But while you kept your secrets, you could lie in my arms and let me fuck you. Let me fill you. Let me claim you as my mate and talk nonsense about forever? Did you plan a hundred ways to betray me while my cock was inside you? While I was filling you with my seed, feeding your Ardor with my life force, were you consumed with plans to leave me behind?"

"I didn't—I'm sorry. I don't know. I didn't know you, Thor. You're a Jax. I got arrested, and then you showed up at the station to save me, and then—"

"Then we spent the night in bed together. Then you screamed my name and begged me to fill you. And you still said nothing of who you really were. You listened as I promised you forever and you lied to me, Princess."

"You're a Jax," she countered.

And there was the crux of the issue. "Yes. I am a Jax. My family has been loyal to the true queens for thousands of years. And you're mine, Faith. My mate. I don't care what your sister believes. I know the truth. I am innocent of this."

"I need proof, Thor."

"Release me and you will have it. I will not stop until I have found the traitor."

She shook her head. "They'll never let you go. Not now. They are convinced you are guilty."

"With all due respect, I don't give a shit about any of them. All I care about is what you think. What you believe. What is that?"

Her laugh was bitter, like a strangled cry coming from her throat as she paced before me. Back and forth. Shaking. With rage? Hurt?

Need?

"I don't know what to believe anymore." The hurt in her eyes made me feel as if she ripped my heart from my chest and stomped it beneath her heel. Still, she paced. Back and forth, faster and faster, her breath speeding as well. Her nipples were hard points beneath the smooth fabric of her gown. She wrung her hands together, twisting and contorting her fingers as if the pain of such abuse would distract her from what she needed.

There was no escaping this. Not for either of us.

She knew the answer, knew the truth, but perhaps needed some coaxing. Someone to soothe her in the basest of ways. To clear her mind so she could decide. For herself. Not for her sister, not for the crown.

Faith alone.

"Come here." I made the words gentle, but still a command. She needed, I would provide.

She froze in place, but looked down at me with those unfathomable dark eyes. "What?"

"Come here." I rattled the chains, flexed strongly, pulling against them to prove I could not escape their hold. "I cannot hurt you if that is what you fear. Come here, mate, and take what you need."

The flush on her cheeks darkened to a deep crimson, but I held her gaze. I knew what she needed. We both knew. And chained or not, I did not want her taking what she needed to soothe her Ardor from another male. She was mine. Mine to care for. Mine to fuck.

Her Ardor was mine to feed. No one else's. Her body would take my heat, my energy, my seed, and my life force would fill her up. My cock would stretch her open, fuck her. Fill her. Mine.

I was innocent of the crimes her sister had laid against me. Eventually, I would prove I spoke the truth. I would prove myself worthy of her trust. Faith *would* be mine. Forever.

But first, I would give her the soothing she required so she could think clearly, at least for a time, until her Ardor drove her yet again.

"Come here, love." I calmed myself, relaxed my muscles, let a smile curve my lips. "I understand why you were afraid to tell me the truth. But I am not a traitor. I will prove it, I promise you. And when I do, I'm never letting you go. You are mine, my princess. My mate. So come here. Climb onto my lap, lift that pretty dress and ride my cock like I know you want to. Take me, Faith. Take what you want."

She eyed me, then laughed. "You're crazy. This is insane."

That was better. She wasn't mad any longer. She thought *me* slightly insane. I was. For her.

"You need me and I want you to take what you need. I'll give it to you. Not from a consort. *Me*. My cock is yours mate. Look at it. See how hard it is. That's all for you. It's only ever been this way for you and you know that. Look at my hands. Shackled. I can't touch you. Can't do anything but feel the wet clench of your pussy as you surround my cock. Use it. Use me. We will both love it."

She bit her lip, thinking. But I knew her body, recognized the look in her eyes when she was about to give me what I wanted.

Control. Surrender.

Mine. She was mine, even as I was restrained.

"Come. Here." The command was firm this time, from a male to his mate, a mate who suffered. Who needed.

"This is insane," she repeated. Her words were barely more than a whisper, but she turned to face me, stepped forward, lifted her skirt so I had a brief glimpse of her ankles and climbed onto the small, flat mattress. Her knees settled on either side of my thighs. My arms moved automatically, to pull her close, press her body to mine, but the sharp bite of manacles against my flesh forced me to hold still, afraid to startle her by struggling further. My cock was hard and firm against her stomach, the fabric of my pants the only thing between us. Already, I could feel the wet heat of her core, even through my prisoner's garb.

"Kiss me, Faith. Forget this place, where we are. Forget about everything else and let me fill you up."

Her breath was coming in little pants and her cheeks were flushed. Her eyes were so dark, heated with her Ardor's need. "God, you make me crazy."

I hoped that was a good thing and leaned forward to claim her lips with my own.

Her small hands moved down my body, between us, and freed my cock as I kissed her, reveled in the taste of her on my tongue. It was addictive. Feminine. I'd never get enough.

I groaned. She moaned. Softened for me as she lifted higher on her knees, then settled down onto my hard cock. We both shuddered at the feel of it. Fuck, her pussy lips wrapped around the crown before I sank in, opening her up. She was so wet, my entry was easy. She kissed me once more before her mouth moved to linger on my jaw before she nuzzled my neck, her hot breath fanning my skin.

"Thor," she almost whimpered. She was seated right on my lap, completely filled with my cock. She remained still, and I wasn't sure if I could survive the delicious feel of her.

There were tears in that voice, pain. Uncertainty. And yet she'd let me in, joined us as one.

"It's all right," I murmured. "Do it. Feel me. Let me take care of you. Please, Faith. Please." I was begging now. Begging her to move. To ride me. To take my energy and fill herself up. I wanted to be part of her forever. I wanted to know that it was my life force that made her strong. Whole. "Please, baby. Move. Take me."

Pinned to the wall like an insect, I felt powerless. Helpless, and yet powerful, for I was the one to give this to her. The one to make her pussy all but drip with her need. Her inner walls clench and clutch my cock. My energy transferring to her, giving her the relief she needed.

If, when we were done here, Faith walked away from me, I knew, somehow I knew, that I'd lose her forever.

"I can't do this." She leaned back, sitting harder on my cock, taking me deeper, not in pleasure, but as a side effect. She gasped as I bottomed out. I yanked against the chains, desperate to break free. To hold her to me.

No! Fuck, no. I was crammed inside her tight pussy, and yet I was losing her.

I lost my mind, just for a moment, knowing she was mentally drifting away. "No!" I pulled with all my might against the restraints, blood running from fresh cuts at my wrists.

She pulled her head back, eyes wide on my arms. "Stop it! Right now."

Faith kissed me. Hard. Over and over until I stopped struggling. "Hold still. Okay? Just trust me for a minute."

She held my gaze, those dark brown eyes no longer sad, but filled with resolve. To leave me? Kill me? Fuck me senseless. I had no idea. But she needed me to hold still, so I would, no matter the cost. Sweat dripped from my brow as I nodded. She grinned and kissed me again. Slower. Deeper. Buried her fingers in my hair and tugged just hard enough to let me know she was already riding the edge of release.

She shifted her hips and moved on my cock, moaning with pleasure. Heat built between us and I felt the sweet release of tension in my body as she drained the excess energy from me, claiming it for her own. Feeding her Ardor. "Maybe we should try this again someday. Tying each other up." Lifting her hips, she slid back down, taking me deeper still. "Under different circumstances, of course."

"Mate, what are you talking about?" She had me so confused, so wound up, I had no idea what was going on.

"This." Reaching up, she somehow released the bolts from the wall, the manacles dropping to hang with a soft clinking sound along the stone. The restraints around my ankles collapsed as well, falling to the floor with a thud.

I was free.

The door was open.

And my mate was riding my cock. Hard. And calling out my name as if I were a god. As if I were the life force she needed to breathe instead of the traitor she thought me to be.

3

P*rincess Faith, The Royal Dungeons*

I MISSED THIS. I missed Thor. God, it had only been a couple of hours, but I was frantic. Desperate to come. He felt so good. *This* felt so good. The connection was intense. I didn't care if it was because of my Ardor and his awakening. I'd felt nothing like it. Knew I never would again.

I held onto his shoulders as I rode him, used him for my own pleasure. But he wasn't suffering. I watched him as he realized what I'd done. It was a slow process because I was circling my hips, rubbing my clit against him as he did so.

"Why?" he breathed, his hands going to my hips, squeezing.

His dark gray-blue eyes held mine with an intensity I couldn't break.

"I believe you."

He breathed raggedly once, twice, then his hand slid around to my front so his thumb played over my clit. My eyes fell closed.

"Look at me," he commanded, and I did as he wished. Held his gaze.

"Come, mate. Come now."

I did, for I loved to obey him. Silly, really, since I held all the control. I'd been able to use him for my Ardor. He'd offered and I'd gladly taken. But then I accepted what I'd already known. My heart, my head finally synced. Thor was innocent. I knew it. Felt it. Believed it. *Breathed* it.

And so I'd released him. Given him the obvious proof that I trusted him. It was the two of us now against the world. Everyone—including Trinity—believed him guilty. Thor had believed I'd been the traitor, and he'd saved me anyway. Vowed to protect me from Lord Wyse and that horrible Optimus unit, no matter the cost.

He was honorable, and he was mine, willing to risk defying everyone to keep me when he thought I was nothing. A servant. He would fight for me now, as well. Fight for us. So I would, too. I'd take a leap of faith. I'd love him.

Love burst through me like there had been a dam holding it back. And with it, heightened senses. Every touch meant more. Every kiss. Every shift of my hips and his, either one of us loving the other. I'd never experienced anything like this. Like him.

Pleasure flooded me. Swamped me, all but drowned me, but I had an anchor in Thor. I couldn't fall because he was there to catch me. Hold me. Keep me together as my body fell apart, as my Ardor took in his very essence and eased the hunger consuming me, as I found the most blissful pleasure.

I cried out, milked him. I felt him thicken, lengthen impossibly further within me as he came. His hands tightened on my hips as he thrust up one time. Filling me. Emptying his balls with his seed and giving it all to me.

"Mate," he growled.

I was panting, sweating, trying to catch my breath.

"Again," he demanded.

I nodded, definitely not done. His cock didn't flag inside me, and when he began to rock his hips, I knew he was instantly ready to fuck some more. His seed slipped between us, coated our skin. My body was still soaring, so close to another peak that I cried out, on the edge within moments. Shuddering. Begging.

"Yes. Please. More."

His hands came up, tugged down the bodice of my dress, exposed my breasts to him. "Where is that fancy, sexy as fuck, undergarment?"

"I came bare," I breathed as he latched on to one nipple. My hands went into his hair, tangled, as I arched my back and offered more, rubbed my clit against him. Spread my knees so that my body opened wider. I wanted more. Everything he could give me. And more still. There would never be enough.

He groaned as he switched to the other nipple, so neglected. I rolled my hips and slowly fucked him as he didn't let up. The pleasure of his mouth sent pulses of heat to my pussy. I held on with a soft groan, holding back, riding the edge all over again. I wanted this to last forever.

When his teeth grazed my nipple, then gently bit down, I came again, startling me. It wasn't powerful like the last one, but the heat spread through me, like a thick syrup. Warmth and pleasure seeped into my bones, and I moaned his name.

"Must we continue this here? I much prefer to tuck you beneath me on a more sumptuous mattress."

His words reminded me of our surroundings. I was a princess. If I wanted Thor to be free of this dungeon and in my bed, no one could stop me.

"My rooms. Yes. Now."

"We must separate, mate."

"No. Never again. Everyone is against us. You are a Jax. I am a Herakles. We are star-crossed lovers." I thought of Shakespeare's *Romeo and Juliet*, but knew we would not die for our love.

"The world be damned. We will go to your rooms, but unless you wish me to carry you through the palace with your legs about my waist, cock buried deep for everyone to witness, I will have to pull out."

"I don't care," I said, lifting and circling my hips, ready to come once more. God, would the pleasure ever stop?

"You do, mate. What we share is private. Just for us. I wish to keep your cries of pleasure just for me. I want no one else to see what you look like as you find your pleasure, as my seed fills you up. As your Ardor is soothed."

"One more then. I want to come once more, then we'll go to my rooms."

With my breasts bare, his hands settled on my hips once more. He brought his legs up, knees bent so I was cradled between him and his thighs.

"My mate, my princess. As you wish, but know this, we won't be leaving your bed until your Ardor is gone. If we are to fight the world together, then I will set you free."

҉

THOR, The Royal Palace

IT TOOK two days to end Faith's Ardor. I wasn't complaining. Hell, no. Two days of keeping her naked, writhing, and alone together in her rooms. There was no doubt her sister knew what we were up to. I'd been expecting guards to burst through the doors at any time and drag me from her bed.

But when they came knocking, our visitors were Trinity and Leo, not armed guards. And Faith very firmly told her sister to "*leave us alone*". After that, my beautiful mate ordered trays of food to be left in the hallway for us. Two days of sleeping, fucking, talking, bathing together in her luxurious private suite. Laughing. Loving. More fucking.

Kissing.

Touching.

If she hadn't already owned my heart, she did now. I was fully and truly smitten. And delighted to discover that Faith was wickedly intelligent, and did not hesitate to challenge me at every turn. She loved to laugh, and loved to torment our visiting queen's guards when they'd delivered our food, especially the brutish one named Nix. She teased him and laughed, but he handled it better than the rest of them. The young ones had stopped coming to our door, unable to cope with my mate's determination to chat with them and ask for news. She was mischievous, like my father's cats, full of a joy for life I'd never imagined could exist before I met her.

And I never wanted to lose her. And to that end, I kept no secrets. I told her everything I knew, everything I suspected, and everything I'd done over the last few weeks. She asked questions, a lot of them, but I answered them all.

And then I took her again. Fed her Ardor. Made her mine.

If the question was truly personal, or difficult to answer, I demanded an orgasm from her body as payment.

I didn't have to worry about myself. Simply being inside her pussy was enough to drive me half mad with lust. No, I had to worry about the opposite—holding back—prolonging both our pleasure.

Being a princess had its benefits, and this luxurious suite of rooms was something even I'd never seen before. My family was wealthy, but the palace looked like something out of a children's storybook. Art on every wall. Carpet so thick one could sleep on it without discomfort. Or fuck. Or both, as we had done many times since locking ourselves in this private oasis. We had conversations on that floor, with her lying atop me, my cock still inside her, neither of us willing to give up the physical connection.

In here there were no rules, no family members, no history

or soldiers trying to kill us. Just Faith and me. Mates. Just us, learning about each other.

Faith told me of growing up on Earth, of her sisters, her father who was an Earthling and was still there. Of her interest in animals and her refusal to eat them. Of so many things. I, in turn, shared as well.

By the time the Ardor finally broke, we'd slept for hours to recover. I felt confident in our connection. That she was my mate. Truly mine.

And, in the end, she realized the truth; I knew there was a traitor within my parents' home, but I had no idea who it was. Neither did she.

And though we agreed to return there once more, I refused to let her go posing as a servant. She was mine, and I would not have her waiting hand and foot on my father when we had dozens of others who could do the task. No, she was my mate and would be treated with respect and honor. Not as much as she might receive from others when they discovered she was a princess, but enough for now.

As for me, I held no other in higher regard. She'd traveled blindly halfway across the galaxy to save her mother. She'd left her sisters and managed to infiltrate my parents' home in a matter of days, serving as closely to my father as one could expect. She was resourceful and clever, and I admired her courage. I was honored that my cock had chosen her, for my heart and mind agreed. Faith was perfect.

The instant she'd released the restraints she'd become mine. Her decision had been made, her fate sealed. I'd vowed then that we would fight the world together and I'd meant it. Even with her sister currently in charge of the entire planet, Trinity didn't matter to me. Not in this. She had no power to change the way I felt about Faith, and no sway over what we did. Who we loved.

We would find the real traitor before Princess Trinity and her people could. No one in her circle of guards knew my house—or its servants—better than I did. She was a new arrival, and although I believed Nix, Leo and their queen's guard had spies in every house, whoever they had implanted in my parents' home had missed all the warning signs with Zel. And allowed the Jax name to be placed in danger. And that, I could not forgive.

I was innocent in this and Faith believed me, but no one else would. So far, Princess Trinity had downplayed the Jax family's involvement in her kidnapping. But if I couldn't give her answers, and soon, that would change.

The people were hungry for answers. And if we couldn't give them the truth, they would manufacture their own theories, believe the lies our enemies might spread through the world. It would endanger not just my family, but Princess Trinity and Faith as well.

That I could not allow. Faith and I would work—together this time—to root out the mole once and for all. That was the first step to finding Queen Celene and clearing my family name, for I was convinced the traitor in my house would have information we needed to save the queen. Once the elder royal was found, Faith would be third in line to the throne. Which was better than second.

The further from the seat of power, the better, as far as I was concerned. She wanted a simple life, children, a family. She didn't want the crown. It wasn't her. And I did not want her to be the target of every power-hungry, crazed lunatic on Alera.

I wanted her happy, safe, and protected, and in my bed.

And as I helped Faith dress—no fancy dress this time, but simple clothing with the sexy-as-fuck underthings beneath that were only for me to see and know about, I felt contentment wash through me, a peace and completeness I'd never felt before. In the past, something inside me had been empty. Hungry. Looking at Faith, I let the heaviness of happiness melt me into something new, something softer in this moment, and pulled her into my arms. Not to fuck, but to hold her close, absorb the peace and satisfaction I felt whenever she was near.

Love. This was love. She would be my greatest source of strength for what was to come next. And my greatest weakness.

Reluctant, I let her go and waited as the S-Gen machine made clothes for me. I looked to Faith, who was eyeing me as if her Ardor had returned.

"I'm really going to miss seeing you naked all the time."

I grinned. "It will all be beneath, my love. Just waiting for you."

She sighed. "I wish... I wish we knew where my mom is. She's been waiting to return to Alera with us all this time. Waiting to be queen. Once she does, we can just be simple princess and mate. Nothing more."

I went over to her, my cock rising again just looking at her, brushed her long hair back from her face. If I had my way, she'd never wear it up again. "Simple princess and mate? I doubt we will ever be simple."

Her head tilted into my palm and she rubbed her soft skin against me like one of my father's Zebcats. Her eyes drifted closed for a moment before she looked up at me. I saw all the emotions I'd been feeling reflected there. Love. Peace. She was mine now. Truly mine. "Fine. Not simple. Danger-free. How about that?"

I smiled. "Yes, I will agree to that. No danger." The S-Gen machine beeped, signaling my clothing was ready. I stepped away, for if I didn't do so, we'd never get out of these rooms.

I dressed quickly in a warrior's uniform with my family crest on the sleeves. I did not want to go before Princess Trinity and her mate, and her guards, looking like a pompous lord in silk and fluff. But I did not want to appear weak, either. I'd settled on the uniform reserved for the head of my family's military forces. Each family kept their own standing armies. Mine was quite large, spread out over dozens of my family's estates. As my father's heir, I was, indeed, their commander.

Normally, I did not rub that fact in other lords' or ladies' faces. Today, I wanted to go before Faith's sister with my power on display. I was not weak. Neither was my family. I would not beg. Faith was mine. My goal was to make sure Trinity's mate, Leo, recognized what I said without words—that Faith was mine to protect, and I would die defending her.

She smiled as I tugged the hem of my sleeve into place and walked to me, taking my hand. "I always did have a thing for men in uniform."

I grabbed her. Kissed her. Hard. "Not men, mate. Me."

Her soft laughter made my heart feel like it had wings, flapping beneath my ribs, trying to escape. "Yes, Thor. Only you. You are named after a Nordic god, after all."

That took me aback. Me? Named for a god? In no pantheon I'd ever heard of was there a god named Thordis. It was a family name, going back hundreds of years. "Perhaps it is because I am a god when I am between your thighs."

I thought she would deny me the admission. Instead, her cheeks turned a delightful shade of pink and she bit her lower lip. The look she gave me made my cock roar to life. "True. You are."

"Mate, stop looking at me in such a manner or we shall never leave this room."

She laughed then, the sound wild and free. "My Ardor is over."

I pulled her closer, making sure she could feel the hard length of my cock pressed between us. "What about *my* Ardor?"

"You don't have an Ardor, Thor."

I lowered my head and kissed her neck. "I beg to differ, mate. Tell my cock your lies."

She held me tight, turning her head to the side to give me better access. It was a blatant invitation, and I was all too eager to accept it. "We must go speak to your sister. She may be content to allow you this time with me, but I promise you, her mate will not wait much longer."

"He can kiss my ass."

Lowering my hand, I squeezed her bottom, lifted her into my cock, tormenting myself. "No, mate. No one will have his lips on this body but me."

Reluctantly, I let her go. The upper floor of the palace was much fancier than the dungeons below. While my parents' mansion was ornate, gaudy even, the rooms were simply furnished, with clean lines and tasteful colors. The palace?

I could see that Lady Radella had put her own stamp upon the rooms. Much like the lady, everything I'd seen so far was bold. Bright colors. Orange and red next to vibrant blue or shining silver. There was no restful energy here, but a frantic need to express herself, like a beautiful, colorful bird locked in a cage.

If my mate asked, I would live here with her, but I longed to abandon both this palace and my apartment and find a home. Some place that belonged to both of us, with room for the children I hoped would someday come.

Someday, when we were danger-free.

Holding her hand in mine, we made our way down the hallway and found Princess Trinity and Leo in the royal salon. They were having their lunch in a small dining room, the table only seating eight, unlike the formal one below which could accommodate up to eighty. They looked up when we entered and after I offered a nod of respect, I noticed they weren't alone. Nix sat across from Leo. The two men's uniform coats were hooked over the back of their chairs and the princess was dressed in simple clothing, similar to Faith's. I'd only seen Princess Trinity in formal wear and she looked quite different with her blonde hair pulled back at her nape in a tail and her face free of makeup.

"All better?" the princess—fuck, it was going to be hard to

differentiate the sisters since they were *both* princesses—asked Faith, a knowing smile curling the corner of her mouth.

"Much." Ignoring the glares of the males as if they did not exist, Faith walked to the table and sat next to Leo before I could offer her a chair. I remained standing behind her, still uncertain of our welcome as Faith reached and grabbed a small piece of fruit from a platter and popped it in her mouth. "How's it hanging, Leo?"

Nix, who had been watching me as if I would slit Faith's throat at any moment, blinked quickly and turned to stare at my mate. Clearly, he was not yet used to these new princesses from Earth.

"Do you refer to my cock, little sister? It is unhappy at the moment."

Nix choked on his food. Trinity laughed. "Later, mate. We can not stay in bed all day and night."

"Actually, we could."

Trinity shook her head as Nix busied himself with his food. I'd never seen an assassin blush, but if I had to guess—

"Sorry about your blue balls, Leo. I'm sure Trin will take care of it for you later."

Blue balls? Why would Leoron's balls be blue? I assumed my mate referred to his testicles. And, if they were truly blue, how was my mate aware of this strange coloration?

Luckily, Leo spoke before I could torment myself with the answer to that question. "I fucked your sister until she screamed this morning. My balls are not blue."

"Good to know. And thanks for all the food you had delivered. Marathon sex can really give you an appetite."

Trinity lounged back in her chair in a very unroyal fashion. "You're welcome. Is your Ardor over?"

"Done." Faith patted the seat next to her and looked up at me for a moment. "Sit down, Thor." Clearly, she didn't seem bothered by her sister and the others knowing what we'd been up to these past two days. In fact, she was all but taunting everyone with it. I wasn't bothered in the least that everyone knew we'd been fucking. As Faith had said, like rabbits, a furry animal from Earth who must go at it constantly. There would be no doubt in anyone's mind that we were mates.

She turned back to her sister the moment I was seated. "So, what have we missed? Have you heard from my twin?"

"No. I have not. I thought we might try to get a hold of her today. I'm getting worried."

Faith glanced from her sister to Nix, then back. Trinity met her gaze as I watched and nodded. "You can trust him."

"You sure about that?" Faith turned to Nix. "No offense, but the last two times I saw you, you were trying to kill us, and then you dragged my mate off to prison."

Nix had the good sense to look contrite. "My apologies, Your Highness. In the first instance, I was trying to save your life, not end it."

She seemed fine with that. "And in the second?" Rage colored her voice. "I believe you owe Thor an apology. Like now." Pure steel in her tone, and Nix actually sat back to study her, a look of surprise on his face.

"Faith—" Trinity began.

Faith held up her hand, palm facing her sister. "Talk to the hand, Trin." She didn't even look at the princess, but stared at Nix. "Well?"

He bowed his chin to her, then looked me in the eye. "My apologies, Lord Jax. I was simply following orders and believed Princess Faith was in danger."

Fuck me. I couldn't believe it. "Apology accepted."

Trinity sat back, her arms crossed, but she kept her mouth shut.

Sitting between the two sisters, Leo waited, taking his cue from his mate.

Good. These males should not underestimate my mate, nor her sister. They were beautiful, but I had learned that they were also highly intelligent and more stubborn than any male

I'd ever encountered. And I had yet to meet Destiny, my mate's twin. She had told me about Destiny during our time together, and about their escapades growing up.

Destiny sounded like the most volatile of the three sisters and I very much looked forward to meeting her.

Faith popped another piece of fruit into her mouth and patted me on the thigh. "Good, now that that's settled, can we get ahold of Des? I'm worried. She's in the viper's pit."

"While I know what she's up to, *generally,* I don't know where she is." Leo looked at my mate, his brows raised in question.

"You don't know?" Faith leaned back, pressing her back into me. Happy to respond, I pulled her—and her chair—closer to me and wrapped an arm around her.

Trinity shook her head. "I kept my vow to Mother and told no one of our plans."

"Holy shit, Trin. Not even sharing with your mate. Wow. You are a hard-ass, rule follower, just like Dad."

"Nothing new there," Trinity said. "And Leo understands."

I glanced at him and wasn't so sure, but at least he was patient. Probably had to be with these ladies in charge.

Faith shook her head. "That's... wow. Which is why you'll be a better queen someday than I could ever be." She rubbed my arm absently, petting me where it was wrapped around her waist. "I was supposed to get into the Jax house. Destiny was supposed to join the clerical order."

"What?" Nix sat up straighter, concern on his brow. "The clerics? Leo, you knew about this?"

He nodded, but that didn't seem to appease the guard.

"That is not acceptable."

Trinity sipped her drink. "No shit, Sherlock. But we didn't have a choice. Our mom was kidnapped from Earth by someone who knew where to look. Based on the politics of the time—when my biological father was murdered—she suspected the Jax house and the Clerics. The plan was to divide and conquer and all that."

Nix shook his head, muttering to himself. "Insane. Females are insane. What were you thinking?"

"That we needed to save our mother," Faith answered. She turned back to Trinity. "Do you know where Destiny is? Can we reach her?"

"Yes. The citadel will support us in this."

Faith nodded, as if that made complete sense. Which, of course, it did not. The citadel was a building with some spires and pretty flowers on the outside. But I wasn't going to argue. It was well-known lore that the royals believed the citadel to be more.

The rest of us humored them.

"Do it then," Faith said. "I won't feel right until I know she's okay."

Trinity nodded and rose from her seat. She walked to an empty screen along one wall and pressed her palm to the wall. The screen wavered for a moment, as if liquid waves flowed beneath the surface. There was no picture, but I distinctly heard a female's whispered voice.

"Jesus! About fucking time. Just a sec."

Faith chuckled. "Yep. That's Destiny."

Trinity turned from the still empty screen and met Faith's gaze, smiling. "I'd say she's fine, at least right now."

"Thank god."

Trinity sat back down and we all turned toward the screen as it flickered, then turned dark. Barely visible, Faith's twin sister looked as if she were speaking into a small screen. "Trin? Faith? Can you hear me?"

Faith looked down at her palm, at the small scar I'd noticed there, and rubbed at it as if it ached. "Yes, we can hear you."

Nix leaned forward, squinting at the screen as if trying to discover who the mysterious third princess might be. We could see her outline, hear her voice, but she was in a very dark room, her features obscured, as if the communication itself was protecting her identity.

"Leo? Is that you?"

"Yes, Destiny. I am very happy to see you are well."

"I'm alive, if that's what you mean," she grumbled.

Nix shifted even farther forward. "It is dark, Your Highness."

"Really? I hadn't noticed." Her tone of voice clearly indicated the opposite. "I don't have a lot of time to ask who you are. What's been going on there? Oh, and Trin? Fucking loved the dress. Can't fight for shit in that thing, though, could you? What have I told you about that?"

Trinity leaned back into her seat with a sigh. "It was pretty, Destiny."

"Cinderella style. What the fuck happened, anyway? How'd you let that guy Zel get the drop on you?"

"How do you know of these events?" Nix asked.

"I'm in the order, not dead. They do get the news feeds here."

I knew Faith well, and recognized a bit of her in her twin sister. Enough to know that Destiny was, most likely, rolling her eyes at Nix at this very moment.

"We are fine, Des," Faith called. "What about you? Any luck?"

"No. But there has been some buzzing lately about prisoner movements. I'm hoping I don't have to try to seduce the answer out of one of these asshole clerics."

"You shall do no such thing," Nix ordered.

Destiny cleared her throat, her face becoming just distinct enough that we could see her eyes as she scowled at him. "Who are you, anyway? Trin, who is this guy?"

"I am a member of the queen's guard, and loyal servant to Alera."

Destiny moved back again—back from what, I had no idea.

It was as if she held a small communication device in her hand. "Whatever."

Nix stood, clearly bothered by the princess's curt tone and blasé attitude.

Destiny ignored him. "Look, I have to go. They're moving their prisoners around, and I heard they are transporting their high value assets in the next day or two. I'll try to get in there. See who they've got. One of them could be Mom."

"Be careful," Faith said.

"Love you guys. Just in case—you know—"

"Don't even say it, Des. Don't. Just don't." Trinity stood as well. Faith's fingertips dug into my arm and her breathing raced.

"Destiny, if you die, I swear to god, I'm going to hunt you down and kill you again." That was my sweet-tempered, loving female.

Destiny tilted her head and I could practically see her mind working, calculating odds. "Keep your fingers crossed then." A loud thumping noise sounded, as if someone knocked on a door behind the princess. "I gotta go. Like now. Love you."

The screen went blank. Trinity sat back down, her head in her hands. Nix stared at the screen, as if he could force Destiny to return by strength of will alone.

"Shit," Trinity said.

"She's going to do something crazy," Faith added.

Nix turned from the screen to stare at my mate. "Where is she?"

Faith shrugged, her small body moving against mine, and I was never more grateful to have her close. Safe. "I don't know. Wherever the new recruits go for the clerics. Somewhere in the city."

He turned to Trinity, who looked up at last and agreed. "We have no idea. That was part of the plan. If one of us got caught, the other two would have no information to give our enemies."

"Fuck." Nix sat, but his fingers drummed a steady beat on the tabletop as if he could not sit still.

"Well, the news is about to get even better." Leo spoke, breaking the tense silence. "Thordis, I'm sorry to have to tell you, but your apartment has been ransacked."

I glanced at Nix, who held up his hands. "It wasn't me or anyone in the queen's guard. In fact, quite the opposite. We were the ones who found it destroyed when we returned to have your doors repaired. Someone was searching for something."

"Or someone," Leo added, eyeing Faith.

She was about to put another piece of fruit in her mouth, but she froze. "Me? Who knew I was with Thor?"

Trinity shrugged. "Everyone in the queen's guard. Me and Leo, of course. Lord and Lady Jax, I would assume, since they were the ones who'd had Faith sent off with the police in the first place."

"I didn't tell my parents anything. I'd been alone when I decided to go after you." I put my hand on Faith's shoulder. Squeezed. "No doubt Lord Wyse, or someone in the Optimus unit told them I dropped the charges and took you away from there."

"You're welcome to remain here. Obviously the palace is big enough for all of us." Trinity looked at Faith, waiting for an answer. Not me, Faith.

I was offended—for a brief moment—then conceded that the princess was correct. Where Faith was, so would I be. If that was here, or in my parents' home, as we'd discussed before leaving our rooms.

Faith looked to me. Smiled. "Actually, we're going to stay at the Jax mansion."

Princess Trinity frowned as I relaxed, content that my mate had not changed her mind and would remain by my side as we hunted for the traitor. "Are you sure that's a good idea? Lord Wyse already arrested you once."

"Exactly, which is why we're *not* staying here," Faith countered. "And he doesn't know I'm a princess. No one outside of this room knows the truth. We have to go back and catch the traitor."

Trinity shook her head. "It's too dangerous."

"Princess Trinity," I began, but she held up her hand.

"I think, considering what you and my sister have been up to, you can all me Trinity. At least in private."

I didn't see a trace of her previous hostility and anger toward me. I had no idea what she and Faith had talked about while I was chained in their dungeon—or if they'd talked at all —but she seemed to have come to a decision not to hate me. Perhaps, if Faith believed in me, Trinity had decided to trust her sister's judgment.

I offered a slight head nod of respect, then continued. "Trinity, as you're well aware, the traitor in the Jax household has yet to be identified. Faith and I will return there... together, to discover who it is once and for all."

"That is a dangerous proposition," Leo commented.

"As Faith is my mate, I do not want her far from my side. I'm sure you understand, Captain. But as a Jax, it is crucial I clear my family's name."

"Thor's my mate, Leo. You can relate to that. I believe in him and want him free from this. The traitor wants to harm our family, and his as well. We can only be together, in peace, once we learn the truth and free my mother."

"But your safety, princess," Nix said. He'd been quiet since Destiny had signed off. But all of the conversation had been a family discussion, which he was not a part of. His job was to see to the safety of the royals and that included my mate.

"I will keep her safe," I vowed.

Leo stood, came over to me. He was slightly taller and definitely formidable. But I would stand up to him and anyone else who tried to separate me from my mate. "If anything happens to her, I will flay you alive."

"If anything happens to Faith, Captain, I will already be dead."

He eyed me, considered, then nodded.

"Very well. May your mission be successful."

"And by all that is holy, Faith," Trinity said, grinning. "Try to be quiet when you come. I mean, you want your in-laws hearing that?"

Leo put his hand to his chest. "I'm her in-law, as you Earth people call it. I heard it. I found it very inspirational."

Trinity struck him on the shoulder, but she was smiling. "Shut-up, Leo. Seriously."

Faith stood and I followed, made peace with the fact that I was mating a royal, a princess, and this would be my role in life. To be at her side. To go where she wandered. To protect her. Love her. Support her.

I was content.

Faith walked around the table and hugged her sister from behind, since Trinity was still seated at the table. Leo winked at Faith as we went by. The traitor was out there. It was time to find out who it was. Together.

4

T *hor, The Jax Mansion*

"I HAVE A BAD FEELING ABOUT THIS," Faith whispered. Her fingers clenched mine as we walked through the front door of the Jax mansion. I'd done it thousands of times over my entire life, but it was different now. I held my mate's hand, and I wasn't letting go. I wasn't alone. I was... whole.

Someday, this would become our home. I'd already begun to take over business tasks for my father, but moving into this oversized, ornate place? I wasn't ready for that.

One step at a time. And that meant telling my parents Faith was mine. I dreaded it, perhaps as much as she, but I wasn't going to tell her that. I worried she would misconstrue a lack of eagerness for a confrontation as a disinterest in her.

I wasn't hesitant to share that we were mates to my parents because I wasn't proud of her, of what we now shared, but because I didn't have time for whatever argument was going to come from it. I knew my parents, knew their high hopes for a match for me didn't include the upstairs maid. Their ambitions —at least my mother's—aimed high.

I was all for a highborn mate. The goddesses awakened my cock for Faith. At the time, I'd thought her a maid, not a princess. I hadn't cared who she was, just that she was *mine*. My mother couldn't get any more *highborn* than princess. If it were destined, then so be it. Maid, princess, it mattered not. My cock knew, grew and there was no going back. There would be no one else. Ever. And the days we'd spent together since, fucking, talking, loving and laughing only confirmed that we belonged together.

I wasn't changing my mind—as if I could—no matter my parents' feelings on the matter. And I was sure our arrival wouldn't be met with open arms or even happiness from my mother. She'd been parading females she deemed worthy in front of me for years.

A servant like she believed Faith to be would not be accept-able to her. And I knew her stubborn ways. She would not change her mind. Therefore, I'd rather spend the time fucking my mate than fighting with my parents.

"Trust me, everything's going to be fine," I replied, walking down the central hallway to find them. The conversation with my mother would probably be less than pleasant, but I wouldn't let anything hurt my mate, even barbed words.

My mother didn't remain still from morning until night— only my father could pin her down and that was usually beneath him—but he would be in his office. He was predictable enough that I knew he'd be reading at this time of day.

"Hello, Father," I said, finding him just where I'd expected, in his favorite chair, book in hand.

He looked up and smiled, then his eyes widened at the sight of us together. The last time he'd seen Faith, she'd been taken from this very room in handcuffs by the police. "Son. Faith. What a surprise."

He didn't look upset, perhaps a little confused. The Zebcats came prancing into the room and came right to Faith, rubbed themselves on her ankles. Their familiar loud purr filled the room. Faith stared at the animals, then looked to Father wide-eyed.

"I've never seen them do that before," I said, stunned.

"Animals like me," Faith replied with a small shrug. The corner of her mouth tipped up, pleased at the welcome. She didn't move, just let the creatures do what they wanted before they abandoned her and went over to my father. They hopped up in his lap expecting to be petted.

"I told you they were a good judge of character," Father replied, smiling. His hand stroked down the bigger animal's back.

"I hope you agree with your pets, because Faith and I are mates." There was no delaying the truth. I was proud of it and my cock swelled, as if it wanted my father to have visible proof. I shifted so that that evidence was blocked partially by Faith. My words were enough.

My father smiled and pushed the animals off his lap so he could stand.

"You and Faith? Why that's wonderful—"

"What?" My mother's sharp word cut off my father. We turned as she came into the room. Her eyes were wide and she looked... enraged. Just as Faith had expected. "You're mates? With *her*?"

Mother looked down her nose at Faith. We'd agreed we would keep her true identity a secret and I was glad of it. It was the only way she could remain here, otherwise, she would be stalked by our news agencies eager for a story. The entire planet would seek to devour every bit of information they could. She was a princess. We would be mobbed out of curiosity alone and that would most definitely place my mate in more danger. It was clear now, looking back, why she hadn't told me who she was. Why we were sneaked in and out of the palace through convoluted secret passages instead of the main entrance.

My mother's anger could be resolved with just three words. *Meet Princess Faith.* But I wasn't going to do that. Faith's true nature was obvious to anyone with a passing interest. And I wanted my mother to love Faith because of who she was on the inside, not because she was royalty. No doubt Mother would be thrilled once she learned the truth, preening and fawning all over her, glad to have the closest of connections to the palace.

"Yes, Mother. *Her.* She awakened me."

Her eyes widened in surprise. "Awakened?" she asked, the word almost whispered reverently. It was a big deal. A *really* big deal to her. Which was absolutely ridiculous since it was my cock.

"Then you are not thinking clearly, obviously. No wonder you dropped the charges and took her away before she could be properly questioned by Lord Wyse. The awakening has destroyed your judgment."

"My judgment is fine," I replied, trying to remain calm. "Faith is mine, Mother. My mate."

I felt the way Faith tensed next to me, her muscles rigid and her breath quick, yet she remained silent with a pleasant expression upon her face. There was nothing for her to say. She didn't need to defend herself.

"Not only is she a maid, but I found her, personally, snooping in my room." My mother spoke as if I hadn't even responded. "Instead of being in your bed, she should be in *jail.* Because of your awakening, she hasn't even been formally questioned!"

"Interrogated, you mean," I countered. "She's not in jail simply because my cock is ruling my head, Mother. Faith is innocent and I will not allow her to spend a moment with the Optimus unit. *That* is the reason I got her out of there."

"My lord, you see how the awakening has clouded your son's judgment?" she implored to my father.

"The Zebcats like Faith and they have an excellent judge of character."

Mother sniffed, clearly wishing he'd backed her up instead of being his usual carefree self. They balanced each other well, most of the time. "You think those beasts should decide whether or not this traitor goes to jail?" She turned to me, pointed at Faith. "Let the professionals have their turn with her. Then, after a suitable period of time, you'll be thinking clearly again and seeing reason."

Meaning I'll see some other female who suited me better. With my cock awakened, I could have anyone now. Could fuck any female who would have me with wild abandon. But I wanted no other.

This conversation was only making me angry. I didn't hit women, ever, but this was the first time I had any inclination to do so. The very thought I'd abandon and betray Faith...

I sighed, realized this was just how my mother was. Always had been, always would be. She thought she was doing what was best for me, but no. For the first time, I was telling her no. And all her hopes for the match of *her* dreams were gone.

There would be no reasoning with her. This talk only proved that Faith's predictions were right. Our mating wasn't good news.

But we weren't here to get their blessing. We were here to find the real traitor. Then we could get on with our lives... outside of this mansion.

"My apartment has been ransacked," I told them.

My mother immediately looked to Faith, as if she'd done it.

"I assure you, Mother, Faith has a solid alibi."

My mother flushed red with anger or embarrassment—I didn't care which—and pursed her lips as she made the correct inference.

"We will stay here in my old room until my place can be cleaned up, until the damage can be fixed."

"Wonderful," my father commented. One of the Zebcats

returned and he bent down to pick the big thing up. "Dinner is at the usual time. It will be good to have you back here again. Faith, too."

Father winked at Faith and my mother sighed.

I took his opening for us to leave and nodded to both my parents. I didn't say more, for we'd only end the discussion in a verbal war. Faith was right at my side. It wasn't until we were upstairs, my bedroom door closed behind us, did she let go of my hand.

"Your mother doesn't like me."

Understatement of the century. I studied her to see if she were bothered by that. Tears perhaps. Or anger. I saw neither.

"To her, maintaining the Jax lineage is at the top of her personal to-do list. It's her duty to see the next generation be flawless," I explained. It didn't make her actions right, but at least understandable.

"Yeah, well, clearly an Aleran princess isn't good enough," she replied, tucking her hair behind her ears.

"She *thinks* you're a maid." I went over-to her, stroked her hair. Silky soft. "She's a snob, nothing more."

"You're protecting her," she countered. Faith didn't say the words harshly, but as fact.

Was I? "Perhaps a little. She is my mother, but that doesn't mean I choose her over you. Absolutely not. I'm just explaining why she's so bitter toward you. If I were awakened by the baker's daughter, she'd probably feel the same way. It's not *you* personally. She's been throwing women of her choosing in my path since I was twenty with the hopes one of these eligible females would awaken me. Nothing, until a snoopy maid appeared." I tapped her nose.

She smiled and put a hand on my chest. My cock stirred from that simple touch.

"It makes sense, I *am* hot."

"You're overly warm?" I asked, studying her. Her cheeks weren't flushed and she wasn't sweating.

She laughed. "No, you silly. I'm sexy. Alluring. So desirable I made your cock come awake."

I grinned. "You did do that." Then my smile fell away. "You are sexy and alluring to only me."

One dark brow arched. "Jealous?"

"Absolutely."

"Well, what's our plan for finding the traitor? I'm not too thrilled to stay here forever. It feels like high school all over again."

"You sneaked boys into your parents' house?" Her mouth opened as if to answer but I covered it with my palm. "Never mind. I don't want to know the answer."

My action was proof I was totally jealous of any male in her life. Before me, on fucking Earth or even now, just looking at her. She was, as they said on Earth... hot.

She reached up took my hand from my mouth and turned it so my palm faced her. Leaning forward, she took the tip of my finger into her mouth. Sucked.

"Holy fuck," I whispered at the hot, wet suction. And that was just my finger.

Lower, my cock hardened, jealous. Seemed I was filled with envy.

"What is that for?" I asked, my voice a harsh rasp. She destroyed me so easily.

Pulling back, she looked up at me. "Your mother hates me." She shrugged. "That's fine, but we might as well make sure she's bothered by something I'm actually doing."

"Like what?"

"Riding your cock. And, as my sister accused, screaming your name when I come with your mouth on me."

"I'll fuck you, princess. But first, I want my cock in your mouth feeling that sweet pull, the swirl of that tongue."

She smiled then, waggled her eyebrows up and down. "I've got something new we can try."

Pre-cum seeped from the tip at the very idea of something

new. I was a very eager pupil to whatever Faith wished to teach me. Everything we'd done so far had been adventurous and sexy as fuck. "It involves you sucking my cock?"

She took my hand, tugged me toward the bed. "And you licking my pussy. At the same time."

I stopped in my tracks as I thought of how to do that. It took a second and then I grinned. Fuck, yes.

"The last time I ate your pussy, you screamed," I warned. "I doubt you can be quiet. In fact, it's my mission to make you yell my name every time you come."

Faith tugged her shirt over her head and she stood there in just a pink version of that sexy bra I couldn't resist. She glanced at the closed bedroom door. "Exactly."

Faith

"Not only are you going to be a maid and a traitor, but you're also going to be a vixen who defiles an innocent virgin."

I worked off my pants next, watched Thor following my every move. I felt powerful, sexy and definitely a vixen. "That's me. It's going to be pretty hard for me to suck your cock if it's in your pants."

That got him moving, his clothes a pile on the floor before I could get my socks off.

God, he was gorgeous. No wonder I was a defiler of virgins. Awakened or not, he was totally worth jumping. And to think he was all mine. That huge cock too. Long and thick, it curved upward to bump his navel. The crown looked like a big mushroom cap, but was an appealing pink color. The slit at the top had a bead of pre-cum and I knew that was all for me.

Now that my Ardor was over, I could look at him more clearly. Oh, I still ogled him with lust-filled eyes, but I was no longer in pain. Needy desperation to be fucked. Now, I was just a horny slut who wanted to suck my mate's cock.

Giving blow jobs wasn't really my thing. I didn't do it for just anyone and it was so impersonal. But with Thor, I felt empowered by how I could make him practically lose his mind. Fortunately, his awakening had tapered off. Now, when his cock was hard, I knew it was truly for me, not because he'd first found his mate.

I loved that he was hard all the time, eager for me. And I loved knowing that he hadn't been with anyone else, that everything we'd done together had been a first for him. Just like sixty-nine. By the look on his face when he'd figured out what I wanted to do, it wasn't something they'd taught in those boys' sex-ed classes.

It was time for a little hands-on sex-ed of our own.

"Where do you want me, mate?" he asked, heat and eagerness in his gaze.

I pointed to the bed. "Lie down on your back."

He winked. "Bossy and you have to do all the work? I like it."

As he grabbed the blankets and yanked them down the bed, I said, "Oh, you'll be doing a lot of the work."

When the bed was bare except for the bottom sheet, he glanced at me. "My goal here is to make you scream. If it pisses my mother off in the process, it'll only be an added benefit."

He dropped down on the bed, hands tucked behind his head, elbows splayed out.

His cock aimed straight up, bobbing, as if waiting for me. Every inch of him was perfect. Long-limbed, well-defined muscles, a smattering of dark hair. Flat, dark nipples. Perfection, and he was all mine.

I climbed up so I straddled his waist, kissed him. His cock was pressed between us. He lowered his arms so his hands cupped my bottom, pulled me up higher. His tongue found mine, mimicked what I hoped we'd be doing in round two.

Because round one was going to happen as soon as he stopped kissing me. Which I wasn't in any rush to end because Thor could really kiss. My nipples were hard pressed against him and my pussy was wet. Very wet. No doubt he could feel it.

"Mate," he breathed. Nothing more. I knew he was ready, eager for what was to come. I pushed up onto my hands which made my breasts hang down right in front of him.

He groaned before letting go of my butt.

"Ready?" I asked.

He let his arms fall wide, indicating he was at my mercy. Carefully, I shifted, turning around to face away from him, making sure I didn't kick him in the face as I went.

I positioned myself on my hands and knees facing his feet, but I looked down right at his very eager cock.

"Oh fuck, mate, look at you."

He was looking right at my pussy. I wasn't all that prudish—obviously since I was all but sitting on his face—but I did feel a touch exposed.

Then a finger slid through my folds and I moaned. Yeah, I was no longer nervous about what he thought. In fact, I had no thought at all.

"Is all this for me?"

I wasn't sure if he was referring to how wet I was or my pussy itself so I just nodded. My long hair fell like a curtain and brushed over his cock and balls. He hissed.

His fingers circled over my clit, slid over me, dipped inside, as if he were seeing me for the first time. This wasn't the case since he'd gone down on me before, in front of an entire group of queen's guards even. He'd seen me before.

"I love it when you touch me," I said, giving him guidance, letting him know I was into anything he wanted to do.

"Here?" he asked, swirling around my clit.

"Yes."

"Here? he asked again, this time slipping two fingers into

me and curving so he stroked over my G-spot. I bucked my hips which made him pull out.

I whimpered.

"What about here?" he asked one last time, his slick fingers brushing over the tight swirl of my ass.

"Thor!" I shouted, the touch a complete surprise. We hadn't gone there... yet and I hadn't expected it right now.

"Oh, you like that?"

I could hear the desire in his voice, but the wonder, too. He was learning my hot buttons and based on the way pre-cum all but seeped from his slit, it was turning him on

"Yes," I replied, because he would know anything else I said would be a lie.

"We'll have to play there, explore more... one day. But now, you have a different lesson for me, don't you?"

My bottom hole tingled and nerve endings I didn't even know existed came to life from that brief play. I liked it and I wanted more. But he was right. I had other plans and that was to get us both off.

Big hands settled on my hips and tugged me backward, right onto Thor's face. His mouth was open and his tongue slid all the way across my pussy.

"Oh my god." My eyes fell closed and I groaned, the hot feel of his mouth on me something I loved. Loved. LOVED.

"Mate, I believe you're supposed to be doing something too."

I opened my eyes, looked down and took in his cock, all eager and angry colored and weeping with its need. I licked at the tip, the flavor of his pre-cum bursting on my tongue.

He groaned and more slipped from him.

"This?" I asked, then licked him from base to tip.

"Fuck, yes."

He attacked my pussy then, going at me with a fervor of a new-to-sixty-nine virgin. Little did he know he was going to have to pace himself.

I took his crown into my mouth, sucked on it like I would a lollipop, then went down. Took him as deep as I could go, then gripped the base.

I had to shift my hands so I was balanced and began to suck and stroke at the same time.

Slurping and sucking, groans and moans filled the room. It was sexy and dark, wild and incredible.

Even without the Ardor, I'd been close to coming ever since the last orgasm he gave me. The way Thor thickened in my grip, coated my tongue with an endless stream of pre-cum, I knew he was close too.

Perhaps it was the gentleman in him, but he slipped a finger inside me as he flicked my clit in the way he knew I loved. The way he'd learned would set me off like a firework at Fourth of July.

I had to come off of him so I could breathe, coming so hard I did, indeed, scream. It was his name I shouted so everyone in the Jax house could hear. There would be no question by everyone in the mansion, and maybe even the one next door, what we were up to.

When I finally came down from the pleasure, it was my turn to attack, I gripped the base and stroked, twisted and lifted as I suctioned the crown, my tongue moving in circles to get beneath the ridge.

He came too, thrusting his hips up and filling my mouth with his seed. It was salty and I kept him shallow so he coated my tongue, avoiding my gag reflex. Thor called out my name, his hands all but ripping the sheet on the bed.

I lifted up so I was kneeling on top of his lower belly, wiped my mouth with the back of my hand and glanced down at him over my shoulder.

"Mate. We have until dinner." His hand slid along my bottom so the thumb tipped down to press gently against my back entrance. "Nap, then I'm playing here."

I turned about, lowered myself down so I was tucked into

his side, my head on his shoulder. His hand cupped my hip. He was damp with sweat and we smelled of sex. Wild, abandoned, fucking.

I smiled, thinking of what he wanted to do later. I'd never done any butt stuff, so I couldn't be any kind of a teacher. I was looking forward to us figuring it out together.

5

F *aith*

LADY JAX HATED ME. That's all there was to it.

I tried small talk. I tried talking about Lord Jax's Zebcats—one of which was curled up around my feet at the moment much to Lord Jax's shock and delight—and I tried talking about the food, the house, the freaking weather.

She was Thor's mother. I really wanted her to like me. It was kind of stupid, but I did. By snooping about her house, I'd set myself up to be on her enemy list. And then being a *maid* who'd gotten her sharp claws into her only son... yeah, I was her worst enemy. It wasn't as if I'd seduced him, stripped naked and forced his cock to awaken and then somehow "fall" into my pussy. No, Thor had *some* responsibility for all that. And yet I was branded the harlot. Virgin ravager.

Whatever.

I was stuck in this uncomfortable situation of my own making, partially intentional and partially completely out of my control—and madly, stupidly in love with her son. Yeah, that was the part that had been out of my control.

He sat beside me, looking so good I had little interest in the food I knew we were about to enjoy. I was sure it would be wonderful, as I'd been sampling bits and pieces from the kitchen during my time here as a servant, but I smelled burning meat, which generally made my stomach churn with nausea.

I loved animals. All animals. The thought of eating one made me ill. The smell of one cooking?

Well, if I thought nothing would ever curb my sexual desire for my new mate, this had proven me wrong. Charred flesh killed the sexy right out of me. So did the sight of Thor's mother. Her glare. Yeah, she'd heard us having sex earlier.

No question.

I took a sip of wine and tried to smile at Lady Jax. Again.

"This wine is lovely." I wasn't much of a wine fan. Sweet. White. Not much taste to it. That was about the only thing I could take. This was a dark, blood red and tasted like tree bark and pepper left to rot in a vat of vinegar. It was hard not to grimace, which would only irritate the woman even further.

No. Not a fan. The woman or the wine. I sipped it anyway, forced myself to smile at my future mother-in-law and tried not to shudder as she poured herself a third glass from the crystal decanter near her elbow.

"It's the finest wine, from Atlan." Thor leapt on the opportunity to fill the stifling silence in the intimate dining room. This was the family's private table, not the larger room that was for guests and sat twenty. I knew that well since I'd had to polish the glossy surface every day I'd worked in the house. This room was small, but decadent. Large double doors on three sides closed us in like donuts in a box, the large glass ceiling overhead offered a view screen to the stars. It would have been romantic, any other time, or at least with only Thor in the room with me. The stars twinkling overhead, the muffled sounds of the Zebcats purring made it almost possible to forget Lady Jax. Almost.

"I don't drink anything else," she replied. "That's something you should know, Faith, if you're going to be part of this family. We do not accept anything less than the best."

The woman raised her brow and looked down her nose at me, her intention clear. She did not believe I was the *best* option for her prodigal, oh-so-beloved son, and she wanted me to know her opinion.

Message received. Jeez. I wondered if this was what it felt like for every woman brought before a judgmental, over-protective mother-in-law. From what Thor had said, *he* hadn't brought any other woman home with him. Hadn't told his parents before me that he'd found his mate. Not like guys on Earth who might change their minds ten times over. No, I'd awakened Thor and that was the end of it. I was his mate. Period.

But I remembered Thor saying Lady Jax had brought women to him in the hopes one of them would awaken him. Nope. Hadn't worked. Until me.

Ha!

I had to admit, Thor was fantastic. And gorgeous. And smart. Honorable. Fucking amazing in bed.

Rich.

But I wasn't after his money. I didn't need it. In fact, compared to my family, they were paupers. I'd seen my mother's palace, and been told that my mother owned several more homes scattered on different continents on the planet, all nearly as large.

We were richer than I could fathom. Me, Trinity and Destiny. And back on Earth, Trinity had struggled to pay off her student loans from law school, Destiny worked at her martial arts gym about fifty hours a week, and I'd barely scraped by enough on odd jobs to keep myself respectable.

No, I was a bazillionaire. And while I wasn't sure how much

money we had exactly, I knew it was a lot. Technically, from what I understood, we owned the entire planet.

Which was just crazy. Who owned a damn planet?

Me.

Double ha! I should tell the witch with the scornful, disappointed expression on her face. I wasn't going to give her what she wanted. A higher place in society. God, she'd probably keel over from the new social standing alone. It was probably her ultimate dream—her only son mated to a *princess.*

And yet she looked at me, most likely thinking about the best way to toss me out into the back alley with the rest of the trash.

Thor's warm hand slid onto my thigh beneath the table, and I was grateful for the contact. One, it broke my depressing, bitter train of thought. And two? It was Thor. Touching me. Always a win.

"How was your day, Father?" Thor asked.

"Fine. Fine." He popped a spoon-filled bite of something that shook like jelly but was thick, black, and smelled like burned peaches into his mouth. Gross. "And you? Any word from the guards on who broke into your apartment?"

That got monster-mother's gaze off me and onto her son. "What break in?"

Thor sighed and leaned back in his chair, slumping like a scolded ten-year-old. "It's nothing, Mother. I'm taking care of it."

"What do you mean, nothing?" she asked.

Clearly, she didn't like that someone messed with him. For once, I agreed with her, but I wasn't going to say that.

"Someone broke into your home? I may have retired from the Optimus unit, but I still have connections. You know that. You should have told me at once." There was real worry in her voice. She loved her son beyond all reason, which I could respect.

I could win her over eventually with the fact that we both

loved Thor, right?

Thor squeezed my thigh and I relaxed. "And have old man Coburt sticking his nose in my business? No thank you, Mother. I've told you before, I don't care for Lord Wyse, or his style of investigation."

She frowned at him, her gaze darting to me—the elephant in the room. Lord Wyse had fully intended to take me to some prison and interrogate me. Thor had saved me from that, which probably pissed his mother off on top of everything else. Surely, she'd wished Thor had left me with the Optimus unit, especially since she knew what they did to bad guys.

I didn't have to win over Thor's mother. Or his father. Or his cousins or uncles or staff. I had Thor's heart. He was mine and I was his. That was all I needed. It wasn't like we were going to live with his parents for long. God, if there was a motivator to find the real traitor, it was that alone. I wanted Thor, in a place of our own, without parents looming or judging or just plain-old hating.

If Lady Jax came around, great. If not? Well, I still had Thor. And our future, which I hoped would include a couple of Zebcats of my own, and maybe a set of twin girls to run around and tackle Daddy when he came home from work.

I had a lot to learn about his job, too. And that was after we managed to catch the traitor. If we caught him.

We'd only been in the house a few hours, and we'd been naked and fucking almost the entire time. That wasn't the best way to root out a traitor, but it had certainly made me feel good. Because of our afternoon in bed, we were no closer to figuring out who had been behind the attack on Trinity. It was frustrating, all of it except the part about being with Thor as his mate. That was extremely... pleasant. Much more so than sneaking around on my off hours and cleaning up after his father. Now I had someone to snoop with, and we didn't have to be all that secretive about it.

The Zebcat at my feet stretched, then rubbed its whiskered

chin against my ankles, the purring noise louder than any I'd heard before.

Thor's mother scoffed, looked under the table and glared at her mate. "You know I don't like to have animals in the dining room. They're filthy."

"Life's filthy, love. You like it a little *dirty*." He smiled and waggled his eyebrows at her, which made her cheeks flush pink as she looked down at her plate.

I did *not* want to know.

"Back to the discussion at hand, Mother." Clearly, Thor didn't want to have his parents talk—even thinly veiled—about their sex life over dinner. "I need to see the work schedule for the day the comm was placed in my room, the day of the royal reception."

"I'm looking, dear, but you know how things are around here," his mother replied. "Sometimes the schedule is on the computer system, and sometimes it's not. I've asked the head maid to find it. She will."

"When?"

"I don't know, dear." Lady Jax put down her glass and patted her lips with her napkin. "She's busy. These things take time."

Thor slammed his glass of wine down on the table. "No. They do not. I want the schedule, and I want to see it tonight. It's been too long already."

She tilted her head at him, her expression serious. Placating. "Of course. If that is what you wish. I'll ask her about it immediately after dinner." Her gaze darted to me, and the scowl returned to her face. "I could bring it by your bedroom, if I know you're going to be—available."

Available? As in *not fucking your new mate's brains out and making her scream your name.*

I smiled at her, and it wasn't exactly friendly. But it wasn't mean either. I *did* want her to like me. But I had no intention of giving back her son. He was mine now. And she would just have to put on her big girl panties and deal with it.

The servants came into the room and went like ghosts, bringing soup, a crisp, fruity salad and more wine. Always more wine. Since I didn't have more than the one sip, my glass remained full, but the youngest of them was observant enough to refill my water glass instead.

Thank god. Some of the crackers and side dishes were dry, and swallowing fermented tree bark was not my thing.

When the main dish arrived, the burned smell I'd identified earlier intensified. Lady Jax rose and went to a side table, where the steaming dish had been set, and left behind, by the kitchen staff.

Thor's mother was beaming, then lovingly glanced over her shoulder at Lord Jax. "I made your favorite, dear!"

"You know how to keep your mate happy." His smile was endearing, and full of true contentment, even as he patted his stomach in obvious eagerness for the stinky dish. It *almost* made up for the stench of burning flesh.

I looked at Thor, who grinned at me, tracing my lower lip with his thumb. "My mother comes from a land far from here where this dish is a delicacy. The recipe is very old, passed down for generations."

I swallowed. Hard. Oh, shit. There was no way. No way. Whatever it was, I would vomit all over the table if I tried to eat it. "Thor, I don't eat meat." I mouthed the words to him, made less sound than a whisper.

I'd messed with Lady Jax enough. Offending her and where she'd grown up might push the woman over the edge. Especially if I threw up. Not a good impression.

His mother laid a plate of steaming dead body parts in front of me, then went back to fill plates for everyone else. Three small chunks of charred... something with a coating of dark sauce.

"Don't worry," Thor whispered. "You don't have to eat it."

"That's right, you don't eat any of your animal friends," Lord Jax murmured. He, too, didn't want to upset his mate. He winked at me as his mate returned and placed an identical plate in front of him.

When she turned her back again, Lord Jax reached over and speared two chunks of meat from my plate onto his fork and stuffed every bite into his mouth with a huge, self-satisfied grin on his face.

"There," he said, cheeks full. "Good job cleaning your plate."

The words were garbled since his mouth was so full, a bit of sauce on his lip.

I put my hand on his and whispered, "Thank you."

God, he really was adorable and he also knew his mate's unhappiness. I wasn't sure if he were trying to smooth things over with me, or with her. I knew where Thor's charm came from. And it definitely was *not* his mother.

She set a plate in front of Thor as well and went back to the sidebar to serve herself. By the time she sat down with her own plate before her, Lord Jax had emptied my plate, and both her mate and her son only had one piece left.

Her smile was brilliant. "I see my boys were hungry." She glanced at my plate as well, eyes rounding when she saw that my plate, too, was bare. "And you, Faith. Did you like the dish? It's a family tradition. I made them to honor you and Thor and your mating."

I smiled. She was trying. That was something. "Thank you. They were delicious."

Preening, she looked down at her plate and I glanced at my future father-in-law, who winked at me with a grin. We were both happy. He got a double serving, and I didn't have to eat a single bite. *And* Lady Jax was pleased.

When the plates were cleared, Thor's father rose and lifted his glass. "To you, Faith. I have never seen my son so happy. Welcome to the family."

"Thank you." I lifted my glass and managed to swallow a bit of the wine. Sometimes, a girl had to do what a girl had to do. A sip of the bitter wine was better than any of the meat. "I am happy as well."

"We all are, dear," Thor's mother added. I doubted her words were sincere, but I wasn't going to call her on it. I'd take the words for now.

Thor's hand was back on my thigh and I leaned into his side. Happy. Content.

Thor's father swayed, as if he'd had two bottles of wine, not two glasses.

"Are you all right?" I asked.

Lady Jax looked up from the table, where she'd been staring at her wine glass, rotating the base on the table, around, and around, and around. Thinking. "My lord?"

"Fine. Fine. I'm—" He toppled, falling hard to the floor. The Zebcat closest to him hissed in alarm as his master nearly fell on top of him.

"Father!" Thor jumped from his seat as Lady Jax fell from hers, landing on her knees next to her mate.

"My love!" She shook her mate as Thor settled on the opposite side of his father's unconscious body. I loomed over them, not sure what to do. Lord Jax was flushed, sweating. Unmoving. Ten seconds ago he'd been fine and now...

The lead servant stuck his head into the room, probably hearing the loud thud of Lord Jax falling. Thor yelled at him, "Summon the healers, now! And get me a ReGen wand."

"At once, my lord." The door closed behind the servant and we were alone in the room, the elder Lord Jax's labored breathing a garbled sound I'd never heard before, as if his lungs were full of fluid.

"Father?" Thor rolled his father onto his back and the old man's eyes were glazed over, like glass. Staring, unseeing, at the ceiling. "Father?"

"My love?" Lady Jax screamed, shaking his shoulder. "What have you done? What have you done?"

Shit. I had no idea what to do. All I could do was watch.

Until Lady Jax stood and pointed at me. "You. You did this!"

I stared at her wide-eyed. Me?

"Did what?" I took a step back as she moved forward, all kinds of crazy on her face. Veins popped out at her temples, her gaze narrow and the fiercest I'd ever seen. She glanced at the table, grabbed her husband's knife and waved it at me. Was she planning on stabbing me? With her mate dying on the floor?

"You! You poisoned him!"

"What?" Holy shit. I put a chair between us and kept backing up. "I don't know what you're talking about. I didn't. I would never—"

"Enough, Mother!" Thor said, putting his hand on his father's shoulder. "Stop this. Get the ReGen wand!"

She took a step around the end of the table and looked down at my empty plate, then back up at me, her gaze no longer lucid. "You poisoned him."

I moved further away, putting two chairs between us. I didn't want to go kung fu on Thor's mom, but this was getting real. Fast.

Poisoned? As if.

I could see she why she wouldn't like me. I *had* been snooping around her bedroom. And now I was her son's mate. That was reasonable. But this? This just made me angry.

I could feel the power building inside me like a grenade about to go off. If she came at me with that knife, I wasn't going to be able to stop whatever was inside me from kicking her ass.

Then she'd never like me. Never. Not even giving her cute grandkids would be able to save me from a life of scorn and disappointment from her.

"Mother!" Thor stood now, walked to her and ripped the knife from her hand. "I said enough. Stop this. Father needs help." He glanced down at the prostrate man.

She shook her head and leaned into her son. "Nothing is going to help him now. Nothing." She sobbed, her shoulders shaking like she was breaking.

A servant brought in the wand and Thor took it, dropped beside his dad and began waving the blue light over him.

"He'll be all right," Thor said as he worked. "I'm sure the medical team will be here any moment. We don't even know what's wrong. A ReGen pod will have him back here chasing you around the house in no time."

She shook her head, spun on her heel and turned back to me. Pointed. Livid. "You did this. If you live a thousand years, I want you to know this was your doing."

Her words were like a dagger in my gut, but I stood tall and kept my chin up. She hated me. So be it. But I wasn't going to give up on Thor because of that.

"What are you talking about?" I asked. "I told you I wasn't the traitor. We'll find who's messing with the Jax family. Set things right."

"No." Her hands shaking, she reached into a pocket of her gown and pulled out a small vial. "Things will never be right." She glanced over her shoulder at Lord Jax's unconscious body.

She opened her mouth and tipped the contents of the container onto her tongue. What the hell was she doing? I didn't understand what I was seeing, what was happening so quickly.

Thor, who'd been checking on his father, saw her as the final drop fell.

Between one second and the next he was beside her, throwing the vial away from her to shatter against the wall across the room. "Mother! What have you done?"

He was wild with fear. With anger. With surprise.

She looked up at him, her shoulders sagging in defeat. "It was supposed to be her." Her legs gave way, as if they could no longer hold her weight, and she slipped to her knees. Thor tried to catch her, but she'd gone boneless. Weak.

"I'm sorry, my son. It was supposed to be her, not your father."

6

T *hor*

MY BLOOD RAN COLD. The truth was obvious now. Every grue-some bit.

"It was you," I said, kneeling before my mother. From my position, I could also see my father, only a few feet beyond. I could no longer hear his ragged breathing, no longer see his crest rising. He was dead.

My mother had killed him.

But that death, the poison she'd drunk, wasn't meant for her mate, my father.

It had been for Faith.

I glanced up at my mate, my body filled with horror at the shock of this. My father, dead. My mother, a traitor to the queen, to the throne, to my mate.

To me. She'd betrayed us all in a relentless pursuit of power. And for what? Did my father not provide enough for her? All these years, all the business deals I had overseen, the wealth and properties and armies. None of it mattered to my mother. She wanted power. And recognition.

I had no doubt now, that if she could, she would have placed herself on the throne and walked around with the crown on her head.

And Faith? Goddess. What was she thinking now? I had protested my innocence, sworn to her that my family was not involved.

I'd lied to her. Been wrong. My own blood had tried to kill her, under my roof. Under my care. And my mother had very nearly succeeded.

Faith stood looking down at my mother. Frozen, her face wide-eyed with horror. She knew.

Mother's breathing was becoming more labored, her forehead now dotted with sweat. Whatever poison was in the vial, it was fast-acting. It hadn't been more than five minutes since my father ate the meat from Faith's plate. And now he was dead.

And so the clock was ticking. I had to get the truth out of my mother, the fucking traitor, before she, too, was dead.

My heart shattered, torn in two. How could I love my mother, and hate her this much? "Mother? What have you done?"

"I told Zel what to do. It was me. I'm sorry."

She gave orders to Zel to kidnap Trinity? "Goddess, mother. Why?"

This made no sense. I knew her to be ruthless in protecting her own, but this? Trinity had nothing to do with... anything.

"Lord Wyse promised me a place in the new government."

"New govern—"

"Lord Wyse is the queen's first cousin," Faith said, cutting me off. "But his daughter failed to light a spire."

Holy fuck. "Lord Wyse kidnapped the queen? He hasn't killed her, the spire is still lit. So, he went after Princess Trinity as well? Why?"

Mother's breathing became more ragged. "Yes. Lord Wyse."

Lord Wyse, the fucker. I'd kill him myself. Hunt him down and strip the skin from his body. Kill him slowly. Make him suffer. For this. For the death of my father. My mother. For trying to kill my mate.

"Why did you do this?" I asked, knowing her time was almost up. "Why?" I asked, ready to shake her for the answer.

"Son. Love you. Only the best. For you. Sorry. Forgive me," she wheezed, then fell unconscious.

Faith dropped down across from me, took Mother's hand. Not that it mattered now. She wouldn't awaken, not if she passed as my father had done. Wouldn't know Faith was touching her, holding her as she died.

I stared at both my parents. Dead and dying. Poisoned. Faith was the one to be unbreathing on the floor, not either of them.

"Lord Wyse wants the crown," Faith said. She was looking down at my mother, but thinking aloud.

"Mother was the traitor in the Jax household," I replied, stating the obvious, now that she lay seconds from death between us. "While you'd been snooping about, she'd been the one to contact Zel, help him to kidnap Trinity—most likely to take her somewhere and have her killed. She must have been the one to send Zel along with the other guards to collect you from the transport center."

"She didn't know who we were, that was obvious. If she knew I was a princess, she'd have been thrilled for us to be mated." Faith's words rang true and a bitter pain settled in my chest. I was not worthy of this female. A traitor's blood ran in my veins. I was what Leo had feared, a traitor to the queen. A danger to Faith, and her sisters.

I laughed, although it was completely without humor. My parents were dead before us. What a ruthless plot that had just unfolded. "Mother wanted power. She'd been greedy for it. And yet she had it before her all along. The highest power of the land. She'd done it for me, but all she had to do was love you. She didn't even know her son was mated to the princess."

Faith was quiet, for my tragic words couldn't ring any more true.

"Lord Wyse must have known who you were," I said, finally, thinking of that bastard.

Faith shook her head. "No. That makes no sense. He would have said as much in that interrogation room. He knew I had no Aleran records, but not that I was from Earth, or that I was a princess. God, he'd have killed me right away if he'd known."

And to think, when I'd arrived at the station, he'd been taking her away, to some level of the Optimus building meant for the worst criminals on Alera. Had he really intended to take her there? Or somewhere to kill her? While Faith might not have talked, upon her death, her spire would have gone dark. He'd have known then, had probably been willing to risk an innocent life for the chance to kill a royal. To remove anyone in the way of his gaining the throne.

"Or later, when he came to my apartment to find us." I avoided sharing my other thoughts. "But it was empty, so he must have ransacked it looking for a clue as to where we went."

"You think Lord Wyse did that?" Her face was pale, her eyes haunted.

"Who else?" Who the fuck else?

"Then if Lord Wyse doesn't know I'm a princess, then there must be someone else in on all this."

"Zel, dead. Mother, dead. There are many people in play here. Lord Wyse, too, perhaps is just a pawn. This is more sinister than I ever imagined."

Faith set Mother's hand down, laid it gently on her unmoving chest.

I looked to my father. Dead. The pain was great, but I was too numb. Too overwhelmed. Mother was part of a master plot to overthrow the crown.

And I was mated to that crown. To Faith.

The Jax name was destroyed. I glanced at Faith. My mate.

I was like the plague for her. If she touched me, if she claimed me as her own, she'd be ruined. The planet would hate my family, what my mother had done.

If she stayed with me, she would be judged harshly. We would not be left in peace. Not ever.

No. I couldn't let that happen. I would protect her with my life, and that meant cutting her from it.

I stood, albeit shakily.

"Call your sister. Leave."

She looked up at me. Frowned. "What?"

I put my hands on my hips, my heart aching, tearing in two. "I am not worthy to be your mate. Look at this!" I said spreading my hands out. "My parents are dead. Poisoned. My mother is a traitor to the throne. To *you*. You can not align yourself with me, or my family. You must go and tell no one of our mating."

Faith hopped up quickly, came over to me, but I held my hand out, keeping her at a distance. I couldn't let her near me. Never again. I would destroy her.

"What are you talking about? You're my mate!" she looked frantic now, unshed tears making her eyes glassy.

I pointed at the table. "You almost died! Goddess, if you'd taken a bite of that meat, you'd be dead. Do you know how close you came? I can't let that happen to you."

"You didn't do it, your mother did," she replied.

The knife dug deeper. "Exactly. My *mother*."

"And... and I'm sorry, but she's gone. Thor, I love you. We'll get through this together."

I shook my head. "No, we won't. We won't be able to say Lord Wyse was involved. You, the lowly maid. Me, the head of the ruined house of Jax. It will only make me and my family name look worse, trying to pass the blame on someone like the Inspector Optimi. My family land, the title, the money will all be stripped away. I won't even have the honor of my name left. You shouldn't be tainted by that."

There was no honor left in the Jax household. But I would give what was left of mine to Faith. I went over to the wall comms unit. Called Nix.

"What are you doing?" she cried, coming to me, grabbing my hand. Squeezing. Her eyes were pleading, tears streamed down her face.

"What's happened, Thordis?" Nix's voice came through the unit clearly. I would only contact him if something bad happened. He knew it. I knew it.

"Come to the Jax household at once," I replied. "Protect Princess Faith."

At that, I ended the call, cupped Faith's jaw with my hand. Felt her heat one last time. My thumb swiped away a tear, then I couldn't help myself. I stole one last kiss, one last touch of her lips against mine, one last teasing breath of her flower scent.

And then I strode through the door and out of the mansion. Out of Faith's life, for I would destroy her. Perhaps I already had.

BOOK 6

PROLOGUE

Q*ueen Celene, Aleran Dungeon*

THIS NEWEST PRISON cell they transported me to was in Mytikas. I couldn't see outside, as there were no windows in the square room, but I knew what home smelled like, even after all these years.

The Aleran flowers that surrounded the citadel grew randomly throughout the city in a multitude of colors. The petals close to the honored building were nearly translucent and delicate. But farther away, they changed based on the environment in a way our scientists had never understood.

I knew it was the citadel itself that made them change, that they were part of the consciousness of the intelligence that designed them. Strange as it sounded, they were the citadel's nerves within the city.

And their scent was unmistakable. Sweet. Comforting.

Home. It smelled like home.

A fresh set of clothing awaited me once more, and I didn't

bother arguing, changing quickly into what looked like the uniform of a low-level cleric. The basic black pants were comfortable, the white, silver and black pattern on the tunic symmetrical on the outside. Within, it was soft and warm. Thank the goddess they were warm. The dress they'd made me wear on the spaceship for a while had been thin and cold.

But then, making me uncomfortable seemed to be part of their plan. Until now. For included with the uniform were a thick pair of socks and comfortable boots.

I could have been preparing for a walk in the mountains with my husband on Earth.

Adam Jones. I missed him. Knew he was so far away. Unreachable. The emptiness inside me was even more profound than when my Aleran mate, the king, had been murdered.

That had been a young love. Passionate, but short-lived. We'd only been mated a few months when the attack occurred. When he'd been killed, and I fled Alera for Earth.

I'd mourned my mate and what could have been, what *should* have been. Time softened the ache and the goddess had put Adam in my path. A surprising twist in my destiny. With Adam, our love had been aged by years of struggle and shared victory. By raising three daughters. By life. He was part of me, and the longer I sat, isolated by my captors, the more my thoughts turned not to saving Alera, but to him.

I would leave Alera when the time came, step down and allow Trinity and her sisters to lead if that's what I had to do to feel his arms around me once more. If he could not come to me, I would return to Earth. To my life there.

He was my true mate. Not in the Aleran way, but in every way that counted. Heart, body and soul.

The door slid open and I hastily wiped the tear from my cheek. I was ruthless with my emotions so not to show weakness to these traitors.

"More news about your daughters, Celene. Would you like

to hear?" A cleric I'd never seen before walked into the room; behind him, the scar-faced man stood with a scowl and his arms crossed.

Damn it, he was baiting me, but I could not resist. I was desperate to know how my girls were doing. "Yes."

He came in and sat on the small bed I'd been given, so close our thighs touched. I scooted away from the contact and he chuckled, as if my disgust amused him. They had yet to touch me sexually to get me to talk. I had to assume, since I was fully clothed, even down to boots, that kind of torture would not begin now.

I wondered why none had tried to force themselves upon me. To get me pregnant. It would be the easiest way to ensure their DNA would become royal. Perhaps they discovered from the ReGen wand scans that I was no longer fertile. For once, early menopause was a blessing.

"Your daughter, Faith, was arrested by the Optimus unit and headed for interrogation."

He knew her name. There was no reason to deny her existence now. But there was no reason to respond either. Whatever he meant to tell me would be designed to torment me with worry. A worry I welcomed.

"She was arrested for snooping through Lady Jax's private rooms. However, the Jax family refused to press charges, and Thordis Jax himself came to remove her from custody."

Again, I waited. More was coming, I could feel the tension thrumming through his body like an electric charge in the air.

"Your daughter then returned to their home, and now Lord and Lady Jax are both dead. Poisoned."

Lord and Lady Jax were dead?

"That is troubling news," I said, spitting out the words as I considered the implications.

"Yes. Your daughter will not fare well in our care, I'm afraid."

I glanced up at him. "What are you talking about?"

"She was a traitor who seduced Thordis Jax into bringing her into his bed and his home where she poisoned his parents. Her plan was to set up his well-respected family to fall and it worked. She will answer for her crimes, Celene."

Faith, poison people? Maybe with her horrible cooking. People would go hungry because it was always burnt, but kill them? Impossible. And so I said as much.

"She did not poison anyone."

A new voice came from the doorway and the scar-faced man stepped aside. It grated on my nerves even more now than it had when we were both young. My cousin, Lord Wyse, now leader of the Optimus unit, if his clothing was any indication, stood before me with the same emotionless face I remembered. "Faith Jones Herakles is a traitor and a murderer, Celene. I will make sure to send her your regards."

"No!" I didn't want her to worry about me if she were held by the Optimus unit. She had enough on her mind as it was.

The cleric rose and walked out the door, leaving me with my cousin.

"I should have tried harder to kill you, Celene. You're like a needle in my boot, a constant irritation."

"You haven't changed, Coburt. Still sneaking around in the shadows like a snake." We'd grown up together. While he was a decade older, royal circles were small.

"Where is Destiny?" he asked.

I froze. Shit. How did he know Destiny's name? I shook my head and stared at the wall, giving him nothing. If he didn't know where she was, then she was still safe.

"I had men on Earth, Celene. They asked around. I know you have three daughters. I know Faith and Destiny are half-human twins. I know your pathetic human male is hiding from your own government, waiting for word from you."

"Don't you touch him, Coburt, or I will send you to the depths of the lowest hells myself," I hissed, my hands clenched in my lap. He had lived with me for over twenty-five years, knew Aleran ways, at least tangentially. But he was still an Earthling.

His laugh was not reassuring. "As of an hour ago, you are no longer my problem."

The door slid closed behind him.

What the hell did that mean?

I dropped onto my side on the thin cot, pulling the blanket up over me.

Damn him.

Damn him to hell.

I hoped my daughters killed him slowly.

And they would succeed. Coburt Wyse would die.

I simply could not think of anything else.

Thordis Jax, Jax Mountain Lodge

THE ALERAN MALE I had bound to the chair bled, not from any torture or abuse he'd suffered at my hands, but from his attempts to claw his way through the metal binding cuffs that held him. He'd been here for a day and had told me nothing.

That was about to change.

"Where is the queen?" I asked.

"I don't know what you are talking about," he spit out. "Release me. You'll rot in the Optimus unit's dungeons for this. Let me go. I demand it." Of course he did.

"Yet you are the one tied up. This isn't a dungeon," I glanced around the servants' room on the top floor of the lodge. We only used the retreat a few weeks a year and there were only two servants who remained year round. They lived in a small house elsewhere on the property. This room was sparse. A bed, a table and chair. A chair that the bastard was tied to now. On the wall behind me was a vid display, recording everything that was happening. He glanced up often, saw himself on the screen.

"But I promise you, I will be ruthless with you if you don't begin to talk."

He was noble. Rich. A spoiled son of a wealthy family. And my mate's distant cousin. I took a moment to think of the royal family tree. Queen Celene's mother had one sister, Zetta. She had a son, Coburt, now known as Lord Wyse. Lord Wyse and his mate had Radella. When Queen Celene disappeared decades ago, Radella moved into the palace with her mate, Danoth. A few years later, they had a son. Pawl. The little fucker before me.

It seemed the evil didn't fall too far from the tree, for I'd grown to hate Pawl's grandfather, Lord Wyse, Inspector Optimi of the Optimus unit, who I now suspected of trying not just to arrest and interrogate my mate but murder her in cold blood. My mother, with her dying breath, had given him up.

He was my enemy. An enemy to all Alera, and yet he held one of the most powerful positions in the land.

He would kill Faith—and her sisters—if given the chance. He'd had several now, and fortunately, they had not been successful.

My purpose in life changed the moment my mother confessed her sins and then died in my arms. My one goal now was to make sure Faith was safe. My mother had tried to poison my mate, the female I loved beyond all thought or reason, and then confessed her sins as my father lay dead in Faith's stead.

I'd lost everything in a matter of moments. My family. My honor. The wealth and status of the Jax family would be stripped from us. Even if I did not spend the rest of my life rotting in a prison cell, I would be a disgrace to the entire planet. The only Jax who remained alive, to carry the burden of my mother's sins. All of Alera would judge me for my bloodline, if not for my deeds.

And Faith. Fuck, my heart ached for my mate. My cock

longed to sink into her warmth, to fill her again with my seed as she came, milking it from my balls. She deserved more than just a skilled fuck and a male whose soul was not stained by such a terrible legacy. And children who wouldn't be tainted. She was a fucking princess. While she was not direct heir to the throne—Trinity would become queen after their mother—she was royal through and through.

I was not worthy of Faith. But I could protect her. And that is what I would do—at all costs. If that meant torture and murder of the lying bastard before me—her fucking cousin—then I would bury my disgust and do what was necessary. I was not a killer, I was a noble, a man of business and law.

But for Faith, exceptions must be made. I didn't give a shit if Pawl's murder was recorded for the queen's guard to discover. My life was over without her. As long as she was safe, nothing mattered.

"Where is Queen Celene?" I sat in a chair facing the young idiot, watching his gaze as he looked at me with the eyes of a liar and a cheat. They narrowed as I reclined in my chair, arms crossed, completely at ease as far as he could see. Inside, I seethed with the need to rip his head from his shoulders and unleash the pain within me as violence against my enemies.

That didn't work well when one of those enemies was my own mother.

Fuck me. Pawl may be the grandson of a traitor, but I was the son of one as well.

"I told you, I don't know," he repeated. "I have no idea what you are talking about."

Lies. Lies. Lies. I sighed and lifted a comm sphere from my pocket. Holding it into the air, I activated the holographic images I had stored there for this purpose and made sure to hold it up to be clearly within line of sight of the recording device on the wall.

As soon as I had walked away from Faith I'd made the call to Nix to ensure her safety. But the moment I watched the assassin's arrival and stepped foot off Jax property, I'd been on a mission. Get to the truth, to the mastermind. My mother, while guilty, had been a pawn. Just like Zel. I'd known where to go, to dig. I'd paid some very large bribes to some lower level members of the Optimus unit who didn't care for Lord Wyse's style of leadership, but I'd finally found what I needed—Lord Wyse's orders to Pawl, giving him instructions just a few weeks ago to leave the planet and go where?

Earth.

Coincidence? No.

I played the recording, watched Pawl's eyes widen as he realized exactly what I had found. Not only did it prove his guilt, but his father, Danoth, had been with him when he received the order from Lord Wyse. It seemed evil ran in the family.

In the comms, there had been no mention of the queen by name, no direct orders, nothing substantial. Nothing I could take to Princess Trinity or the Optimus unit that was strong enough evidence to take down their leader.

But I knew. I *knew*, and I wasn't above breaking the law to protect what was mine. Faith. For her, I'd kill a thousand males just like this one.

"I don't think you understand me, Pawl." I leaned forward, slipping the holographic comm back into the pocket of one of my best tunic jackets. I looked like I'd just come from the palace. Well-dressed. Powerful. Connected. It was all part of my plan, even though I hadn't slept since I'd walked out of the Jax mansion and out of Faith's life.

I didn't expect her to forgive me. I'd left Faith with my parents' dead bodies—fuck, had it really happened? Any moment now, I expected the news of what had happened last night in my family home to spread like a wildfire. Announcements would be made, my family shame exposed to the world, my family name worthless after hundreds—no thousands—of years of loyal service to the queen and her royal bloodline.

All because my mother wanted more.

More. More money. Power. Prestige. Status.

Now she was dead and had nothing. Not only was I, her precious son, not going to be a powerful ruler, I would be a penniless orphan and an outcast once my mother's treachery became known. I could only imagine what had occurred inside that dining room once Nix and the other guards arrived to find my mother and father lying dead in the dining room, and my mate, tear-streaked and broken, kneeling beside them.

I left the Jax mansion knowing Faith would be safe, protected by Trinity and all her royal power, by the warriors Nix and Leo, and by Leo's father. I knew that what I planned would place Faith in danger. And I didn't want her to see me like this—desperate and angry and willing to kill. I'd lost my entire family, my parents, my home, my life. I would *not* see Faith fall. I could give her up, save her from the monster these traitors forced me to become, but I would not risk her life, or expose her to the kind of evil pulsing through the veins of the coward before me.

I'd yet to hear anything through the news sources of my family's downfall, but it was only a matter of time. The truth would come out and I would be ruined.

Before then, I intended to make sure that Faith—and her family—were out of danger, even if I had to cut Pawl into pieces to do it.

"Faith Herakles is my mate. So let me be clear. I will let you sit in your own piss and feces for days. I will flay the flesh from your body one small strip at a time as I kill you and smile when you scream. I will let you rot, tied to that chair, as maggots eat out your eyes. I will do the same to your traitorous parents."

"Wait. Wait!" he said, tugging at his restraints. "My mother has nothing to do with this. She's innocent. Weak. She's been content to live in the palace and throw parties, but nothing more. Please, I beg you to believe me. My mother knows nothing."

"Ah, so it is your father and grandfather who have raised you to be a traitor. You follow in their evil footsteps."

He remained silent, even pinched his lips together. But there was no denying the truth of the holographic message I'd just replayed for him and the camera.

"Faith is mine. Where is her mother? Where did you take the queen after you dragged her from her bed like an animal?"

"Thor, you're insane. What are you doing?" he asked, instead of answering my question. "We've been friend for years. We grew up together." Sweat ran from his temple, down his cheek and into the creases in his neck. I watched the slide of liquid, oddly detached. Numb. My parents were dead. My life was in ruins. Worse, Faith could never be mine. I would not drag her down with me. I would watch her take another male as her mate, raise a family, live and breathe and love another.

Numb was better than the pain I had locked away at the idea of her in the arms of another. I wondered if I'd ever feel again.

"We grew up together, but we were never friends." I slid a jeweled dagger—my mother's dagger—from my boot. It was a work of art. Polished platinum, it was a ceremonial piece, not meant for battle, but bestowed upon her with honor when she had retired from the Optimus unit after four decades of service. The blade was not made for war, but it was wickedly sharp. To prove the point, I walked around Pawl until I stood behind him and placed the dagger on the side of his ear. Slicing up toward the ceiling of the dark room, I cut the hair along that side of his head on a single sweep, chuckling out loud as the dark strands fluttered in a scattered mess onto Pawl's lap.

"Thor?"

"Faith is my mate. Lord Wyse—your fucking grandfather— tried to have her killed. He sent you to Earth. What do you think Trinity and the royal guard will do to you when they find out *you* kidnapped the fucking queen!"

"Thor!" he repeated, this time his tone pleading.

I ignored it and continued. "Lord Wyse is the reason my parents are dead. My mate will be dead if he's not stopped. What value do you believe I place on your miserable life?"

He exhaled shakily. "None."

"Now you understand." I pressed the flat of the blade to his sweat covered cheek and waited.

"I don't know where the queen is now. But I know who does."

Now we were getting somewhere. "Tell me."

"He's Lord Wyse's personal guard. His name is Marish. He has a scar on his face, from the corner of his mouth to his neck, like a hook. He went with me to Earth. When we transported back, he took her. I don't know where. I went home—"

"To take out Trinity."

He was shaking now, the fingers of his hands trembling against the arms of the chair. "Yes. I was sent home, back to the palace, but they transported somewhere else. I don't know where they took her. I swear I don't."

Damn it. I believed him. I knew I wouldn't trust such information to a male of his low caliber. "And Lord Wyse? Why does he want the queen now? After all these years? Why not leave her alone on Earth?"

"He needs the royal gemstones. He wants to be king."

The idea was ridiculous. "Alera has never had a king. Not in thousands of years."

"Tell that to him," he countered. Now that he was talking, he'd relaxed, a bit of his arrogance settling back around his shoulders. He even had the nerve to smile as he continued, telling me of his plans to seduce Trinity when she first arrived at his parent's home, how he'd learned of her Ardor from Lord Wyse and decided to take matters into his own hands. He'd intended to fuck and murder his own cousin. But he'd been late arriving back at the palace and the royal consort had slipped into her bed first.

"You thought, what? That you'd mate your own cousin? Do you fuck your mother as well?"

That had made him angry, and he puffed up, face turning red as he cursed at the male. "No. Fuck you, Thor. Insult my mother again and I'll—"

"What? Go on. Do tell." I pressed the flat of my knife into his cheek so that the meat covering his bones edged over the blade, a shallow sliver slicing open from the pressure, just enough to make him wince. "Thor. No. I wasn't going to fuck her. I do not need a mate. I said I'd seduce her into bed. Get her alone. Then kill her."

"Lord Wyse needs all four heirs to die, and all four spires to darken before the people will accept him as their new king. Kill Trinity in her bed and there are only three to go." I said it aloud as I worked through the ludicrous plans. I lifted the blade and didn't even try to pretend the sight of that small sliver of blood didn't please me. This bastard had every intention of murdering Faith's sister, had kidnapped her mother, and would, without hesitation, have moved on to Faith next. He deserved to die. But not yet. I needed more information first. "Take them out one by one?"

He nodded. "Exactly. It wasn't like my father could seduce her. Trinity had already met him and he's too old for her. Seduction wouldn't work."

"And after?"

"After, it was brought to light that Leo is her mate. Since then, he hasn't left her side... or her bed. *Their* bed. I had no chance again."

"But Zel did, at the royal reception."

He nodded but didn't say anything. I knew what happened there, when Trinity had been taken prisoner and nearly killed by one of my mother's guards. I had already left the reception for the night and, thank the goddess, Leo and Nix had been there to save her. Otherwise, that would have been one more sin, one more death my family was responsible for. I didn't want or need to hear Pawl's account of that evening. But Trinity did.

I walked over to a chair and sat, facing him once more, the bloodied dagger twirling in my hand. "You should be thankful, Pawl, for I have no doubt Leo would have made quick work of you if you dared crawl into Princess Trinity's bed. Especially if you had tried to kill her."

I saw agreement in his eyes, the hint of fear at the thought of being ripped to pieces by Leo. "I told you about Marish and the queen. What else to you want from me? Let me go! I haven't killed anyone. I'm not a murderer. You have to let me go."

"Do I?" I sighed deeply and slid my thumb carefully along the edge of the blade collecting the scant remains of his blood into a small drop. He watched, his eyes glued to the movement as I smeared the blood between my fingertips. "I will promise not to kill you, on one condition."

"Yes. Whatever you want. Anything. Just let me go."

"Start talking, Pawl. And start at the beginning. What do you know about the events that led to the king's death twenty-seven years ago?"

"I wasn't even born then."

"But your father and Lord Wyse were adults. And you, now their trusted confidant. Their assassin."

"I didn't kill anyone."

"You kidnapped the queen."

He sighed, perhaps resigned that his involvement couldn't be concealed any longer, that talking was the only way to save his sorry life. He talked for over an hour and answered my questions. When he was done, I had the information I needed to move forward. He knew more than I did, but not much more. And I still had no idea where to find the queen. But it was a start.

"Thank you, Pawl." I stood and walked toward the door.

"Wait! What? Where are you going? You said you'd let me go! You can't leave me here!"

"I said I wouldn't kill you. And I won't. But you are a threat to me and mine. Did you really think I would let you leave? To run off and warn your father? Your grandfather?"

He blabbered like a fool, begging for his mother, for the guards, for anyone to come save him. I was not a cold-blooded killer, but I could not let him go. Not yet. Not until the queen was found and my mate was out of danger.

I should simply slit his throat and be done with it. But he didn't deserve such an easy death.

No, he deserved to suffer.

I pointed to the vid screen and his eyes flared wide. I'd gotten what I needed from him. I typed in my commands and the data was sent to the palace, specifically to Leo's father, the head of the royal guard. "You'll be fine until the royal guards show up. It might take some time for them to figure out where you are, but you'll be alive. For now. But it is a centuries-old tradition on Alera to execute traitors."

"Wait! No!" He howled as I closed the door behind me with a very soft click.

F aith, *The Royal Palace, Alera*

"You're back a lot faster than I expected," Trinity said, coming into the bedroom Nix had found for me in the palace.

I was in bed, but I'd barely slept. The early morning light came through the large window, the pale blue curtains softening it even more. This room was smaller than the one I'd shared with Thor, but no less sumptuous, somewhere on the second floor of the palace.

I had yet to come through the main entrance, being snuck in, once again, through the secret passages. I was still a secret. And now, between realities.

After the insanity of the night before, Nix and I decided we'd keep my existence quiet until we had time to think. While I'd been mated to Thor—no question it had been more than just fucking—that information had only been shared with his parents outside of the palace.

And they were dead.

My mating was a secret, my status as princess was a secret.

I didn't exist on Alera.

I felt like a ghost. As if I were lost, adrift. Alone.

"Yeah, well, it seems rooting out the traitor was easier than I thought," I replied drily. I tucked the blanket up higher about my ears.

Trinity came over from the doorway and sat on the edge of the bed. Her hair was up in a sloppy bun and she had on what looked like an Aleran version of sweats. Gray, loose pants and a hoodie sweatshirt without the front kangaroo pocket. It looked comfortable, but not very attractive. Almost like prison garb. Clearly, she hadn't grasped the power of the S-Gen machine. But she was the reigning princess, so her time was probably best used elsewhere—doing royal stuff.

Whatever that meant.

I, however, had all the time in the world. I could be her personal S-Gen machine dress designer. Groaning, I pulled the blanket all the way up and over my head.

An instant later, it was tugged down.

"Nix gave me an update and I wanted to kill both of you. Why didn't you call me?"

"Because having the princess and her mate—no way Leo'd let you go to a murder/suicide by yourself—arrive at the Jax home late at night would have been impossible to keep quiet."

"I thought Destiny was the sarcastic one," she replied.

When I didn't say anything—because what could I say?—Trinity continued.

"Fine, give me the 411."

"What did Nix tell you?" I asked.

She rolled her eyes and moved further onto the bed, crossed her legs. "I want to hear the details from you. Two dead bodies and no explanations from you? What the hell happened, Faith? And where's Thor? He was all caveman about you before, so where is he? Spill."

I did not need the reminder that just a short time ago Thor had been at my side, pledging to protect me and make me his forever. Fighting back tears, I pushed up so I was propped against the pillows and fancy headboard. "Turns out, Lady Jax is... was the traitor. While it was Lord Jax who'd sent the guards and consort to meet us at the transport center, Lady Jax was the one who made sure Zel was in the group."

Trinity's jaw clenched. "So, he's the one who almost killed Destiny."

"Yes. I don't know if Lady Jax actually ordered Zel to kidnap you at your big reception, or if it was Lord Wyse. I don't know how they talked him into any of it. Maybe they guilted him, threatened him, whatever, to finish the job he'd started."

"But Leo killed him that night."

"Right. After that, you were too well-protected and I guess trying to kill you was tabled for later. So Lady Jax decided to go after me. A *different* problem."

"She knew you were a princess?"

I shook my head.

"Definitely not. She wanted power and she wanted it through a strong match for Thor. Honor to the Jax name. If she'd known I was a princess, obviously that would have given her all that. Instead, she found me, a maid, far too low-class for what her son's mate should be. To make it even worse, I got caught snooping around in their house. She had me arrested. Everyone knew I was up to something, even the police. She wanted me out of Thor's life. And, knowing what I know now, she was probably worried that I had actually found something. So, kill me and she took care of two problems at once. She could keep her traitorous actions hidden and force Thor to choose someone else."

"Destiny will kill her."

"She's already dead. She tried to poison me at dinner."

"Holy shit, Faith," Trinity whispered, grabbing my hand and squeezing. Hard. "Did you eat or drink any poison? Are you all right?" Her pale gaze roved over me, but it wasn't like poison would make me bleed or I would have a huge gash in my forehead.

"Yeah, I'm fine. She hated me and didn't bother learning anything about her son's mate. Lady Jax poisoned some fancy meat dish."

She sighed hard, in total relief. "I thought you being a vegetarian was a total pain in the ass growing up. I will never, ever, say a bad thing about it again."

I couldn't help but smile. But it was a small smile. Weak effort, even for me. "Yeah, well, Lord Jax and I got along. He knew I didn't eat meat and he must've thought he was saving me from the embarrassment of not eating a special dish Lady Jax made in honor of my mating with Thor. He ate my portion like a kid on Christmas morning, Trin. I can still see his smile, and the wink he gave me when Lady Jax's back was turned. And poor Thor. His mother poisoned her mate—*his* father— instead of me. Lord Jax dropped dead on the dining room floor. God, that was horrible. When she realized what she'd done, she was beside herself. She took some of the poison, drank it right in front of us, before Thor could stop her."

"Holy shit, Faith. It's like... it's like ninth grade English class. *Romeo and Juliet*."

I stared at her wide-eyed for a moment. "You weren't there. Trust me, if you'd been there, you wouldn't be spouting starcrossed lovers shit right now. It was beyond awful. I liked Lord Jax. He was a simple man, but he was always kind to me. Unlike his wife."

She looked contrite. "Sorry, you're right."

"I can't believe she tried to kill me because she thought I wasn't good enough for her son."

"Well, that's total bullshit. You're amazing. And smart. And beautiful. And a god damn princess. Besides, that bitch doesn't matter anymore. She's dead, and obviously, Thor disagrees." Trinity said the last with such confidence I couldn't hold back a small sob.

"He told me to forget him, Trin. He looked at the bodies, stood up, and told me not to tell anyone we were mates and forget him. Move on. He called Nix and he left me there to wait for him. Why? Why did he do that?" The tears were rolling now and I couldn't stop them.

Trinity put on her very best big sister face, the one I realized in that moment that I'd relied on my entire life. "He loves you. I saw it in his eyes. He must have said something else."

"He said his family would be dishonored. That he'd lose everything and that I shouldn't be associated with someone like him." I wiped away my tears, anger building inside me, threatening to burst. "I don't give a shit about money or who his parents are. Doesn't he know that?"

"No, hon, he doesn't. You've known him a few days. He knows nothing about Earth. He grew up here. A freaking *lord*. With castles and titles and status and money. He has no clue who we really are. None of them do."

She squeezed my hand and as I stared into her eyes, seeing nothing but compassion and a stubborn streak that matched mine, I made a decision. "I'm not giving him up."

"Of course you're not. You have the full support of the royal family." Her grin was pure mischief and I loved her more than ever. "We're really fucking rich, Faith. Leo's been showing me the books, and it's insane. We have estates on every continent, business holdings, wildlife reserves, royal forests, we even own crap in outer space. Space stations and asteroid mines and some other stuff I don't understand. We're strong, and we'll help you keep him. Protect him. He's family now. Okay?"

The sigh that rolled through me was real this time. No more worrying. No more indecision, although I had no idea how an asteroid mine could make things right with Thor. But, he was mine. He could just fucking deal because I wasn't giving him up. "Okay."

Trin sat back and crossed her arms. "If Lady Jax was the traitor, and she's dead, that means... what? I'm confused."

"Lord Wyse is the man behind the curtain."

"And who's pulling out book analogies now?" she countered.

"There's a big difference between a Shakespearean tragedy and the Wizard from *The Wizard of Oz.*"

She sniffed, lifted her chin. "Mrs. Gomez would be totally proud of me for remembering that play."

"Yeah, she'd have given you a B instead of a C."

Trinity rolled her eyes. English hadn't been her best class. Not because she wasn't a fantastic student—as law school had more than proven—but because she'd thought the play was stupid, Juliet an idiot, and the whole feud between the families ridiculous and not worthy of her time. She was still stubborn like that.

"So, what about Lord Wyse?" she asked.

"He's the mastermind. Lady Jax told Thor right before she died. It was a fucking horror movie, Trin, complete with death rattle confessions." I shuddered.

For a second, she froze, mouth open, brain spinning.

"Lord Wyse?" she stood, paced in front of my bed. "He's Mom's cousin. Radella's dad."

"Exactly. Radella was the top of the royal heap after mom disappeared. Which is why you found her living in mom's palace. They're the most powerful and connected royal descendants, without us in the picture."

She studied the carpet at her feet as she paced. "So he was behind the attack that killed my biological father and forced Mom to run. But he kept looking for her? Found Mom on Earth, kidnapped her—which still doesn't make sense. Then he heard about a transport from Earth, connects the dots and wants us dead. When that attack failed, he worked with Lady Jax to make Zel come after me again at the reception?"

"I guess." Trinity was the analyst, not me. And I was so heartsick over losing Thor that I could barely think straight.

"And when that failed, she tried to poison you? That doesn't make sense. She didn't know who you were."

Trinity was right. Lady Jax had no idea. And it seemed a pretty bold move for someone like her to make.

"What was she going to do after you were dead, Faith? That's cold-blooded murder. Not to be gross, but there would have been a body. Evidence. How was she planning on getting away with it?" Her pacing increased, and I sat up straighter, adjusting my pillows. So much raw energy and aggression pouring off her that she was making me nervous. My hands balled into fists and I felt the weird urge to go Kung Fu swirling in my gut.

She stopped dead in her tracks, her head snapping up, and I held my breath. Jeez, she was a stress-case.

"Lord Wyse."

"What about him?"

"You said she told Thor he was behind everything."

"She said his name. That was about it. She wasn't in very good shape." That was an understatement. But I hadn't been watching her too closely. I'd been focused on Thor, on the lines of pain etched into his cheeks and around his eyes. Of the way his shoulders hunched and his voice cracked as he watched first his father, then his mother, die right in front of him. God. I couldn't even imagine.

I wrapped my arms around my stomach and rocked gently, fighting down nausea, wishing I could hold Thor close and rock him. Pet him. Touch him. He was hurting and he was out there alone. I should be with him. That stupid asshole. What the fuck was he thinking, leaving me like that? I'd Kung Fu the crap out of him once he was back in my bed, where he belonged.

I was having a meltdown, but Trinity didn't notice. And her voice was crisp, cool, completely under control. "What's his reasoning? To what, get us out of the picture? But if that's all he wanted, he would have left us alone. Mom was gone for almost thirty years. There was no reason to think she'd ever come back. So, why risk everything now?"

"He can't be king if she's alive," I countered. "The citadel knows. Her spire was still lit, so the whole planet knew she was still alive."

She couldn't argue with that.

"But why kidnap her? He could have just killed her on Earth. Much easier."

I shrugged, for I had no answer.

"Didn't he have you in custody?" she asked.

"Lord Wyse?" I nodded. "He was about to take me to some special place at the Optimus unit, but Thor got me out of there."

"Oh shit, that was close, wasn't it?" She paused. "That means Wyse knows you're a princess."

I thought back to my time with the Optimus unit, and reviewed every word I could remember. "He did seem very interested in the fact that there was no official record of my existence."

"Exactly. He's not stupid. And he could have taken your DNA off of anything to test it. They had full access to the Jax house. I'm sure Lady Jax would give him anything he asked for. A hairbrush. Toothbrush. Clothes. Whatever. He must have figured it out."

"Probably." I didn't have proof to say officially. "Which means he was most likely the one who ransacked Thor's apartments, hoping we'd be there so he could get me back into custody. He was going to take me to some horrible torture chamber or something. He said as much."

"So, I'm sure he's looking for Destiny. God, Faith. You were so close to being—" She stopped, apparently unable to complete the thought. Being a good little sister, I did it for her.

"Dead. One princess down, two to go."

She scowled. "That's not funny."

"No. But we're both still alive and Destiny is still hiding out as a nun." I thought of the pain on Thor's face. The shock and confusion in Lord Jax's eyes as he'd fallen victim to the poison. About what everything Mom must have gone through all those years ago. "But now we know. Now we go after him. Bring him down and get Mom back."

She laughed. "Right, arrest the head of the Optimus unit."

"You *are* the princess," I countered. "And if he kills Mom—"

"Don't even say it."

"If he kills Mom, you're the new queen and I'm the runner-up."

"He'd going to try again to get to you. To kill you. You're still a princess."

"But only a few people know about me. Lord Wyse won't tell anyone. It'll be easier for him to kill me if I'm an unknown rather than a princess."

Trinity sat back down, some of her frustration falling away. "It is a pain being the center of attention."

I rolled my eyes. "Whatever. Pretty gowns, a gorgeous hunk at your side. Total pain."

She smiled then. "Total."

It hadn't even been a day since Thor and I left the palace for the Jax mansion, but still, I missed Trinity, so I said as much, then added, "I miss Earth. Well, not Earth exactly, but our life there. Mom. Dad. Even Destiny."

Trinity squeezed my hand again and smiled wistfully.

"Me, too. But I've got Leo now and Mom will be found. Maybe Dad will come here... after we get things sorted out."

I thought of Dad on Alera, as Mom's king. It was hard to picture, but so was everything else that had happened since Mom had been kidnapped.

"Destiny's a freaking nun. Talk about weird," I said.

Trinity laughed. "There's a story there. And you've got Thor, a mate. Hot sex all the time."

Her sly smile fell away when I didn't say anything, didn't return the devilish look.

"So, the real question is, where is Thor?" She looked around, as if he were hiding behind the drapes. "He knows what we know, Faith. So where would he go?"

"I have no freaking clue. He left me and that was that. I haven't seen him or heard from him at all."

Until I said the words, it hadn't been really true. He'd walked out, needed space. His parents had just died in the most awful of ways. He discovered his mother was a traitor to not only their family, but to the throne. To all of Alera.

I could see that. God, I thought moving to Alera was a life change. But he'd had his whole life turned upside down within minutes. Over dinner. He'd lost everything. At least, he thought he had. I had news for him in the mating department. "Men. I swear to God, Trin. I want to kill him."

"Um... what?" she laughed after she realized I wasn't going to say more.

For some reason, the tears were gone. Completely gone. I couldn't cry about this any longer. I had no idea why. It was ripping me in two, this heartache, but there were no tears. "He's a Jax and now that Lady Jax is a traitor, he doesn't want to... to *taint* me with that. Even if I find him, he's not going to want to be with me."

"That's bullshit. He couldn't keep his hands off you." She frowned. "And he wasn't the traitor in the family."

"No, but the Jax name will be in ruins as soon as word gets out, and it wouldn't be good for *Princess Faith* to shack up with someone so dishonorable." I played with the lace edging of the blanket. Mindlessly.

"Whatever. Go get him. Tell him he's wrong."

"This is like déjà vu, Trin. I mean, we were having a similar conversation just the other day. I went to the dungeon and rescued him. His name was in ruins then. Not as bad as it will be after this, obviously, but I'd believed him innocent when even you thought otherwise. I wanted to be with him anyway."

"And now?"

"Now I want to be with him, but it isn't for me to decide. I can't sway him with BDSM makeup sex again."

Her eyes widened and her mouth fell open.

"I have no idea what that means... exactly." She held up her hand. "I don't want to know. Yes, I do, but that's a rabbit hole we can't go down right now."

I sighed. "I'm not going after him again. He's my mate. He knew it the second he saw me and had to coax me into the idea."

"Using BDSM makeup sex," she countered.

The corner of my mouth turned up. "And other persuasive ways, yes. He's changed his mind."

"So change it back."

I shook my head. "He has to want me more than family honor. He has to want me more than idle gossip. He has to want *me* and to make a family with *me* more than anything. Besides, I need to get to Lord Wyse and take him down." I wanted to do my newfound Kung Fu shit on Lord Wyse. Big time. He had Mom. He'd hurt Thor. He'd tried to kill Trinity and me. He was going down.

"What? You're just going to march into Lord Wyse's office and wrestle him to the ground?" she wondered. "I don't think that's much of a plan, little sister."

I shrugged, then shook my head. "No. But there is one thing you can do, one thing I need your help with."

"Anything. Tell me what I can do."

I considered for a moment, but there was no other way. "Send Nix and your boys to bring Thor here before he can do anything stupid. Don't let him talk to the police or the reporters —or whatever they're called here. Keep him safe, even if you have to lock him up in the dungeon."

"Is this for the good of the planet, or your sex life?"

That made me laugh, and it felt good. "Both."

Trinity tilted her head, her thinking eyes staring at me, glassy, bright. It was like I could literally see the analytical wheels spinning in her head. "I'm with you, but what exactly are you going to do?"

I smiled. "I'm going to introduce myself to the entire planet, and then I'm going to lie to them to protect my mate."

Her grin was contagious, even though this situation was anything but funny. "You're turning into a regular politician, Faith. Who knew you could be so sly?"

She was right. I was the bluntly honest one of the three of us. I said whatever I wanted, whenever I wanted. It drove Destiny crazy and had made Trinity sigh and shake her head on more than one occasion. But for once, I was going to be a bit more like my sisters than I'd ever thought I could be.

Because Thor was mine. Sadly, nothing was going to bring back his parents. Nothing. But I could protect him, whether he wanted me to or not.

"Where's the closest S-Gen machine? I need to get to work."

"On what?"

"If I'm going to meet the people, I need to look like a princess."

Trinity squeezed my hand and moved as if she intended to get up and leave me, so I held tight and made sure she saw the determination in my eyes. "Thor's mine. Bring him here before he does something stupid, okay?"

"I'll send Leo and Nix."

"Send a whole battalion. Thor's stubborn."

That made my sister laugh, the sound the happiest I'd ever heard her. "My dear sister, you really haven't spent much time with my mate. No problem. Trust me."

"Yeah, well, you don't know Thor. Tell Leo to take set his ion blaster to stun. Hell, take tranquilizer darts or something. He's going to need them."

Trinity was still laughing when she left me alone with the S-gen machine. I had two hours to get ready. After that, Trinity said she'd send in the hair stylist and makeup guru to help me look like a royal, like a woman who knew her place and power on this world.

In other words, like a complete stranger.

And by then, Thor should be in royal custody as well. Trinity assured me that Leo would make sure he looked his part.

I had a gown to make. And not just any gown, but a fucking badass, do-not-mess-with-me, princess gown.

Thor hadn't seen me in full battle mode. Not yet. I didn't need a uniform and body armor. No, I would fight in a killer dress with heels.

He might be a dumbass and leave me because of honor, but Thor was mine, and I would do whatever it took to protect him.

3

T hordis Jax, Jax Mountain Lodge

I MADE it three steps out the front door of the lodge when Leo stepped in front of me, blocking my path.

"Where the fuck do you think you're going?" he asked.

"Get out of my way, Leo." He might be bigger than me, but I had anger on my side.

"Not happening. Let's go." He thumbed over his shoulder.

"How did you find me?" I'd just sent the message with Pawl's confession to Leo's father a couple of minutes earlier. This lodge was remote, over an hour's drive from the city. How had Leo arrived so quickly? It was impossible.

"You sent us directions along with Pawl's confession. Thanks for that, by the way."

"My pleasure." And it was. Every threat to Faith would be dealt with one by one. "But I should have had an hour or more."

Leo tapped a small item on his chest and I squinted, confused. "A transport beacon? How the hell did you get that?"

The small buttons were very valuable, hard to come by, and monitored by the Interstellar Fleet. Finding one on Alera was damn near impossible.

Leo held up another button, clearly meant for me. "Trinity is personal friends with Prime Nial."

Fuck. *Of course*, she was. Wasn't that just fucking perfect. "I have business to attend to, Leo. Get out of my way."

"Faith's at the palace. She's upset. Which means Trinity is upset. And that, Lord Jax, means you aren't going anywhere."

A new argument was on my lips when both Nix and Leo's father came into view, flanking me on both sides, each wearing a transport button as well. *Shit.* They had me surrounded, the only option for escape was to head back into the lodge. And that wasn't happening. I had things to do. "Listen, Leo. I'm doing everything now to *protect* Faith, not hurt her."

"I know," he said calmly, as if being a mated male himself he understood.

"My family is a disgrace. My mother was a traitor. She tried to have Trinity killed and tried to poison my—" I stopped myself before I used that word. I couldn't say that word ever again. "She tried to poison Princess Faith on Lord Wyse's orders. He has to be stopped."

"I know," he repeated. "And you're still coming with me to the palace."

"I can't take down Wyse from the fucking palace." My voice was calm, but inside I was roiling with rage. Aggression. I had to get out of here and protect my mate. The need was critical, primal, more important than breathing. "Don't get in my way."

"Too late," he countered. "And it's not me standing in your way. Fuck that. If it were up to me, we'd be blasters firing, straight in the front door of the Optimus unit. We'd kill him and be done with it."

Both Nix and Leo's father nodded.

"Then let's go."

Nix stepped closer, but it was Leo's father who spoke. "It's not up to us, Thor. Trinity and Faith are in charge, and they have other plans."

No fucking way. Run. I had to run. They didn't want to kill me, that was clear. If they had, I'd already be dead. Which meant they wouldn't be willing to use lethal force to stop my escape.

I'd go back inside. Head for the roof. From there, I could track their locations and—

"Don't even think about it, Thor," Leo warned. "Faith needs you. She's your mate. You are not going to fuck this up."

"I've already fucked it up by being a Jax. I'm ruined. She's not mine. She must choose another."

He sighed. "Well, she disagrees. So let's go."

I moved faster than I ever had before. Pivot. Turn. Door open.

A sharp pain struck my ass cheek, followed by a burning sensation in my muscles.

Before I could process that, my feet refused to move like I wanted them to and I fell, smashing into the door on my way down. Twisting, I felt an odd projectile sticking out of my flesh. I pulled it free to see a needle on the end of an odd dart. I had never seen anything like it. "What... the... fuck?"

My voice sounded far away, down the end of a tunnel, and the sky was spinning.

"One going to be enough?" Nix asked as all three of them loomed over me.

One what? And why was that bastard laughing?

Leo's father squatted beside me, no menace in him, just curiosity. "Looks like it."

"I like this weapon." That was Nix and I turned my head just far enough to see the fuzzy outline of some kind of short rifle resting over his shoulder.

My lips went numb and I blinked several times, trying to keep my eyes open. It wasn't fucking working. "Leo? What the fuck have you—"

My tongue was too thick to finish the sentence.

"Tranquilizer gun." Leo grinned and stared at the weapon I had to assume Nix had fired at my ass. "Better than the stun setting on an ion pistol."

"Impressive," Leo's father commented.

"Let's transport him out of here. Trinity said to strip him naked and tie him down on Faith's bed." That was Leo.

"Shooting him in the ass was fun, but stripping him naked?" Leo replied. "Not the best part of the job."

The last thing I heard was Leo's laughter and then everything went black.

FAITH, The Citadel

TRINITY NODDED to me and said two words, "Got him."

Just like that, I could breathe again. Thor was safe. The news reporters, or whatever they were called here, were practically piled on top of each other around the perimeter of the citadel's deadly border. A nice feature to ensure they didn't get too close. Eagerness was one thing, hounding another.

Trinity had been busy while I'd been getting ready. They'd been broadcasting my imminent appearance for the better part of an hour. Everyone on Alera who didn't live in a cave knew the next princess was about to be introduced to the people. Live. At any moment.

Time for part two of my plan.

The gown I wore was blood red, a deep, dark color that I hoped would convey my message to Lord Wyse or anyone else who threatened my family. I was royal. Strong. And no longer a scared little girl, but a woman full of her own power. The material did not shimmer like satin as I'd remembered seeing Trinity's do, but absorbed light like velvet. The top half of the gown was sheer, a network of blood-red Aleran flowers covering the juicy bits, trailing over my bare shoulders and back, down my arms like living, breathing fire. And the skirt did not balloon into a mess three or four times wider than my body, but hung like a dagger, straight and strong and fearless.

This wasn't a modest garment. No. I had to go as I planned to proceed. Trinity might be the heir apparent, but no one should fuck with the runner up.

My hair was pulled away from my face, matching Aleran flower pins sparkling in the mass of curls that fell down my back. I'd told Trinity to go bold with the makeup as well, and my lips were bright red, my eyes dark and dramatic, lined and piled with more layers of eyeshadow than I'd ever worn in my life.

Ridiculous, yes, to fawn over my looks when Alera should respect me for my brain and the blood that flowed through my veins. But it was a publicity stunt. Not for the Aleran people, but for Lord Fucking Wyse and any of the others who messed with my family.

I stood looking in the small compact mirror Trinity had handed me and looked at an alien staring back. A beautiful, fierce, frightening bitch who looked like she'd be just as happy to kill me as invite me over for tea.

Good. Trinity was blonde and beautiful and perfect. I didn't need to sell that model. I needed to scare our enemies into making stupid mistakes.

Where was Destiny when I needed her? She was dramatic for all three of us. She could pull this off without even trying. This was so not my department, but for Thor? For him, I'd do anything.

"You ready?" Trinity asked, taking the compact and tucking it away into some hidden pocket of her dress. She looked fabulous as well, but her gown was light and sparkling, golden and feminine and soft. Her hair fell in soft waves around her face, making her look young and innocent. Angelic. Fragile. Delicate.

As if. But that, too, was part of our plan. The planet at large had only seen her once in person. Heard her speak once when she originally introduced herself. And she'd been perfect. At the royal reception, where a select group celebrated with her, she'd again been perfect. Beautiful and diplomatic and well-spoken. Everything a princess should be.

Time to put a little rattle into the masses and shake things up. We might be sisters, but we weren't clones. And yeah, Destiny and I were twins, but wait until they got a load of her. Inwardly, I laughed.

Prior to our arrival on Alera, there had been battles for control of areas outside the capital city. Leo had told us of raids and skirmishes for control of outposts and towns. Not full-out war. Not yet. Luckily, our arrival seemed to have stopped all that as everyone reassessed their positions. Their standing. There were new power players in town, and not just our mom, but the three of us. And as long as we weren't afraid to play, we were pretty much guaranteed to win. We had the spires to prove it. The blood in our veins, too. Time to start acting like it.

"Ready."

"You look like a vampire goddess with blood flowers growing out of your skin."

Only Trinity could make me laugh at a time like this. "Sounds perfect."

"Yep." She grinned. "Leo's got Thor. He's safe *and* he's watching."

"Him and everyone else on the planet," I murmured, taking a deep breath.

"That is what you wanted, resident badass."

She was right. No second thoughts. Not now. "Let's do this."

A quick hug and we walked out of the building, side by side, to face the cameras.

4

T *hor, The Royal Palace*

THE WORST PART about being knocked unconscious by some kind of pointed... dart by two males I considered friends wasn't the fact that they'd been ordered to restrain me. Naked. To Faith's bed. That, I found bittersweet, for I could still smell her in the sheets and her scent was driving me half mad. And that was the worst part. My cock was rock hard as I stared at the large screen on the wall, Faith a vision in red. She looked more beautiful and fiercer than I'd ever seen her. She looked like a queen, and goddess help me if seeing her glowing with power and intent didn't make my cock harder than it had ever been.

She was mine, that magnificent female. My mate. While the royal consort who was with me as attendant—babysitter more like it—had put a towel over my waist as a ridiculous attempt to protect my modesty, it was tented so much that it looked like a family of zebcats could set up a den beneath. I looked like a fool. Obscene. And the restraints around my wrists did not improve my mood. My mate was out there, facing the entire planet alone. I couldn't be with her, not anymore, but I could protect her from the shadows, watch over her and make sure she was safe.

Leo and Nix robbed me of that right. Left me buck naked and tied up... and without my mate. We'd fucked as I'd been restrained before and that had been hot. But this? Torturous and miserable.

"I'm going to kill Leo and Nix," I muttered to myself.

Even in my drugged haze, I remembered their tone had been filled with humor when they mentioned tying me to Faith's bed. Apparently, they'd been serious and I'd awoken with my arms tied to the headboard of a thick, sumptuous bed. Faith's bed. Naked and with the fucking royal consort in a chair he'd pulled up beside me. The fact he was stuck supervising me burned my pride more than my current state of undress. The large video screen on the wall showed Faith, larger than life, gorgeous as fuck. Regal, confident, commanding.

I wasn't embarrassed. Fuck, no. That was my mate on the screen and my cock throbbed to be back inside her. Just this glimpse was enough to make my balls ache, to have pre-cum spreading a wet spot on the fucking towel.

The consort heard my threat, of course, and deigned to take his hungry eyes off my female long enough to issue a warning. "I wouldn't mess with either of them, Lord Jax. I assure you, I am just thankful to be alive. Captain Turaya could have killed me with his bare hands for touching his mate."

I turned my head, looked at the male in his fancy royal robes. It was his job to satisfy the females of the royal family. He wasn't keeping himself busy with Trinity and there was no fucking way he would satisfy Faith, so I would have to assume their cousin Radella received his services. Instantly, I felt sorry for him.

"You could at least cover me with a blanket," I muttered.

I was bare except for the towel. Leo and Nix must have

dumped me, stripped me and tied me up without getting the covers out from under me.

The consort stood and went to a cabinet, pulled out a white sheet and spread it over me. It did nothing to hide my obvious desire for my mate.

"That female is lovely," he commented. I growled. He held up a hand and was about to say more, but Faith spoke. In perfect Aleran.

"Citizens of Alera. As you all know, Queen Celene was attacked twenty-seven years ago in a coup to overthrow the royal family. She escaped. Her mate, Princess Trinity's father, your king, did not."

Trinity stood behind Faith's left shoulder wearing a golden gown that sparkled with every bit of light that found the dress. Behind Trinity? The citadel itself, the spires brightly lit far above them. No one else stood upon that sacred ground. There would be no argument as to Faith's identity, nor her royal bloodline. The sisters were almost too beautiful to be real and I was held in their thrall, hanging on every word Faith spoke, as, I was sure, was the rest of Alera. When Faith looked back over her shoulder at her sister, Trinity nodded and Faith too a deep breath, as if fortifying herself.

Here it comes. The truth. The downfall of my family. And even that could not make my desire for Faith wane. My cock didn't care about titles or wealth or honor. It wanted one thing, and one thing only – the same thing I wanted—Faith.

But to protect her, we would never have her again.

I hadn't allowed emotion to overcome me when my mother's betrayal broke something inside that would never heal. When she'd accidentally murdered my father and then suffered remorse so keen that she'd taken her own life. I had not shed a single tear.

But now, watching Faith, my beautiful, kind, intelligent, courageous mate, I had nowhere to go, no activity with which to occupy my mind, and the tears streamed silently from the corners of my eyes to soak her pillow. Pain gutted me, ripping my soul into pieces. I would let her go, because it was the honorable thing to do. And I would have nothing.

So be it.

Her smile made me forget to breathe. "What you do not know is how our mother, Queen Celene, escaped that night with the help of two loyal guards, one of whom stands among the royal guard today, Captain Travin Turaya. He was a young man at the time, and he protected our mother, escorted her to a secret location where she transported off Alera to protect the one thing that mattered to her above all others—the future of Alera. What you do not know is that Queen Celene was already pregnant with Princess Trinity that fateful night. But she knew her enemies would not stop searching for her. She was young, and alone. So she fled to a distant planet, a planet so small and insignificant that no one would think to search for her there. That planet has been my family's home for the last twenty-seven years."

I started breathing again, my lips numb and tingling. The consort shifted in his seat, staring with rapt attention at the screen. This was more information than anyone had received so far, and the media and camera teams broadcasting live across the entire planet were silent. Dead silent. No one wanted to miss a single word of explanation. We'd been starving for the truth for almost thirty years.

"As you all know, Queen Celene was young and beautiful. When she arrived on Earth, she met and fell in love with another man, my father, an amazing, strong and honorable man named Adam Buchanan. My mother told him the truth about her past and he chose to hide her by assuming a new identity. Adam and Celene Jones. He knew, as we did, that the day would come when we would return to Alera and right the wrongs committed against the royal family and the people of this beautiful planet. He adopted Princess Trinity as his own and together, he and Queen Celene lived a peaceful life and had two more daughters. We were taught about duty and honor, about what it would mean to return and claim the throne. We were taught to speak the language of our home world and value the history and traditions of a proud people. I am honored to stand before you next to my sister and introduce myself to you. I am Faith Jones Herakles, of both Earth and Alera. I am Queen Celene's second daughter, Princess Trinity's sister. *I am Princess Faith."*

The crowd clapped and cheered, the reporters began to shout questions at her all at once. The chaos was astonishing, but the barrier surrounding the citadel easily held them back as none wanted to die crossing it. And when Faith held up her hand, silence fell quickly as we were all hungry for more.

She paused then, the camera zooming in close. I'd never seen her with makeup. It only made her eyes even more striking, her lips look fuller. More kissable.

"We lived in peace for many years, planning our return. But true to Queen Celene's fears, our enemies never stopped looking for her. And a few weeks ago, they finally found us. My mother was dragged from her bed and taken. Kidnapped. Princess Trinity and I transported to Alera to find our mother, *our queen,* and to bring those criminals who masterminded not only the original attack, but her recent kidnapping, to justice."

She paused again but there was no eruption of questions this time. It appeared everyone was in shock. The consort turned to me, his eyes huge in his face and I realized just how young he was. "Is it true? Was the queen kidnapped?"

I nodded. "Yes." I knew that much. Faith had told me much in our time together

"People of Alera, we call upon you now for assistance. Our mother, your queen, is still missing. We fear she is being tortured, or worse, although her spire is still lit." Faith looked up into the sky as everyone else did, seeing the truth of those words. "But now, we finally have information on her perpetrator, on those behind the attack twenty-seven years ago, on a male among you who wanted the crown for himself."

The crowd gasped, as did the consort next to me, as if such a thing were beyond their imagination. "Who?" The consort asked aloud. "Who would do such a thing? A king? We do not want a king. We have never had a king. Males protect their mates and their people, they do not rule. If males were meant to rule, the citadel would not have chosen the females among us." He was mumbling to himself, so I ignored him, imagined that many watching were having the same reaction.

The image panned wide and I clearly saw that Faith and Trinity stood within the Citadel's perimeter that only those of royal blood could pass without being killed. I had recognized their placement before, but this would show people all over the planet, those who had never set foot in the royal capital of Mytikas, exactly where these two powerful women stood. It proved their royal status without having to say a word. Those in the crowd—and it was a large one—gazed at her with rapt attention. I didn't blame them. I couldn't look away either. She was about to destroy my mother, my family, in front of everyone.

No. Not Faith. My mother had done that to herself. To us.

"Prior to our arrival on Alera, it was decided that I would remain hidden, a secret, so I could move freely among you and discover these traitors. They have now been identified and I will announce who they are. Once I do, I expect every citizen of Alera to assist us in apprehending these murderers. They tried to kill Queen Celene, murdered her mate, and have caused countless deaths among you during the resulting battles for power in the queen's absence."

She tipped her chin up and smiled, not a brilliant smile, but a kind smile. The type a mother bestows on her innocent child. Magnanimous. Very, very royal.

Goddess, she was breathtaking.

The crowd was loud, talking with each other, then silenced immediately when Faith held up her hand.

"How do you know I really am Princess Trinity's sister? Not a cousin?" She nodded and looked to Trinity. "We don't look much alike, do we?" She pulled something from a pocket of her ruby red dress—it looked fucking stunning on her, highlighting every one of her curves I knew so well—and held it up. "As you can see, this is a med wand." She held it over her finger and the blue light glowed. I saw her eye twitch from the prick I knew had happened and she pulled the unit away. "My blood."

The video zoomed in close so there was no question what she was doing. It was as if I could reach out and touch my mate, to feel her soft skin, to breathe in her specific scent.

She moved the wand back in place. "As you can see, I passed through the citadel's barrier safely. Should there be any doubt, the DNA data from this blood sample..." She paused, waited. "Is being displayed on every Aleran's video feed now." She turned the small unit's display so it faced the cameras. "You can confirm that what you are seeing in my hand matches the data on your personal vid screens. What is also being shown is the DNA coding of Queen Celene, which has been public record for decades."

Everyone could read the data analysis. It was obvious to me, and everyone around the world, that Faith was, indeed, Queen Celene's daughter.

"She really is Princess Faith," the consort said, eyes wide. "Two daughters? Goddess, she is beautiful. Princess Trinity has a mate, but perhaps my services will now be of use to her sister."

I growled and glared at the male, although he was watching the screen and barely noticed, so entranced was he by the beauty on display there.

My beauty. My female. Mine.

No. No. No.

Not mine. Not anymore. And yet, even though the consort

had no idea he was sitting next to Faith's mate, it was a good thing I was restrained.

"It is my honor to be your princess," Faith continued with a slight bow of her head. "While Princess Trinity has been filling in as royal leader of Alera in our mother's absence, it has been my task to find the queen. To rescue her from attackers and bring her back to all of us, and to her rightful place as *your* leader."

The crowd roared and began changing *Queen Celene, Queen Celene,* over and over. Faith let it continue for about a minute, then she held up her hands and an instant silence fell.

"I will not be answering questions today. I have introduced myself, and it is now time to tell you of the traitors and ask for your help in delivering justice to those that betrayed all of us."

Bile rose in my throat. The traitors were my family. I held my breath awaiting her next words.

"We have evidence that Lord Coburt Wyse, inspector Optimi of the Optimus Unit and cousin to Queen Celene, is the mastermind behind the murder of the Queen's mate and the attempted murder of Queen Celene twenty-seven years ago. He is also responsible for the kidnapping of Queen Celene from her home on Earth and the recent attempts on Princess Trinity's life."

No one spoke. No reporter questioned. It was as if everyone on the planet collectively held their breath. Even the consort next to me was transfixed. I, on the other hand, was ready to throw up. Ready to accept the inevitable. The downfall of the Jax family, the end of my mating.

The end of my life, for it would not be worth living without Faith.

"Yesterday, Lord Wyse made an attempt upon my life. I have spent my time since my arrival on Alera within the Jax family. With Lady Jax's history and decades of experience working in the Optimus unit, they were invaluable in helping me root out Lord Wyse." She looked down, swallowed hard. "I am sad to announce that Lord and Lady Jax have both been murdered by Lord Wyse in a failed attempt on my life. They were an honorable pair, offering protection and assistance to an unknown princess despite the great danger to themselves and their great family name. They took me in as their own daughter and blessed my mating with their only son, Thordis Jax. I will miss them greatly. Please mourn with me and my mate, the new Lord Thordis Jax, in this time of grief for the passing of our family."

The consort looked to me, wide-eyed. "Oh shit. Forget what I said. Don't hurt me. I won't touch Princess Faith, I promise."

I didn't look at him, just stared at the screen.

"A full service honoring Lord and Lady Jax will be held in the capital city of Mytikas, and will be conducted by the head of the Clerical Order in a few days' time."

What the fuck was going on? She was lying. On camera and in front of the entire planet. Trinity even put a comforting hand on her shoulder. The crowd was eating this up. So was the consort beside me.

"Congratulations, my lord, on your mating," the consort replied humbly. He fucking bowed, as if I were a royal. Worthy of great honor. "I am sorry for the loss of your parents. They died with honor."

I couldn't think. Couldn't process everything at once. Faith lied. The truth she was sharing with the entire fucking planet wasn't the truth at all. My mother wasn't honorable. She was a traitor and a murderer. The Jax name was tainted.

I was tainted.

And yet she announced their deaths as a point of pride in bringing justice to Alera. She claimed me as her mate, boldly and without hesitation. As far as the people of Alera knew, my parents died protecting the royal family and I was not just mate to the new princess, but the son of brave, self-sacrificing nobles who died defending the crown.

What. The. Fuck?

Why? Why would she do this? My blood was tainted. My family dishonorable. Traitors. She should not look at me without hatred in her eyes, let alone claim me as her own. She needed another. A true warrior. A true servant whose bloodline was true and pure, and loyal to the queen.

No. I was not worthy. Faith had to see reason. I had to talk with her. Now.

"As penance for keeping me here against my will, you will release me and let me go stand with my mate. I belong at her side." If Faith could lie, then so could I.

He shook his head. "I'm sorry, Lord Jax. You may be Princess Faith's mate, but my orders are not only from Captain Turaya and Captain Vennix, but Princess Trinity herself. She is the final word on all things. Until her mother is set free, she is our leader."

I groaned. Fuck. Leave it to the weasel to be loyal now, when I needed him to be a bit less strong of will. Resigned to wait, I stared at Faith on the screen once again as her words made every hair on my body rise in alarm. She was baiting a monster now. Putting a target on her back.

"A royal warrant has been issued for the arrest and detainment of Coburt Wyse." Faith nodded solemnly to her sister and Trinity stepped forward.

"On my orders, the royal guard are, even now as I speak, hunting him down like the rabid dog he is. Coburt Wyse is henceforth stripped of his title of Lord. All of his lands and wealth are passed to his daughter, my cousin, the Lady Radella. Furthermore, Coburt Wyse is stripped of his rank and privilege within the Optimus unit and will stand trial for the murder of my father, the king, attempted murder and kidnapping of Queen Celene, and the murders of Lord and Lady Jax."

Trinity reached backward and Faith slid her hand into her sister's as if she needed comfort for the loss.

Liar. She was a fucking liar. But why? Why would she do this?

Oh, Faith. My Faith. She might be intense and fierce, bejeweled and gorgeous with her makeup and styled hair, that fucking sexy dress. But I knew the real female beneath the act. I knew her vulnerable and naked and fresh-faced. Open and spread wide beneath me. I knew her scent, what she tasted like, what she sounded like when she came, the feel of her pussy when it clamped down on my cock, pulled the cum from my balls. I knew *her*.

And she deserved better than me.

And when I got out of these restraints, she'd understand that, even if it meant she would know the feel of my hand on her ass once more.

5

F *aith*

NIX WAS ALREADY TRACKING down Coburt Wyse. He'd escorted me to the palace as he ordered a group of his men to begin the search. Once I was safe in the palace, he'd left to join them. In this moment, as I stood next to Trinity before the citadel, I finally understood what it meant to be royal, to have responsibilities bigger than anything I'd ever imagined. I didn't belong to myself anymore. I didn't belong to Thor, as much as I wanted to.

I belonged to *them.* To all of Alera. I stared out at the people, the children with their beaming smiles, their parents with faces full of hope and horror—in equal parts.

But hope was winning. Trinity and I represented thousands of years of stability and tradition. Of safety and security, prosperity and peace.

And no old, greedy asshole, who happened to be our mother's cousin, was going to take that away from these people. Even if my mother's spire went out—the very idea made my eyes burn with unshed tears—there were three of us to carry on the bloodline, to ensure the future of the planet.

To have children and pass on the traditions and our royal blood.

My hand crept over my abdomen. I could be pregnant; Thor had given it a good college try, filling me again and again with his seed. I secretly hoped we'd made a baby. *Thor's child.* The thought of a son or daughter with his smile, his eyes, made my heart melt all over again, made me blink back tears for another reason. The dream also hardened my resolve.

I had just lied to billions of people to protect my family. And Thor was mine. End of discussion.

Now I would just have to convince him.

Trinity and I stepped back and disappeared inside the citadel. Per our earlier plan, we met Leo's father and two of the queen's guard near the back entrance—Leo's father knew of its existence, of course—and disappeared into an armored EMV for a quick ride back to the palace.

I knew Thor was there, in my room, waiting for me. Leo had told me as much. I hadn't quite understood the grin on his face when he'd spoken of shooting Thor with a tranquilizer dart, but my nerves rattled around inside my body as we drew closer.

Trinity reached across the bench seat and squeezed my hand. "He loves you. It'll be fine."

To her, I was an open book. She knew I was more nervous about Thor than anything else. The Alerans knew the truth, knew of Lord Wyse's duplicity. He was being hunted and would be found. Now, I could take a moment and deal with Thor.

"I don't know. He's stubborn, Trin."

That made Trinity throw her head back and laugh. "Have you met yourself? Destiny explodes. I argue. But you? You're stubborn as a bull, Faith. You look sweet and innocent, but you're not fooling me. I know you too well. There is no one in the universe more stubborn than you are. Convince him."

Her words were ringing in my ears when I stepped into my bed chamber to find Thor lying on my bed and a strange young man sitting next to him. "Who are you?"

The younger male stood and bowed low. He took my hand, kissing the back. "I am the royal consort. And I am at your service, Your Highness. Anything you need, you need only ask."

I ignored Thor's growl from the bed.

I looked the consort over. He was young, eager to please. I recognized him from the news reports about Trinity's kidnapping and remembered that he had helped save her on the night of the royal reception, when the traitor Zel had kidnapped her. "Thank you for your assistance in saving my sister's life."

He blushed like a teenager. "Thank you, Your Highness. Anything to assist, you need only ask. Anything at all," he repeated, although he gave a furtive glance at Thor.

Thor practically growled from the bed and I was surprised that he had not risen to greet me. Had not shoved the consort's hand from mine.

As tactfully as I could, I slid my hand free and placed it behind my back so the young man would not see me wipe his touch from my skin on the back of my dress. "Thank you. And yes, there is something you can do."

"Anything, Princess."

"Leave us, and tell the guards to block the door. No one gets in here. Not even my sister."

His eyes widened and he was quiet for a moment. "Are you sure, Your Highness—"

I cut him off with a wave of my hand, my eyes on my mate now and nothing else. "Leave. Now."

He bowed and scurried out of the room like a chastised puppy with his tail between his legs. I waited to hear the door click, then walked over to lock it before returning to the side of the bed. It was then I saw the restraints, saw the sheet that covered him, the way his cock tented the thin material. I swallowed, my skin heating.

"They had to tie you down?"

"They did." Thor's gaze devoured me as if he'd been starving for the sight of me. I felt the same. But him being cuffed to the bed, bothered me.

"Why? Are you so desperate to be free of me?" The words hurt. A lot.

"I should not be here." He tugged at the ropes around his wrists, to no avail. But he didn't take his gaze off me. My body. My breasts. My neck. Lips. And finally, my eyes. I caught his gaze and willed him not to look away. The time for games was over.

"You're mine, Thor." I put every ounce of royal conviction into my voice. Maybe him being tied up was a good idea. He had to listen, to hear reason, the stubborn fool. If I had to keep him restrained until he listened to reason—well, that wasn't ideal, but I was desperate. He couldn't leave me. I needed him.

"You should choose another," he replied. "I am not worthy. My family is tainted."

I shook my head, put my hand over my heart. "You're mine. I need you. You promised me, Thor. You promised me forever."

He shook his head, and I noticed the salty remains of tears streaking the side of his face. My heart stuttered.

"That was before—" His voice broke and I choked down pain so I could speak.

"Before what? Before I fell in love with you?" Stubborn, stubborn man. I leaned over and kissed his temple, the remnants of his tears. Then I released the tie on his wrist.

He didn't move, confusion in his eyes. "You have never spoken of love."

I walked around the end of the bed, slowly, the gown I wore making me feel like a phantom wearing a shell as his gaze followed me. This royal beauty was not me. I was simple and plain and preferred to curl up in front of a fireplace with a good book. I was not this complicated, seductive, posturing princess.

This gown was not me. This made up face was not mine. I was an imposter. A fake that I'd shown to all of Alera.

The only time I felt real was in his arms. With his cock buried deep inside me. With my name on his lips and his heartbeat pressed to my ear. He made me feel alive. Real. Whole. And I didn't want to give that up.

Regardless, I was not going to force him. This was not going to be a repeat of the dungeon. I was not ruled by the Ardor any longer. There would be no coercion. No more lies or secrets between us. I released the restraint on his opposite wrist and he was free. I held my breath. Waited. He stared at me. His cock tented the sheet but neither of us moved for long moments, staring at one another.

I wondered what he was thinking, but I didn't dare ask. I'd put my heart on the line, told him the truth, set him free. I was in love with him. That I needed him. If he left me now, he would destroy me, but I would know he wanted honor over me. The Jax name was important to him, but I had to hope I was even more valued.

"Why did you lie, Faith?" he asked. "About my mother. About all of it."

He spoke of my announcement to Alera. He'd seen it.

"I protected what was mine, Thor," I told him. "And you are mine."

He shook his head again. "But what of Trinity? Leo? The royal guard?"

I had to make him understand. Now. There would be no room for error. "And Trinity thinks I'm stubborn," I muttered, then sighed. "Trinity and Leo know the truth. They support my decision. No one else knows, Thor. And no one else ever will."

"But the royal guards," he countered. "I called Nix. He came to my parents' house to be with you after they died, after I left. Then yesterday, he even shot me in the ass with some kind of... dart and left me here. Naked."

"Yes. He knows what happened, saw the bodies himself." I

thought of Lord and Lady Jax dead on their dining room floor. "And he believed everything I told him. As for the tranquilizer gun, it worked, didn't it?"

He frowned, but said nothing. He rose to sit with his back against the headboard at my words. The sheet fell to reveal a very tempting expanse of muscled chest. One small tug, and his cock would be free as well. I curled my fingers in the fabric on the edge of the mattress as Thor spoke. "You lied to Nix? To the royal guard?"

"Yes." I yanked the sheet and there it was, his cock, thick and long and hard. Mine. "That very night. Kneeling over your parents, I heard what you said. I heard and I understood what was at stake."

"And what was that?" He didn't try to cover himself, but let me look my fill, which I took as a very good sign. So was the way his cock bobbed up toward me, hardening even further. A pearly drop of fluid seeped from the tip. I kicked off my shoes, lifted my skirt and crawled toward him.

"You're mine," I said. "I protect what's mine. My sisters will protect us. And my mother. We are family, Thor."

He still didn't touch me. "You could have any male on Alera now. You know that. Thousands of males would come if they thought there was a chance you could awaken them. Even the royal consort. He will see to your every whim, no awakening needed."

"I don't want them, *mate*. I want you." Lifting the skirt to my hips, I closed the distance and settled myself onto his lap. I sighed in relief when his hands found the curve of my waist and he didn't push me away. His touch burned through the thin fabric of my gown, but the hard top of his cock nestled at the entrance of my pussy made me moan his name. I had purposely decided to be bare beneath the gown, this moment a fantasy I'd held close to my heart since the S-Gen machine generated it.

Lowering my lips, I kissed him. Softly. Slowly. I told him

with my lips that I loved him. That he was fragile and precious and protected.

He accepted my touch for a few moments before he took control, his kiss dominant and aggressive, his hands now gripping, holding me to him. Full of lust and love and desperate need.

"Faith." He groaned as I settled my hot, wet pussy on top of him, taking his cock deep. I was wet. Ready. Eager. "Fuck. Goddess, I can't tell you no."

"Then stop trying to push me away and love me."

"Goddess help me, Faith. I do," he said against my lips. "I love you. I know I should let you go, but I can't. Does that make me greedy? Selfish?"

"No. It makes you mine. Stop arguing." I ground my hips against him, rose and took him deep. He loved me. He'd said the words. Now. Despite everything we'd been through, despite his parents' deaths and my new responsibilities as a princess. I squeezed my inner muscles and grinned when he moaned my name, his hands cupping my breasts and squeezing my hard nipples through the fabric of the gown. He closed his eyes and I kissed him. Our tongues tangled, the heat of him, the feel of him beneath me, surrounding me, seeping into me. "You're mine, my lord."

"Yes, Princess."

"Forever," I insisted.

"Forever."

He crushed me to him and took control, lifting his hips off the bed as he pushed me down, driving deep. I clung to him as he pulled my hips closer, rubbing my sensitive clit against his body. He knew what made me hot, what pushed me over the edge. He may have been a virgin before we met, but he knew *me*.

My gown pooled around us like dark roses and I loved the image of us entwined, me in the gown, him naked beneath me.

I'd been so primed, so eager for him, I'd been close to

coming ever since I took him deep inside me. I shuddered as I came apart in his arms, gasping for air as he thrust harder, pushing me higher. I called out his name on a shout as my head fell back and I gave over to the bliss I could only find in his arms.

My pussy stretched around him, the pulsing stronger. Too strong. His whispered words of praise, naughty phrases of promise, kept it all going. When it was over, I collapsed in his arms, my forehead pressed to his chest, struggling to breathe when I knew he was still full, and hard, and thick inside me. He had yet to come.

"I hope you aren't too attached to this dress." His comments came as he ripped the delicate buttons down the back and peeled the top half from me, baring my breasts and shoulders. The remnants pooled around my waist, but I didn't care as he sat up and bent me backward over his forearm. Took my nipples into his hot, wet mouth.

"Thor." I pulled at him, wanting more, needing him to move again. The hot, wet suction of his mouth though pushed me back into desperate need so easily. My pussy wasn't satisfied. No. My body was more alive, more desperate than ever. This wasn't Ardor, but love. The first orgasm was just a warm up and now my body was vibrating with every touch. "Please."

He lifted me and rocked me backward, followed me down so that he was on top of me, buried deep. It was my hands now that went over my head, one of his hands holding my wrists, restraining me just as he wanted. I cried out as he thrust forward, rocking my entire body with the force of his lust. I could only imagine what the consort and the guards could hear from the door. I didn't care. He was mine and everyone could know he satisfied me so well.

"Mine. Mine. Mine." He chanted the words to me between kisses. Mouth. Neck. Shoulder. Nipples. I wanted him everywhere.

He thrust faster, rubbing his body against mine, suckling my nipple, making me crazed.

I came again, but he didn't stop, driving me higher. Faster. Until I lost control and shattered a third time, my fingers clawing at his back, his neck. My heels dug into his ass, pulling him deeper. Demanding more.

"Greedy little princess, aren't you?" he growled. He was grinning as he watched me, his gaze locked on my face, drinking me in. Watching me as he brought me pleasure unlike I'd ever known before. There was love in those eyes. A softness I'd never seen, and it made my body spasm again. For him. Only for him.

"I love you."

"Say it again." He moved. Just enough, and I gasped, closing my eyes.

"No. Open them, love. Say it again. Look at me and say it again."

I couldn't deny him, the words a joy as they sprang from my lips. I stared into his eyes and hid nothing. Squeezed my pussy and clenched him, held him deep. "I love you, Thordis Jax. I love you and I'm never letting you go."

He didn't move, not an inch, but an orgasm rocked through him when I spoke. I felt the hot spurt of his seed as he came. He held my gaze as he emptied into me, as his body claimed mine. We were one now. No more questions. No more uncertainty.

"I love you, Faith. I don't care if you're a princess or a maid, you're mine."

Amen to that.

6

F aith, Transport Center

THE EMV SLID to a stop in front of one of the small, public transport stations and Thor's grip on my hand tightened. Or maybe my hold on him. A few hours ago I'd been in bed with Thor, wrapped in his arms. Warm. Safe. Loved. The queen's guard reported that Lord Wyse had been captured that evening and I'd been content. Happier than I could remember being since before our mother had been kidnapped and we'd left Earth behind.

But then the knock on our bedroom door two hours ago ruined everything. Trinity stood on the other side, her eyes dark and tormented. I'd known before she opened her mouth that something was wrong. Very, very wrong.

Lord Wyse wanted to make a deal, our mother's location for his life.

And Trinity, being the analytical hardass I loved, had agreed, placing our mother's life above the need for vengeance. I admired her strength but wasn't sure I could have made the same choice. Perhaps that was her Aleran blood.

No. It was my father's influence, Trinity's stepfather, and their shared study of the law. Her discipline. Perhaps she'd been shaped by the knowledge that one day, she would be a queen. That hard choices would be an inescapable part of her future life.

But then, I'd seen Lord and Lady Jax die before me, witnessed my mate's agony over that loss. Lord Wyse had tried to kill me, my sisters, and had hurt Thor in a way that would never be fully mended. The fact that Lord Wyse helped kidnap my mother was just the icing on the cake.

I remembered Lord Wyse well, the interrogation, his readiness to drag me to some secret cell to probably torture answers out of me. And kill me, never to be seen again. Never to be known as a princess.

I'd felt the intensity of his intentions, the almost... eagerness to destroy the royal line. And take over.

Trinity had met him as well, but she hadn't been his prisoner, barely escaping his clutches. She'd seen his lies, his falsehood. And Thor had known him since he was a boy. God, Wyse had been trying to take over the throne for almost thirty years —that we knew of—and wore his evil like a coat. I had to wonder if, after so long, he now believed his own lies and justifications for his actions.

Of course, he did.

He was the man behind Lady Jax turning against the queen. The man who had ordered her to send Zel to kill my sister. The man who had made Thor's mother so insane that rather than see her son happy, she'd been so hungry for power, she'd tried to kill me.

She'd killed her own mate instead. Lord Jax had been an innocent in all this and was now dead. The devastation she must have felt, the pain so intense that she'd decided to take her own life rather than live with herself and face her son.

Still, I could forgive her all that. In her own, twisted way, she'd loved Thor beyond what I would consider healthy. But at least I could understand it. What I could not forgive was the pain I saw every time I looked into my mate's eyes. The torment ran deep, at the very core of him. I'd lied to the people of Alera to protect him the best I could, but some things only time could heal. He had yet to begin to mourn.

"You ready?" He spoke to me, his thumb stroking the back of my hand almost absently, as if trying to reassure me, but his gaze was moving rapidly, searching the walkways for anyone who shouldn't be here. He'd lost his parents; he'd vowed he wouldn't lose me.

This was queen's business, with Nix, Leo and his father arriving ahead of us to secure the prisoner and now waiting for us. There were two queen's guard standing at the entrance and they waved to our driver, signaling it was safe for us to go inside.

I took a deep breath, let it out. Knew that it came down to this. Caught, Lord Wyse could tell us where Mom was. We could get her back, get her on the throne. Get Dad here. We could be... free. It could all be fucking over. It was like a soap opera on daytime TV gone bad. *Really* bad.

"I'm ready." I looked from him to my sister, who sat on my opposite side in the back of the large vehicle. Trinity's normally fair skin was flushed pink with what I had to assume was anger. Eagerness to have this finished, too. I recognized that look. Destiny and I had made her angry on more than one occasion growing up, relentless in our teasing and pranks we liked to play. "Trin?"

"I want to gut the asshole, not let him go. He killed Thor's parents in a roundabout way. Zel, too. He put an entire planet in turmoil and killed a king. God, if he hadn't gone after her all those years ago, my dad might still be alive." The display of rage was rare. She was the lawyer. Due process and all that legal jargon she and my dad liked to debate for hours when we'd been back on Earth.

"And I wouldn't be born. Destiny, either. Trin, you can't play the 'what if' game. Let's get him, get Mom back. He's our only link to her."

I think I heard her growl. "I know. But I still hate it."

"We do not need to honor the bargain," Thor said, his voice cold. Resolute. "He does not have to be transported off Alera and given his freedom. Once we have the information on your mother's location, we can detain him. Just in case. Fuck, I say we just kill him. *Slowly.*" Thor turned away from the window and glanced from me to Trinity with a grave look. Outside the vehicle, a group of guards surrounded the EMV. Any moment, they would open our doors and escort us inside. I felt safe, if a bit smothered, but we were seeking out a traitor and murderer. This wasn't a visit to an ice cream shop. I guess we'd all get used to it now that we were royal.

"No. I gave my word. I will not break it." Trinity's voice cracked as she spoke, but it was not sadness I saw in her eyes, but more of that barely suppressed rage. "He tells us where Mom is and then he goes into Prime Nial's custody. Once we have Mom back, he'll be free to go."

I forgot to breathe for a second as her words sank in. "What? When did you contact Prime Nial?"

The lines around her lips and eyes relaxed as she showed the first signs of anything but the intense worry and anger I'd seen since the moment Thor and I walked out of my suite at the palace. "While you two lovebirds were in the shower. Taking your damn time, by the way."

I blushed. I couldn't help it. Thor chuckled, the sound wholly masculine and very satisfied. I glanced at him, saw him relaxed for the first time since we left the palace. It reassured me to know I was his comfort—and I didn't just mean because of the really hot sex.

"I could not allow my mate to go unattended," he replied.

"My new—how do you call it—*sister-in-law*—was well attended by Leo as well?"

"Uh-huh. That would be a nun-ya." Trinity was laughing as the guard opened her door. She stepped out onto the sidewalk and was immediately surrounded by five guards.

Thor tugged on my hand and I looked at him as he spoke. "What is a nun-ya?"

I grinned. "It's Earth slang for 'none of your business'."

Trinity took two steps and looked back into the vehicle at me. "Come on, you two. I think you've had enough orgasms to last at least a week. And my mate is inside. I'm eager to see him."

"As if he hasn't been inside you since you got up this morning," I murmured.

She turned to me, grinned and winked.

The guards around her remained stoic and stone-faced, as if they hadn't just heard every word she said.

I slid off the seat and joined her on the sidewalk, Thor right behind me, his hand settling protectively on my hip. I couldn't look any of the guards in the eye. Good god, did my sister have to be such a pain in the ass? "You sound like Destiny this morning, talking smack."

"I never understood her before, all the sarcastic jabs. Now I do."

"Yeah, she's not that tough to figure out. She was born pissed off and eager to torture everyone else."

"Exactly."

Trinity and I stood toe to toe and I took my opportunity to look at her. Really look. There were lines of worry around her eyes, a thinness to her lips that hadn't existed back on Earth. But then, I knew I didn't look the same either. We'd been wide-eyed and innocent when all this started. Blissfully ignorant of anything beyond our little bubble of life. Not outside of our town, our state. Hell, we were on a different planet. Now, I didn't know what we were. Human. Aleran. Ordinary. Royal.

Whatever we were, we were in this together. That was all that mattered.

"Ready?" I asked.

"You might have to hold me back," Trinity said, her fists clenching at her sides. "Once I see him. God, I hate him. I already want to scratch his eyes out, rip his balls off and shove them down his throat."

"But you made the deal," I reminded her. "He's going to get away with murder. *Literally* murder." I took her hand. "He had your dad killed."

She frowned, glanced away, but then lifted her chin. So resolute. "Yes, he did. And yes, I made a deal. I did it for Mom. She's still alive and I want her to stay that way."

She was so brave, so much stronger than I would ever be. I couldn't argue with her. She'd lost more than me and yet she was willing to do what she had to in order to get Mom back. I gave her a decisive nod of agreement, for arguing with her would get us nowhere. "For Mom."

I laced my arm through hers and looked over my shoulder to make sure Thor was with us. Of course, he was. His hand might have fallen away, but he was there, right next to me, whenever I needed him. "I love you, Thor."

I didn't wait for him to answer me. The words didn't require a response. I loved him, knew he suffered so much because of Lord Wyse as well. That was all. I pulled Trinity along and we entered the transport center with Thor guarding my back, as I knew he always would.

Inside, the mood went from fresh air and teasing to a dark quiet that almost tasted bitter on my tongue. The hum of the transport pad could be felt through the soles of my shoes, but I could hear it as well, the faint buzzing making the hair on the back of my neck and arms stand up and pay attention. It was like being in a static-charged clothes dryer.

Trinity pulled her arm from mine seconds before we

entered the main transport area where Leo, Nix and the rest of the guards waited with Lord Wyse.

I remembered him vividly from when we were in front of the police station. Things were different, for I was no longer in handcuffs and he was the one in custody. It was obvious now; I knew why he had been so reluctant to release me to Thor's custody that day. He'd said there was no record of me on Alera and probably assumed I was one of the princesses. He'd been so close. *Too close.*

Then, he'd worn the uniform of the Inspector Optimi, the formal lines had made him appear stronger, taller, a force to be reckoned with. Now, he wore dull gray pants and a dark green tunic. Simple. Average. His boots were black and well worn. In just a few days, his shoulders had thinned with age, the tunic hanging from his frame outlining the sharp angles and bony bits sticking up on his back and shoulders. His face was overly thin, as if he'd been malnourished or was sick. He looked like hell. Old. Weak.

Had he been using a ReGen pod or something to hold off some kind of sickness? Or had the stress of the last few days taken a toll on his body?

How the hell had this old man caused so many problems? Or was this another ruse of his to gain our sympathy, to make us forget what he'd done?

He bowed low and kept his head lowered as Trinity approached him. He was standing alone and I had no doubt he'd been frisked for weapons, but both Leo and Nix were close enough to take him down before he could lay a finger on my sister, if that was his intention.

Based on the no nonsense glare coming from Leo, if Wyse tried anything, he was an idiot and would be dead before his body hit the floor. I don't know how Trinity convinced her mate not to kill Wyse, and I wasn't sure I agreed with the decision, but if there was a chance we could get Mom back, I would let Trinity make the call.

Stepping backward, I reached behind me for my mate. Instantly, Thor's hand closed around mine and he pulled me against him. His heat pressed to my back, the warm strength of him pouring into me. We walked together to the edge of the transport control table where we could hear and see everything, but not be directly involved. I was here to support my sister and find out the truth about our mother.

After everything he'd done, not just to me and my family, but to Thor as well, Lord Wyse didn't exist as far as I was concerned. He was dead to me.

The young Aleran working the transport controls looked up at us, nodding silently before turning back to whatever he was doing. Even though I'd used it to travel from Earth, I had no idea how transport worked. Some super complicated science using wormholes and bending molecules or something. *Star Trek* writers knew what they were talking about. I assumed he was entering coordinates to send Wyse to Prime Nial as his hands flew over the control panel. No one was paying him any attention, so I didn't either, watching as my sister stood before Coburt Wyse with a look on her face I'd seen many times.

It was her no bullshit look. The glare must have been universal because Wyse took a small step away from her, but Nix shoved him forward a bit too hard and the old man fell to his knees before my sister.

No one offered to help him up.

"Lord Wyse, I had to work very hard to convince my mate not to kill you," Trinity told him. "Obviously, I have agreed to your bargain. Tell me where my mother is being held, and by whom, and you will be transported to the Battleship Karter, into the custody of Commander Karter. Once there, they have orders from Prime Nial himself to hold you until my mother has been recovered. Once we confirm the information you give us is truthful, you will be free to go. My one condition is that you never return to Alera. If you do so, you will be executed for treason."

The transport floor vibrated beneath my feet, validation of my sister's words. His transport was imminent, if he just told us what we needed to know. The hair on the back of my neck rose further.

Coburt Wyse lifted his face to Trinity's and opened his mouth to speak, but his glaze flicked in my direction, but to my right. His eyes going round with shock. "No!"

His shout was followed by Wyse raising his arms as if to stop something.

I turned in time to see the transport officer slapping one hand down on a brightly lit area of the panel in front of him, the other held a space blaster aimed at Lord Wyse.

The officer raised the weapon and fired.

Lord Wyse toppled to the floor.

My body took over. Pure instinct drove me. He may have taken out Wyse, but he wouldn't hurt anyone else. I'd been completely useless when we'd been attacked in the suite that first night, but not now. Not after I'd been in the citadel and given some... power. I shoved Thor back to give myself room to move even as I kicked the weapon out of the technician's hand. My leg swung in a wild arc straight out of a Chuck Norris movie. I didn't even know I was that flexible, but the blaster went flying across the room.

Whatever button he'd pushed, the entire room crackled with that pre-transport energy. The floor vibrated even more as three men with black masks and black clothing appeared out of thin air on the raised pad.

They didn't linger, but immediately moved to attack. It was just like in the apartment suite when we'd first arrived on Alera: bad guys coming out of nowhere to attack, although no one came through the windows. This time.

Thor jumped on the nearest one to us. I heard Leo and Nix yelling. Shots being fired with that *Buck Rogers* ping, ping

sound. I couldn't pay them any attention. I had my own problems, because while the traitor—definitely not a transport
technician—in front of me didn't have his gun any longer, he
was twice my size and really, really mad.

It seemed I'd fucked things up. I wasn't sure how. Lord
Wyse had been shot and a bunch of ninjas appeared with the
obvious intent to kill us all. It had been a trap. I had to assume,
since Wyse was most likely dead, that he hadn't been the
mastermind of this little clusterfuck. Someone knew of Wyse's
plan to leave the planet, to give us answers.

The technician had the nerve to grin. He thought he'd won.
Yeah, well, it was time to punch that right off his face.

He took a step toward me and I kicked him again, this time
to the inside of his left knee. His stance widened, buckled a bit
and I turned my kick into a football style punt right into his
crotch.

He shifted at the last second and I only got the inside of his
thigh, which only pissed him off. His right arm came out to
punch me, but I feinted to the left, parried the hand and
punched him in the side of his ribs. I heard one crack. The
action had him leaning in and I took the opportunity to punch
him in the face. Once, then again, like Ali or Mike Tyson.

Jab, cross.

He stepped back, shook his head as if I'd cleaned his clock.
Yeah, fucker. I'm not just a princess; I have serious ninja skills.

We faced off, and I grinned with a strange satisfaction at his
bloodied eye and split lip. I knew I'd blown out his knee and
wrecked his ribs, too.

Frankly, I was surprised he was still standing, ready for
more. Maybe he just didn't like losing to a woman.

But I wasn't just any woman, I was royal, and the citadel
had given me some kind of magical fighting abilities that I was
very, very grateful for at the moment.

As we paused, gauging each other, I noticed the room was
deadly quiet. The floor didn't vibrate and the electric crackle in

the air was gone. I didn't turn to look, but realized everyone was watching the two of us.

"Everyone else is dead," Leo called. "Give up and put your hands on top of your head."

Knowing I had backup, I glanced at the floor. It was true, it was littered with the bodies of the other attackers, all dead. Their bodies were black, motionless lumps on the floor around the transport pad. The queen's guards were circling, squatting down and taking away pistols, ensuring no one could harm us. Thor stood at my side practically bouncing on his toes, waiting for a chance to move into my fight.

Leo had Trinity tucked against his chest, surveying the damage, ion pistol in his free hand.

Nix had his blaster out, pointed right at my opponent.

When the officer saw that, he grinned again, like a fucking Cheshire cat, and raised his hand to the side of his uniform collar where there was a small, metallic button I hadn't noticed before.

"It's a transport beacon! Get him!" Leo shouted.

I didn't know what that was, but I knew it meant escape. "No!" I leaped for him. Nix fired. His blaster fire hit the wall behind where the male's head had been a moment earlier, missing me by inches as I flew through thin air.

It was too late. Instead of tackling a big Aleran who'd been shot, I had launched myself through the air at nothing. He had literally disappeared before my eyes. There one second, then he was gone.

I spun about. No sizzle, no vibrations. Just there and then poof. Vanished. It was like something out of the *Harry Potter* books. Crazy.

"Too late, Nix. Damn it." My sister's voice cut through the silence like a splash of ice water.

Thor pulled me to his chest and smothered me, feeling me everywhere. His hands roamed over my back, my front—which in other times would have been very hot, but now a little awkward—and then cupped my face. "Are you all right? Never do that again, Faith." I looked up at him, his eyes wild. Fierce. "Never. I can't lose you."

I wrapped my arms around him and clung. Now that the adrenaline—and superpowered Kung Fu mania—was wearing off, I felt shaky. And furious. What had just happened? Lord Wyse was about to tell us everything and now he was another body on the floor.

"Did they kill him?" I asked.

"Yes, love. He's dead." Thor kept my cheek firmly to his chest, the beat of his heart calming me, despite the fact that it was racing. "They're all dead."

"Order a hold on all transports to this center. Now!" Nix shouted and one of his men left the room to do his bidding.

"God damn it. Now what?" Trinity pushed Leo away and he let her escape his embrace but kept a hold on her hand, connecting them. It was as if he were afraid one of the dead guys would jump up and get her. "He was supposed to tell us where they're keeping Mom."

She ran a hand through her hair. I don't think I'd ever seen her so mad. She'd made a deal with the devil himself and it hadn't worked out.

Leo looked over the dead bodies, but it was his father and Nix who pulled off the dead men's black masks one by one.

"Do you recognize any of them, Father?" Leo asked.

"No." The older man frowned as he tugged at their clothing. Across the room, Nix did the same.

Nix shoved at one dead man with his boot. "They're not wearing any identifiable uniform."

"No, they're not. But they are marked." Captain Turaya, Leo's father, shoved the sleeve up on a dead man and exposed his wrist. He held the arm up for all of us to see. There, just high enough so the cuff on a shirt would cover it, was a symbol. A dark tattoo.

"What's that?" Trinity asked.

"The mark of the clerics." Leo obviously recognized it because his voice was grim. "Look at the others."

Nix and another soldier checked the other two dead men and found the same identifying mark. "Yes. They all have it," Nix confirmed.

Shit. I wasn't familiar with the clerics, just knew that they were an order that was supposed to be dedicated to protecting the royal bloodline, protecting order and the law. They were not religious at all. All I could think of were the Volturi in the *Twilight* books ruling over all the other vampires. But these dead guys hadn't been protecting us, they'd been trying to kill us. What the hell?

"All of them? They're all clerics?" I asked. I clung to Thor's arm where he'd wrapped it around my waist. My fingertips dug in, hard.

"Faith? What is it?" Thor asked. "They're all dead."

"Yes, but they obviously knew about the deal Trinity made with Lord Wyse. They knew he was going to talk," I said.

"They didn't want him to blab," Trinity added. "Another band of assassins. This time ordered by the clerics. Will we ever get to the top of the ladder of deceit?"

Through her haze of anger, she looked up at me. The moment our gazes locked, I knew she'd thought of the same thing.

"Destiny. Oh, shit. Destiny." Trinity spun to face Leo, the same panic in her eyes that I felt.

Destiny was with the clerics.

"We have to get her out of there," I said. I ignored the dead, stepping over their bodies to get to my sister, hugging her close. "We have to get her out of there right now. Call her. Get Prime Nial to do that insta-dial thing in her head. She has to get out of there."

"I know," Trinity replied. "But shit. Leo? How do I do this? We need to get in touch with her again. To tell her that they're the ones who've got Mom. That they are the bad guys. Now.

Right now." Trinity followed a step behind as Leo moved to the transport controls. "She's in the fucking lion's den."

That made Leo wince. Trinity rarely cussed and seeing her in a panic was even more out of character. But this was our baby sister.

"They'll kill her," I whispered. "Shit. They'll kill her if they catch her."

"I can put in a comm request for Prime Nial from here. But I don't know when or if he'll answer." Leo's hands were already moving over the controls.

Nix moved so silently I'd almost forgotten he was there, until he was so close I could feel the heat of him. "Where is Destiny?" he asked.

Looking up at him, I tightened my grip on Thor as worry for my twin chilled my blood to ice in my body and I started to shiver. "You were there when we talked to her the last time. It was all dark. She didn't say. We don't know. Not exactly."

"What do you mean, you do not know? Where is she?"

"Cut her some slack, Nix. We really don't know." Trinity was bent over the control panel next to her mate, the colored lights from the controls casting her face in a strange green glow.

"If Prime Nial could ping her NPU, then he knows where she is," he countered. His voice was as tense as his entire body.

Nix's words made sense, but right now, right this second, she was out there and in danger. "She was going undercover in the clerical order. We know she got in. But there are at least twenty clerical buildings in Mytikas alone. And she could have left the city, could have gone to another city. She could literally be anywhere on the planet."

"This is Commander Karter. How may I assist?" The Prillon commander's voice filled the room with a distinct lack of anxiety and I calmed immediately, leaning into Thor with a sigh. I wasn't sure why the commander was called instead of the Prime, but I trusted Leo to know what he was doing.

"Thank god," I whispered.

That made Trinity look up at me. "Don't count your chickens, Faith."

"I hate that saying," I grumbled.

Leo ignored both of us. "Commander Karter, this is Leoron Turaya on Alera. I am with Princess Trinity and Princess Faith. There has been an attack and we need to establish communication with their sister, Princess Destiny at once. We were hoping you could assist from Battleship Karter and give us a direct link to her NPU. Her life is in grave danger."

Nix growled and paced, as if he was ready to go after her as soon as he knew her location. I wasn't sure if I should be relieved or fearful. Nix was not a guard to be trifled with, but I knew Destiny would hold her own. Hell, she'd kick his ass into next Tuesday.

7

T *hor*

MY MATE WAS TREMBLING and I fought the fire raging in my blood. So much death. So much betrayal. And now, her twin sister, the one I'd yet to meet, was in danger. I had no idea what they meant about counting strange birds, but I would ask Faith. Later.

Much later.

After I'd stripped her naked, inspected every inch of her perfect body and made love to her until neither of us could move.

While it was obvious these cleric mercenaries had been sent to silence Lord Wyse, I was sure they'd have killed all of us, too, if we hadn't taken them down.

Fuck!

Another attempt on Faith's life. Another clue we now had to follow. Zel, dead. My mother, dead. Wyse, dead. All of them had been pawns of the clerics.

When would this end? When would we find the true

culprit? It was as if we were running and running and never reaching our destination. More death. Never-ending danger. It had to stop.

The silence stretched when Commander Karter did not respond immediately, but Leo held up his hand in a motion for us to wait. He'd been out there in space with the Prillon warriors, fought in the Hive war, and I trusted his judgment.

Nix, however, seemed less patient and I wondered at his scowl and his quiet pacing in front of the control panel. He seemed nearly as emotionally invested as the two sisters, and that made no logical sense. Sure, I was angry about what just happened, but Nix was still obviously agitated, as if his fight weren't over.

He and I had never met Destiny. I'd heard her voice once on the comm call we placed from the palace. Him, too. But I'd never met her. Neither had Nix, that I knew of. But he seemed disoriented, riled. Hanging on by a thread.

"Leo, I have located Destiny's NPU signature. It appears she is in the mountains a few miles outside the city," Karter said through the comms. "I will attempt to patch you through."

"Thank you." Leo nodded to Trinity and stepped back, indicating she should speak.

No formal goodbyes between the males. But that was what I'd heard of the Prillons—they didn't waste time on trivialities or formal nuances. Oh, they had rituals and honor just like the Aleran males, but they sure were abrupt. Since they ran the war with the Hive, they wasted no energy or time for such nonsense.

With Faith in my arms and our enemies dead at our feet, I did not envy the commander the destruction and loneliness of a never-ending war.

"Destiny? Can you hear me? It's Trin." Trinity leaned forward, as if that would help her voice travel through space and into her sister's head a bit faster. "Destiny? It's Trinity." Louder this time.

"Quiet!" Destiny's whispered voice came through loud and clear. And frantic. "I can't talk now."

Faith tensed in my hold.

"Destiny, the clerics have Mom," Trinity continued. "They just tried to kill us."

"I know." Destiny's whisper was quieter now. We could barely hear her.

"What? What do you mean, you know? Why didn't you tell us they were going to ambush us?"

"Not that," she hissed. "That they have Mom."

Trinity glanced my way. It seemed we were a little behind.

"Where are you?" she asked.

"Shhh."

"Where?" Trinity repeated.

"Cell block. Guards. Shut. Up." Destiny's voice was very faint, and very frustrated.

Faith pulled from my arms and I let her go but followed her to the control panel and placed my hand on her back so she'd know I was there. Supporting her. Loving her. As if I were going to let her get more than arm's reach from me.

I'd killed a man with my bare hands tonight. For her.

While she'd been hand-to-hand fighting the transport technician—or cleric disguised as one—I'd wrapped my hands around a mercenary's throat and squeezed until he'd stopped resisting. I'd do it again. He'd been about to shoot my mate and instinct had taken over. Rage. The need to protect. Faith was mine. She'd lied to all the people of Alera to protect me, and now I would spend the rest of my life protecting her. Loving her. Giving her whatever she needed to be happy. I knew she wouldn't be fully content until her mother was found and safe and her sister was away from danger.

"Des, it's Faith. You remember our twin code?"

Two taps sounded through the speaker and Faith sighed with relief and grinned.

"Twin code?" Trinity looked at her sister, frowned. We all looked at Faith. "What twin code?"

"We invented it in kindergarten and used it when we wanted to talk about stuff without people knowing what we were answering," Faith explained.

"Like Morse code?" Trinity asked. I had no fucking clue what that was, but I was intrigued. So was Trinity. Obviously, the sisters didn't tell each other everything.

"Not really," Faith continued. "One for no, two for yes. Right, Des?"

Two taps came through the comm.

"Are you in Mytikas?" Faith asked.

One tap. Holy shit, it was working.

"Are you with the clerics?"

Two.

Fuck. She was in the traitor's den. And not in the city. Where the fuck was she?

Nix leaned forward. "Are you in danger?"

Silence greeted his question, so he asked again.

"Are you in danger, Princess?" His voice had gentled, but not much, and I looked sideways at him, trying to assess his odd behavior. Laser focus, riled and agitated. Unsettled, as if a part of him was missing. If I didn't know better, I'd think Destiny was his mate.

Two taps this time and a shudder passed through Faith. Trinity raised her hand to her forehead and rubbed the skin there as if it were in pain. "Where the hell is she?" she asked the room at large.

Leo's father stepped forward. "The clerical order's main fortress is in the mountains just south of the city. Just beyond the city walls."

Two excited taps—if taps could be excited.

Nix's shoulders rolled back then and he stepped over a dead body. "I am coming." Nix was already walking toward the door when the single tap sounded in the quiet room.

Nix didn't stop, the door to the transport room silently sliding open and he stormed out. He had a mission, it seemed. Get Destiny. He knew she was in danger, knew where she was.

"Too late, Des," Trinity said. "He's coming."

Destiny sighed and we could all hear a rustle of movement. "They're moving prisoners," she whispered. "Love you both. I'm close. Gotta go now. Don't worry about me, I'm fine!"

And just like that, she was gone.

"Fine?" I said, voice loud. "She just tapped that she was in danger and now she's *fine?*"

Trinity slammed her hand down on the control panel and Faith leaned into me as if she couldn't support her own weight.

"Why does she always do this?" Trinity asked. "Mom never should have put her in karate when she was a kid."

"Right. Or Tae Kwon Do. Or boxing. Wilderness survival. She's the badass in the family, remember?" Faith smiled and there was a shimmer of pride in her eyes. She loved her sisters, that was obvious. But talk of Destiny had her straightening her spine and lifting her chin. There was pride in her voice when she spoke of her twin. Pride and love.

"Nix is going after her. He will find her, keep her safe. Drag her ass out of there if need be," Leo added.

"He can try." My mate was grinning, which was a huge improvement from moments ago.

That made me smile in return thinking about what I might do if I was determined to protect Faith, and she was determined not to cooperate. A male could only take so much. "I might actually pity Nix a bit."

"You're not wrong." Trinity looked to me, eyes narrowed in annoyance. "She's a pain in my ass, that's what she is."

"That's no way to talk about my twin," Faith countered.

"You had a secret code and never even told me." Trinity pointed to the blaster indent on the wall where Nix's shot had missed the male that Faith, herself, had been fighting. "You're no better these days. What's with all the karate? I mean,

Destiny's the one with all the self-defense training and now you pull out moves like you're Jean Claude Van Damme."

Faith shrugged. "I went into the citadel normal and came out with Jackie Chan moves. I don't understand it myself, but it's good stuff."

Trinity opened her mouth, looked at me, closed it.

Faith hadn't always been an impressive fighter? It was something she'd acquired inside the sacred building? How?

"Got it." That short answer from Trinity didn't explain a thing, but the sisters seemed to be having a separate conversation. "I'm still going to bitch slap Destiny when she gets back."

"I think Nix is going to take care of that," Faith said and I chuckled, not surprised that my mate had noticed Nix's odd behavior. Indeed, he did seem like a male possessed. And I knew of only one thing that could make a male that crazed.

The guy had tranquilized me, stripped me naked and tied me to a bed to await my mate. I would enjoy watching him suffer a bit.

Trinity was staring at the doorway through which Nix had disappeared. "Maybe." She turned to Leo's father. "I assume the queen's guard will take care of the mess in here? And investigate the men and who they are? Confirm they are really from the clerics?"

Captain Turaya bowed. "Of course. You'll have a report first thing in the morning." He looked to his son. "If you'll escort the princesses back to the palace?"

Leo nodded, hooked his arm about Trinity's waist.

Trinity looked from my mate to me as she leaned her head against Leo's chest. "I need a hot bath, bubbles, candles, and about a gallon of wine. What do you say, Leo? Care to join me?"

"Always." His expression was so content I envied him. But then, I did not, for Faith clung to me with the same love in her eyes.

Faith sighed. "Thor?"

With her saying my name, I knew she asked the same thing.

Would I join her in a bath and whatever came after? It had only been a couple of hours since I had her last, but that was long enough. My balls ached to fill her again.

Fuck, yes.

"Anything for you, love." I leaned down and kissed her cheek, pleased when she leaned into my touch, surprised when she turned in my arms and stood up on her tiptoes to whisper in my ear. I leaned down, intent to know the secret she would give me.

The words she whispered shook me to my soul.

∿

The Jax Mansion

"I feel like I should be out there, getting Destiny away from those people. Out of danger. God, who would have thought being a nun was dangerous," Faith said, pacing the bedroom. All earlier eagerness for a bath and some strange request for bubbles was gone.

I let her pace, let her get her worries out. I wanted to know her problems, share them. Fuck, carry them for her. She was so beautiful. Smart. Caring. Daring. Definitely crazy. She was mated to me. Loved me. Completely insane that she loved me. But thank fuck she did because I couldn't survive without her.

Apparently, my father's zebcats agreed. The moment we'd returned to the mansion, they'd come running and refused to leave Faith's side. Even now, they were curled up on the end of the bed, watching her pace just like I did, and I knew I'd be shoving them off the bed as long as they lived in our home. They had chosen Faith to love, and I could not fault them that choice.

Having those men transport in and threaten her had taken years off my life. Of course, they weren't after her, or Trinity, but Wyse. Still, they were dangerous, they were deadly, and they'd completed their mission. It could have gone differently. They could have killed everyone in the transport room.

I took a deep breath, let it out. Watched the woman I loved worry about her sister.

It was time to make her forget, to take care of her, love her and revel in what we shared. For the rest of our lives.

"You heard her voice. She said she was fine. Nix is going after her."

She'd also said she was in danger, but it was my job to protect and take care of Faith. I'd let Nix deal with Princess Destiny.

She laughed but glanced my way. "She's going to eat him alive."

I gave a little grunt in reply, thinking of Nix trying to boss the third sister around. I hadn't met her, only heard her in conversation. But if she were anything like Trinity or Faith, Nix was going to rip out his hair in frustration within minutes.

I grinned. Good. The fucker tranquilized my ass. Literally. He deserved some torture of the Jones sisters' special variety.

"That may be, but Destiny is Nix's to deal with," I said, sharing my thoughts aloud. "He will do whatever is necessary to keep her safe. You know that."

She sighed, came over to me and wrapped her arms about my waist. Settled her head against my chest. "I know. Still, I'll worry until she's with him. Until our mother is found."

I stroked her hair back from her face. "Then it is my job to distract you."

She pulled back enough to look up at me. "Oh?"

I felt her soft skin beneath my fingers, the beat of her heart as our chests were pressed together, the hard points of her nipples.

"How do you plan to do that?"

I felt her body heat beneath mine. "I could kiss you."

The corner of her mouth tipped up. "That might work."

"On your pussy."

She wiggled her hips and licked her lips, her eyes going dark with a look I would never tire of seeing. "That would definitely work."

I lowered my hand to her belly, felt how soft and lush she was. How different than me. I was all hard angles, rough edges. And she was so much more than I would ever be. She might be small and soft, but she held the power in our mating. She could make life and I had to wonder if she already carried our child. It was possible considering the way I couldn't keep my hands off her. I knew now why the Ardor and awakening combined made for a powerful mix. Surely, every new couple on Alera found themselves with child the first week, if not the first night.

It hadn't been a smooth transition for us. Fuck, my parents dying—I wouldn't think of that now—the traitors in our midst, the dangers, and of course, Faith being a princess. It didn't make for an easy time. Hell, I'd been taken into custody and restrained by guards more since I'd known her than I had in my entire life.

"And your words earlier. Did you mean them?" I thought back to that moment in the transport center when she'd leaned up and whispered in my ear, when she'd made my heart skip a beat and my palms sweat. When I'd been about to explode out of my skin with the need to strip her naked and take her against the wall. I needed her to whisper that promise to me again. I needed to hear it. Was desperate to hear it.

She stilled, came over to me. "That I want your baby growing inside me?"

I nodded, remembering the words she'd whispered in the transport room. "What if... what if we've already made a baby?" I stared down at my big hand where it still rested low on her stomach, imagined a new life stirring under my touch. "Do you feel pregnant?"

She laughed and covered my hand with her own. "That's not exactly how it works."

I lifted my hands to cup her breasts. "Yes, it is." When my thumbs slid over her nipples, teasing them through the fabric of her clothing, she sighed and her eyes fell closed. Her back arched and she pressed herself into my touch. "Sensitive?"

"They always are and you know it." She lifted both hands so they rested atop mine. "Thor, what are you saying? That you want a baby? Now?"

"Yes. I want to fill you with my seed and my child. I want a house full of laughter and chaos and children." I didn't stop brushing my thumbs over her nipples, loved to feel the way they hardened, the way her breathing picked up and her cheeks flushed. "I want a baby. Our baby."

"But... but I thought—I wasn't sure. You don't have to do this now. I know you are worried about the Jax name. You just lost your parents. I can wait. I just—I wanted you to know how I felt. That's why I told you."

"Mate, we've fucked. My seed has filled you up and you're probably pregnant now. We haven't talked about it, so perhaps it's a little late."

She laughed. "A little."

I lifted my hands so they cupped her face, forced her to look at me. To not only hear my words, to see how I felt about them. To know. "I want to make a baby with you. One with your dark eyes, wild hair. She'll be beautiful, but never allowed out of the house until she's thirty."

"What about her Ardor?" she asked.

I growled, thinking of any male touching something so precious.

She laughed again. Fuck, I loved that sound. "What if it's a boy?"

"Then I will teach him to be honorable."

"I thought your honor was ruined?"

I leaned down and kissed her. "You are my honor now, my life. You've seen to that."

She shook her head slightly, for I still held her. "There

was nothing for me to do. You needed to see I believed in you, that you're more than your parents. You're everything to me."

"It will be my honor to be your mate, to make a family with you. A new one."

"Perhaps daughters who might one day rule the world?" she asked.

I kissed her again, softly. Gently. "You rule my world, mate. Always."

Tears spilled from her eyes and I wiped them away with my thumbs. "Boy, you do know how to distract." She offered me a watery smile.

"I think I like the idea of eating your pussy better than making you cry."

She stepped back and I let her. "If you want a baby, that's not how it's done."

"It's not?" I arched a brow and grinned, watched as she tugged off her shirt and let it fall to the floor. She'd dressed in pants and a tunic for the meeting in the transport room, and she looked just as sexy wearing them as when she was adorned with jewels and a fancy gown. My cock, already hardened, pulsed in my pants at the sight of her bare shoulders and belly. I ached to take the rest of her clothing from her and touch her. Kiss her. Everywhere.

She held out her hand. I took it instantly and she led me to the bed where she shooed the zebcats away before pulling me close. "Let me show you."

\|/

FAITH

HE WANTED A BABY? With me? Well, it wasn't going to be with anyone else, that was for damn sure. That gorgeous cock was all mine. Any babies being made would be my doing. And I'd enjoy every hot, sweaty, naughty minute of it.

I thought I'd loved him before. Before he'd said those words. But now, now I knew, with every fiber of my being, that Thor wanted me. I was his mate. He might not be over his parents' deaths yet... I doubted he'd even had a moment to start mourning, but he had definitely come to terms with the fact that his future would not be determined by his parents' mistakes. Especially his mother's. He was honorable, brave, fearless. Fierce. If he felt the need to redeem the Jax name, he could do it by raising good children. Strong and honorable children. A daughter who could possibly rule Alera someday with Jax blood in her veins.

I tugged him to the bed and I sat on the edge so he stood before me. I undid his pants, pushed them down over his slim hips. His cock sprang free, gloriously thick and long, a vein pulsing with life. I leaned forward, licked up the length.

Thor's hips bucked and I grinned, glanced up at him through my lashes.

"This definitely isn't how it's done."

"It isn't?" I asked playfully as I licked up the bead of pre-cum from the broad tip.

He shook his head. "While I love the sweet suction of your mouth, I want your pussy milking the cum from my balls. I want to bury myself deep and fill you."

I whimpered and sucked on the head of him like a lollipop.

He stepped back, waved his finger at me like a kindergarten teacher gently scolding a young student. The heat in his eyes, the wicked grin on his face was all the warning I had before he lifted me up under the arms and tossed me onto the center of the bed. Crawling over me, he pinned my hips with his knees as he leaned down and kissed me.

God, he was such a good kisser. His tongue found mine, dueled, licked. I was lost. So lost I hadn't even noticed him lifting my arms over my head.

When he sat back on his heels and looked down at me, I moved my arms to reach out and pull him back, but I couldn't.

The restraints that had been affixed to the bed to hold him in place earlier now held me. No one had taken them away.

"Ah, this is much better."

My shirt was already gone and my bra had a front clasp. But since I liked frothy confections beneath my clothes to tempt Thor—the way his gaze raked hotly over my chest and his cock pulsed between us, I knew he still liked it all—they weren't any match for his hands. A quick tug here and there and I was bare from the waist up.

"You are at my mercy now. He kissed his way from my neck, down over my collarbone to one breast, then the other, before moving lower. He licked around my belly button as his hands went to my pants, worked them and everything else off.

"Bare and tied to our bed." His hands roamed. Stroked, stoked the heat in my body. My pussy was wet, my thighs slick, my nipples hard. He could see it all. There was no hiding from him, not that I wanted that.

He had all of me.

I arched my back.

His eyes met mine, held. "Greedy, are we?"

I bit my lip, nodded. "Please," I begged.

"Please, what? Touch you? Fill your pussy? Give you all my cum?"

"Yes," I replied. I wanted it all. I knew he'd satisfy me, satisfy both of us.

"Make a baby?"

The look he gave me now was a mix of pure heat and... hope. He wanted this. Needed it.

"Yes." I tugged at the bonds holding my wrists. "Now."

He climbed off the bed, stripped, then spread my thighs wide with one of his, settled at my entrance and slid in. One long, deep stroke and we were joined. He stretched me open, made us one.

He groaned. I moaned.

I'd missed the hot feel of him, how deep he could go.

But he didn't move. I opened my eyes, looked up at him. He was watching me. "I love you."

My heart cracked open then and tears gathered in my eyes. I couldn't stop them and I couldn't hold them back. Didn't want to. I wanted Thor to see them, to know his pain was mine. We were one. "I love you, too."

"I'll be a good father. I give you my word." Such misery in that vow. So much regret.

I clenched my inner walls and willed my heart to show in my eyes, my faith in him, my love. "I know. The best." I could only move my legs and I brought them up around his back, tried to pull him even deeper with my heels against his taut ass. "You're mine, Thor, and I'm a princess. I command you to hurry up and give me exactly what I want."

He grinned, shook his head. "You might be the princess, but I'm in charge now. You're at my mercy."

"Thor," I pleaded. His cock was so big and I was so full—so close to release. This wasn't funny. I needed him to *move*.

"I love the way you say my name when my cock's nice and deep."

He began to move.

I said his name again, this time losing my mind at how he could make me feel. When his hand slipped between us and he brushed a finger over my clit, I cried out his name.

"And now, the way you scream it as you come. You're mine, Faith."

He began to fuck me. Hard. Into the bed. Drilling me. Proving I could do nothing but take whatever he gave me. I took. I came. I cried out his name and it echoed off the walls.

I was his. And when he thickened within me, came on a harsh growl and filled me with his seed, he was mine as well.

We'd struggled and suffered together, lost our way and found each other again. But now, there was no question.

We were one.

Forever.

Thor released my wrists and settled us under the covers. The moment we stilled, my head nestled safely on his chest, the zebcats abandoned their places on the floor and joined us on the large bed. They laid out like they owned the joint, pressed along the entire length my legs and started to purr.

The soft noise fit my mood perfectly. "Seems we already have two children." I loved the cats already and wanted to keep them.

"Whatever you want, love. If you're happy, I'm happy." Thor kissed the top of my head, his naked body next to mine, his hands lovingly stroking my back as his seed –hopefully— created life inside me.

I smiled and wrapped my arm around his chest, squeezing.

"I'm very, very happy."

He kissed me again and I melted into him. Yes. This was happiness.

This was bliss.

WANT MORE? READY FOR DESTINY'S STORY?

READ AN EXCERPT FROM BOOK 7 NOW!

Breaking into the elder cleric's office was strictly forbidden.

I'd heard—again from all that pent-up gossip—that a few hundreds years ago, the offense was punishable by death. Since no one had been caught since, I had no way of knowing whether they'd updated their policy or if no one had ever tried.

"Guess I'll just have to be very, very careful." I whispered the words to no one in particular as I clung to the vines that grew along the tallest tower within the fortress walls. I was like Romeo seeking his Juliet in the high school play.

Glancing left and right to make sure no one saw me... or for maybe one last moment before I did something execution-worthy, I opened a window and pulled myself up, slung my leg, then knee, then the rest of me, through the opening. The office was at least three stories off the ground, but the vines were thick, and I was small. They almost made it too easy.

I landed with barely a sound on the thin carpeting and noticed the room was still nice and warm. The old woman who ran the show had old bones, and she did not like the cold up here in the mountains that surrounded the royal city. But then, with the fortress built eons ago, she didn't have much of a choice but to deal with the weather. The clerical order had formed when the royal bloodline did. The first queen recognized by the citadel had accepted the oath of the first cleric, and so it had begun. Generation after generation, the clerics had served Alera in the matters of law and protection for the realm. They were the scribes and record keepers, and trusted with knowledge known only to a few. Both the clerical order and the royal bloodline were linked to the citadel somehow, but each chose to keep their secrets. The clerics had served the royal family—my family—for millennia.

"Bunch of fucking traitors." Not *all* of them were bad. I'd been training with them, eating with them, pretending to be one of them for two weeks now. I was a novice. A new initiate. And they'd welcomed me into the fold. Most of them were good, solid people. Kind. Friendly. Supportive.

But not all of them. No, someone—or *someones*—within was rotten to the core. Yeah, there was a really bad apple spoiling the whole dang bunch. And I would hunt down the traitors if I died doing it. They still had Mom. They'd tried to kill Trinity and my twin, Faith, more than once.

If they knew who I was, no doubt they'd try to kill me as well. It was obvious we were wanted dead. I grinned, thinking our arrival on Alera must have totally fucked up their plans. Ha!

Moving forward swiftly in the dark, I stubbed my toe on an unexpected outcropping from a chair. I hissed and hopped about. "Damn it." The words were barely more than a grunt, but I heard something move in answer outside. Below me. On the ground.

Then a rustling.

The vines.

Oh, shit.

Someone was climbing the vines. Romeo, himself, this time? I was no Juliet waiting to be whisked away. And fuck it all, they were moving even faster than I had. I didn't have time to go anywhere, and the room's door—which normal people used to come in—would be solidly locked. I had to hide and hope whoever was coming would lead me to another clue about my mother. I knew the clerics had her. Somewhere. The rumor mill was buzzing with whispers and speculation about a very top-secret prisoner. It had to be Mom, or to Alerans, Queen Celene. It just had to be.

Because if it weren't, I'd run into a dead end and we were all screwed. Mom would die. And I just couldn't live with myself if that happened.

Hobbling on my aching toe, I dashed to a corner so dark with shadows it looked black. There I stood, immobile, and waited to see who my unexpected visitor might be. What were the chances of there being two snooping initiates?

The waiting was an agony all its own. I was in tune with my body, keeping my breathing quiet, to try and still my racing heart—yeah, right—and stand as still as possible. The Aleran half of my DNA had decided last week that it was a good time to go into full-blown Ardor. I knew what it was because Trinity'd had it when we'd arrived. Every inch of my skin was sensitive. My nipples ached, the lobes of my breasts felt too full and heavy. They were small, which suited me just fine for fighting. But they felt double their normal size. My pussy was constantly wet and my hearing seemed to have kicked up into some kind of superpower level annoying. Like I was the Bionic Woman all of a sudden. The horny Bionic Woman.

I could hear insects crawling in the walls. Conversations all over the fortress; that was why I knew every bit of gossip that had been circling about. My own heartbeat had sounded like a conga drum inside my head until I'd learned how to ignore it and somehow, that had helped me figure out how to pay attention to what I was hearing when I wanted to, and feel somewhat normal the rest of the time.

Trinity hadn't mentioned super-hearing as being part of her Ardor, but she'd been pretty distracted with Leo, as in naked and having screaming orgasms. Stupid Ardor, screwing with me. It was as if I had no control over my own body any longer. And I wasn't getting off. Damn it.

I was so horny I was close to coming by just rubbing my thighs together. And I heard everything that went on in the place. Everything. Including a few rather sexy encounters that had me squirming and wishing taking care of things myself would actually work. But no. Every orgasm I gave myself just made it worse. I'd quit after two and curled into a ball for a few hours, waiting for the need wrecking me to back off.

It didn't. But I'd been coping. I wasn't sure how much longer I would last before I went insane with lust.

Which was why I'd decided to take this last, desperate chance and break into the elder's office. If I didn't find anything, I'd have to go to the palace and find one of those consort men to take the edge off. Right now, I just *needed* and I was nearly to the point that I didn't much care whose cock I was riding as long as it was hot, hard, and lasted all damn night. Oh yeah. *Hot and hard.*

I was panting when two large, very masculine hands appeared on the window ledge. Nice hands. Long, thick fingers. Inside me. Rubbing me. Fucking me.

Shit. I had to get myself together.

Focusing on my breath, I slowed things down and waited. My eyes had already adjusted to the darkness, so I watched the intruder slide through the window like a cat.

God, for such a large man, he could move. He was strong, that was obvious by the way he handled his entire body weight with just his arms and swung silently to the floor. He landed crouched low, one knee bent as if he were kneeling before a queen. But he wasn't kneeling, his chin was up, his breathing silent—even with my incredible hearing.

He was holding his breath. Listening.

For what?

"Destiny? I know you are in here." His voice was deep. Sensual. The low timbre slid over my skin and I shivered, literally shivered, the tone going straight to my clit and zinging through my body as if he had his mouth on me.

What. The. Fuck?

I didn't move. I didn't dare. And I didn't breathe, either. Holding the air in my lungs as if my life depended on it. I knew that voice. Somehow, I knew it. But from where?

Get Ascension Saga, book 7 now!

THE ASCENSION SAGA

Thank you for joining me on this exciting journey in the Interstellar Brides® universe. The adventure continues...

TRINITY
Book 1
Book 2
Book 3
Volume 1 (Books 1-3)

FAITH
Book 4
Book 5
Book 6
Volume 2 (Books 4-6)

DESTINY
Book 7
Book 8
Book 9
Volume 3 (Books 7-9)

www.AscensionSaga.com

LET'S TALK!

Interested in joining my not-so-secret Facebook Sci-Fi Squad? Share your testing match, make new like-minded sci-fi romance fanatics!

JOIN Here:
https://www.facebook.com/groups/scifisquad/

Want to talk about the Ascension Saga (or any Grace Goodwin book) with others? Join the SPOILER ROOM and spoil away! Your GG BFFs are waiting!

JOIN Here:
https://www.facebook.com/groups/ggspoilerroom/

FIND YOUR MATCH!

YOUR mate is out there. Take the test today and discover your perfect match. Are you ready for a sexy alien mate (or two)?

VOLUNTEER NOW!
interstellarbridesprogram.com

GET A FREE BOOK!

JOIN MY MAILING LIST TO BE THE FIRST TO KNOW OF NEW RELEASES, FREE BOOKS, SPECIAL PRICES AND OTHER AUTHOR GIVEAWAYS.

http://freescifiromance.com

CONNECT WITH GRACE

Interested in joining my not-so-secret Facebook Sci-Fi Squad? Get excerpts, cover reveals and sneak peeks before anyone else. Be part of a closed Facebook group that shares pictures and fun news. JOIN Here: http://bit.ly/SciFiSquad

All of Grace's books can be read as sexy, stand-alone adventures. Her Happily-Ever-Afters are always free from cheating because she writes Alpha males, NOT Alphaholes. (You can figure that one out.) But be careful...she likes her heroes hot and her love scenes hotter. You have been warned...

www.gracegoodwin.com
gracegoodwinauthor@gmail.com

ABOUT GRACE

Grace Goodwin is a *USA Today* and international bestselling author of Sci-Fi & Paranormal romance. Grace believes all women should be treated like princesses, in the bedroom and out of it, and writes love stories where men know how to make their women feel pampered, protected and very well taken care of. Grace hates the snow, loves the mountains (yes, that's a problem) and wishes she could simply download the stories out of her head instead of being forced to type them out. Grace lives in the western US and is a full-time writer, an avid romance reader and an admitted caffeine addict.

ALSO BY GRACE GOODWIN

Her Viken Mates

Fighting For Their Mate

Her Rogue Mates

Claimed By The Vikens

The Commanders' Mate

Interstellar Brides®: The Colony

Surrender to the Cyborgs

Mated to the Cyborgs

Cyborg Seduction

Her Cyborg Beast

Cyborg Fever

Rogue Cyborg

Interstellar Brides®: The Virgins

The Alien's Mate

Claiming His Virgin

His Virgin Mate

His Virgin Bride

Other Books

Their Conquered Bride

Wild Wolf Claiming: A Howl's Romance